CANDACE CAN-CAN COOK

TESSA BURNS

For O! He loves thee far too well to leave thee in thy self-made hell.
A Savior is our Lord!
Hannah Hurnard, *Mountains of Spices*

CHAPTER 1
THE LIBRARY

CANDACE

I t's midsummer. The sky is cotton-candy blue, the temperature low eighties. Crepe-myrtles line the street with vibrant purples and pinks. Glorious! I live in one of the most beautiful places in California. Perfect in so many ways.

Before long, the warmth of summer will morph into the cool crispness of a new season. The sun will shine its signature golden hue, reminding all the trees to conserve their resources and let their leaves fall. I want to be prepared.

My goal? An extravagant turkey dinner with all the fixin's and friends gathered around my table—without alarm. How I long to be able to feed my friends a scrumptious dinner without complaints of something being burnt or not tasting quite right. I'd love my little apartment to be filled with mouthwatering smells wafting from my oven. Melted butter, warm sugar, cinnamon, apple, pumpkin. Comforting aromas that encourage my invitees to partake of my offerings without the need to duck and cover as another pot explodes or, even worse, as their insides detonate from food poisoning.

Cooking? Not my forte. As smart as I'd like to think I am, I just don't have the fortitude to follow a recipe. Which is crazy. I'm an adult. I've lived on my own for years. But somehow, I still haven't been able to hunker down to learn the art of cooking. I'm too impatient, too likely to replace ingredients with what is already in my pantry.

Most of the time, I choose the wrong substitute. I've glanced at cooking shows where creative cooks throw all kinds of odd things together and get rave reviews. Unless they're cooking for Gordon Ramsey. Man, he'd flail me if his presence ever graced my kitchen.

I've made up my mind. This will be the year I learn to cook! I must pursue the skill of cooking with the same tenacity as beekeeping or butterfly charting—both of which are of utmost importance to me. I believe I can save the world by saving bees and butterflies. I'm not so sure my preparing a meal for someone would bring about an important change. But it's time to turn over a new leaf. It's time to prove I'm independent, grown up, and capable of feeding myself and others without some kind of mishap. So here I am, in my clunker Toyota Corolla, driving down a tree-lined avenue to the nearest library, in hot pursuit of the perfect cookbook.

Stopped by a red light, I look toward the sidewalk. A heap of trash, tarps, and dingy tents clutter the landscape. Such an eyesore. They block the view of the gorgeous maple trees that will turn vibrant oranges and fiery reds in a few months. I shake my head. I live in such a beautiful city, yet if I turn down certain streets, this is the scenery I see. Something's not right.

A handful of people huddled in a group catches my eye. They gather in a semicircle around a man in a wheelchair in army green, his hair so unkempt I can't even tell what color it is. I sure hope the girl in leggings and a tank top has something warmer when the weather changes. A guy passes a lit cigarette. As the man in the wheelchair takes a drag, motivation to pursue my own advancement leaks out of my soul like a deflating balloon.

Stop it, Candace! You will always have the poor among you. Isn't that the saying? My job is to live the best life I know how.

But what about them?

A loud honk startles me. I look up. The light has turned green, so I scoot through the intersection. *Just move forward. Toward your goal.*

But what about those people, God?

Something needs to be done. But what? The way they live drives me crazy. It's gotta be a health hazard, not to mention the assault on beauty. Guilt clouds my soul. I'm so uncompassionate.

A sigh escapes as I pull into the asphalt parking lot. Why is the atmosphere so drab? It's still summer, but the sun has lost its luster. Now all the colors are muted gray. Like dirt has been thrown on the canvas of my life.

Geez, Can-Can, get a grip. Let it go. Move on. The only person you can change is you. Go forth and conquer. Find a great cookbook. Learn to cook like a grown up.

I stare through my windshield at the sixties-style gray concrete building. Greenish film tints the glass doors and windows. Maybe it protects the books inside. I haven't been to this library before. Until I graduated, I used the one at my university or the one in my hometown. I'm a big fan of libraries. It's time to make this one my new favorite.

On the glass door, a sad little red and blue flyer dangles as a last surviving piece of tape holds its ground. Something about saving the whales? The letters are faded, but there's a picture of a whale. Yeah, save the whales.

"And the people too," I mutter. A cool burst of air hits my face as I enter the hallowed sanctuary.

I love the aged paper and inky smell of old books. I breathe in the aroma of parchment like I'm returning home to yummy evidence of a special treat created just for me. My eyes scan the shelves as I walk down the sacred aisles. It would be so easy to get lost in all these pages. Light bubbles up from my soul as a rainbow of book spines calls my name and returns color to my world.

A grateful sigh escapes a little too loud.

"Shhh!"

Seems several patrons are cranky pants today. I laugh to myself, making sure I don't shatter the quiet atmosphere for others who hold this sanctuary dear. I can't fault them; I was a cranky pants myself a few minutes ago.

My eyebrows rise as I look up. Ahhh, I'm in the right section. Yay me for pushing past the temptation lining the other shelves.

Do I really want to do this? I reach for the book *Cooking for Amateurs*. Right up my alley.

I need to like to cook, or so I tell myself over and over. A young adult female living on her own should know how to feed herself something other than sandwiches, canned soup, and frozen dinners. Besides, don't I want to be able to invite my friends over without their complaints of "Pizza again?"

I groan.

"Shhh!"

Okay, why is everyone so persnickety on such a lovely, sunny Saturday morning? I can't help myself; I give the lady with the tight bun and stretched face a snarky look. She huffs at me and turns her back to me as she leafs through a saffron-colored hardback. Hugging my find to my chest, I march to the checkout desk.

"Will this do it?" a tall man asks from behind the counter, his dark hair messy.

"I have no idea." I push my glasses up the bridge of my nose. These frames always seem to slide down, but positioning them tightly just gives me a headache. "Do you know if this would be a good choice for a newbie cook?"

He lifts the book closer to his structured face, under his straight nose—probably the most perfect I've ever seen. His brown eyes shine through his black-rimmed glasses as he inspects the cover.

"It depends," he finally says. "What is your purpose with this book?"

It should be obvious. "I want to learn to cook. I want to make a meal for my friends that won't kill them."

He gives a soft chuckle. Our eyes meet. A smile twitches across his face before surrendering to a more studious expression.

"You want to learn to cook?"

"Yes."

"Any experience at all?"

"I can boil water."

He stifles a laugh. It's kind of cute. But should I be offended?

He clears his throat like he's trying to watch what he says. "If you're not opposed to my suggestions, let me go grab other books you

4

might find helpful." I nod and he maneuvers around the counter and glides to the cooking section. His black jeans and gray long-sleeve oxford fit his tall, slim build perfectly. I stare where he disappears into the aisle. When he returns from between the multicolored shelves, he smiles and shakes a couple of books in each hand.

He coasts around the counter and returns to his stalwart position. "I think these will give you a little variety and may help you push beyond the water-boiling stage." He pinches his lips together, in what I presume is his attempt to hold back amusement that I can't cook.

"Thank you," I force out while I slide my borrowed books off the yellowed counter.

When I push through the glass door, that stupid flyer rips off and floats to the ground. Ugh. I bend to pick it up and then take it to the desk where I have to look at the librarian again. I try not to slam the paper on the cheap Formica.

"Thank you," he says. Why does his voice seem almost sultry? "This thing has been on its last leg for a while. But the lead librarian wouldn't let us throw it away." He wads the flyer in his hands. "It has seen its last day. Finally." He shines a big smile at me.

Oh no, Candace. No, no, no. I paste on a straight face, nod my head, and skedaddle out of the library, away from the tall, appealing man.

Wait! I think he's appealing? *No, no, no.*

5

CHAPTER 2
THE LIBRARIAN

HANK

I don't mind my job. It's pleasant to be surrounded by my favorite thing. Books. I love books, often forgetting to eat as I visit other places, learn new skills, or try to solve a mystery. Could be why I'm such a beanpole.

"If you can read, you can do anything." I guess my parents' mantra when I was a kid made an impression, because here I am after earning my degree in my vocation of choice. Librarian.

Not the most glamorous job, I know. Maybe not a sustainable job, in this digital age with all the public resources diminishing. But I'll cross that bridge when I get there. My hope is for people to return to the love of the texture of a book in hand. For now, I make enough money for a single man to survive. And I get to meet interesting people every day. Even one of our town's resident homeless—I mean, unsheltered—comes in and gives my life a little more luster.

Lyle is an interesting guy. Single like me, just trying to survive. We have a friendship of sorts. Yeah, maybe the aroma he brings with him could be worked on. But I really like to hear his life stories when I'm on break. I don't know if they're true. But, man, are they fascinating.

Mrs. Jones, my supervisor, told me to expect a slow day because of some big Save the Whales rally on the other side of town. I squint as the sun shines through the library windows. The weather will be perfect for a swim by the time I get off this afternoon. My apartment has an Olympic-size pool. Tell me that's not a find.

A pleasant gust of air sweeps by the wheeled cart, stacked with scanned books I now need to reshelve. I glance over the top of my thick-rimmed frames as a cute blonde with glasses breezes past and heads straight to the cooking section. I look down at the counter at a copy of *Something Wicked This Way Comes*, I laugh to myself, making sure not to make a sound.

The OFC, the library's Old Fogies Club, is on a roll today. Loud shushes break the typical quiet. Someone is rocking the boat.

Seconds later, I think I identify the culprit as she waltzes up to my counter. She sets a cookbook down. A strand of long blonde hair falls across her face, and she whisks it behind her ear.

"Will this do it?" I ask.

She looks at me with trepidation as her slender pointer finger pushes her glasses up the bridge of her nose. Did she ask if the book is a good choice? I inspect it to buy time to clear the fog clouding my mind.

"What's your purpose with this book?" *O brother, Hank, it's a cookbook. What do you think her purpose is?*

She says something about not killing her friends with her cooking. Though amused, I try not to laugh, since I giggle when I get nervous. Thank goodness my drumming heart can't be seen under my shirt. Or can it?

Focus on your job, Hank. My job is to help this customer find books to best meet her needs. I have some ideas. This book's claim to be for amateurs is false, unless amateurs know how to torch a custard.

By the time I've nearly gained composure, she says she can boil water. I pinch my lips to swallow a chuckle. Everything she says amuses me.

If I search for other cookbooks it might give me a moment to gather my thoughts behind the safety of the bookshelves, out of the sight of her sea-blue eyes. Passing by her, I can't help but calculate I'm about eight inches taller. She must be around five foot six. Probably a couple of years younger than me. She looks the type to frequent a library.

7

Thoughts swim in my head as I scour the shelves for the perfect level of cookbook. Well, maybe slightly underperfect, so she will come back for more. I find a contender and reach over a woman who raises an eyebrow but won't budge. Must be a member of the OFC. Once she figures out I won't give up, she huffs and scoots out of the way. People are funny.

I walk toward my customer, and show her the books I found. I can't discern her expression, but she watches me the whole way to my post behind the counter. A few seconds ago, when I was safe out of view, I wasn't so self-conscious. I draw in a slow deep breath and will my voice steady.

I say something like "I think these may help," and try to give a friendly smile without looking like a dork. Nervous laughter is percolating way too close to the surface. *Please, Lord, help me not make a fool of myself.*

She slides her checked books into her arms and leaves. I hope I'm here when she returns. The forlorn flyer for the whale rally rips off the door as she exits. Her unflashy, perfect form kneels and picks up the paper. She brings it to me, straight-faced as she sets it on the counter.

I notice her subtle beauty, fumble over some stupid comment, and nervously wad the paper in my hands, sure I have a goofy grin on my face. She nods and practically runs out of the library.

My shoulders drop. I watch through the glass window as she marches to a silver Corolla.

When she glances back toward the door, I drop my head and whirl around to a bun-clad customer standing in front of the counter with a perturbed look on her face. Back to reality.

CHAPTER 3
WANTING TO
WANT TO COOK

CANDACE

I set the book with the promising title on my lemony-scented granite countertop. I've purposefully set the stage for success by cleaning. The worn pages of *Cooking for Amateurs* naturally open to the table of contents. This recipe looks encouraging—easy tiramisu.

The picture on page twelve promises a beautiful, decadent dessert. Spongy ladyfingers, creamy layers striped with espresso and cocoa. Wow! Just think how my friends will react when I make this dessert. And I don't even have to cook. Their typical groans will turn to hums of deep content.

I look at page thirteen. How many ingredients do I need?

You've got to be kidding. And how many steps?

Hold the presses! Five steps, but each step has, like, five more things involved. Then there's the warning: "Do this too long and it will fall apart."

Great. This book's title is false advertising. The list of what's involved makes this recipe teeter on the edge of highly proficient, which I am not. Ugh.

I leaf through and look at the pretty pictures. The pages crinkle as I scan page after page to see if any of the recipes could be considered amateur, or somewhat close to my skill level. Nope. Nothing. At least I was able to take in the joy of colorful pictures and the smell of the printed word. Now I'm officially starving. And not for some cheap burger.

Riffling through the contents of my freezer produces slim pickin's. A pot pie and a couple of Lean Cuisine boxes. I really need to learn to cook. I wish so hard I liked to cook. *Please, God, help me learn to like to cook.*

My sisters were my mom's shadow in the kitchen. Me—I played outside, the kid who got nagged to wash my hands and face at every turn, who liked dirt, climbed trees, and collected rocks and bugs in my pockets. I used to get in so much trouble when the dryer vent got clogged with dead roly-poly bugs.

"Sorry for the early death." I touch my lips and throw a kiss up to the sky. "You were my friends, for a moment." I liked to fiddle with their little round bodies as they were probably panicking, stuck in my sweaty stinky pocket. Back then, I didn't understand bugs. Now I do. I absolutely love and respect them. I've finally finished my master's degree and landed my first adult job. I've found my calling. Entomology.

Cooking? Not my calling. But I'm supposed to be grown up and know how to feed myself and those who brave my invitations. Supposed to safely offer something other than take out pizza. So here I am, staring at *Cooking for Amateurs* again.

For amateurs? Ha! I look at the other two books the cute guy found for me.

Wait. Did I say "cute guy"? Did I think "cute guy"? I let out a huff. Yeah, he was kind of cute. Not in an obvious way, but in one of those intriguing ways where you want to keep looking to figure out why you think he's cute. I stare at the stain made on the cupboard next to the stove when canned spaghetti sauce got too exuberant. I wouldn't mind seeing that guy again. I'll have to go back to his library for more cookbooks.

I can't bring myself to go to the library for anything other than a cookbook. Instead of borrowing books, I buy them, hoping my own library will someday rival the one in *Beauty and the Beast*. I'm not there yet, but my bookshelf already holds some jewels I've found. I love the printed-on-paper written word, love savoring the feel of the paper between my fingers as I bend the corner of a page I want to revisit, like knowing exactly where to find favorite passages—how far in, on what side, and how far down the page. I mourn the whole e-book thing. I know. I'm weird. That digital stuff makes my eyes go wonky.

I flip through one of the books picked out by Tall, Dark, and Handsome. I give in to how I feel about him. I'll admit it to myself, just nobody else.

Oh look! This recipe has some possibility. Pasta primavera. The book says I can use mixed frozen veggies, there are fewer than ten ingredients, and only two pots are needed. One for boiling noodles, the other for the vegetables and sauce. I think I can do this. Hope springs eternal. I scour my cupboard.

Bingo! I have a sad little box of spaghetti and some frozen veggies. Not exactly the kind they suggest, but I think they could work. No half-and-half, but I have two percent. No cornstarch, but I have flour. Chicken bouillon. Hmmm, maybe I don't need that this time. I'll get some on my next trip to the grocery store.

Embracing my one cooking claim to fame, I put a pot of water on the stove. But a watched pot doesn't boil, so I ignite the gas flame and grab my latest book obsession, *Percy Jackson*. Yeah, I'm that kind of gal.

Oh my!

Sea creatures.

Monsters.

Percy's on the ground, death eminent—

Pop! Bang!

I jump out of my chair, and send *Percy* flying. What exploded? What smells? My ears are pierced with a high shrill. Smoke? *Oh Lord, not the pot!* I fly to the kitchen, turn off the gas stove, run around to open every window, and fan a towel to push the burnt-metal smell out of my apartment.

The loss of my claim to fame sinks in. I messed up boiling water. My shoulders drop. I'm doomed. I'll never become the cook I think I want to be.

I grab my keys off the catchall table by my front door and leave my stinky apartment.

"You okay, Candy?" Neighbor Bob asks as he waters his gorgeous heirloom tomatoes in his container garden. "I heard the alarm. Another little mishap?"

He means to be empathetic, but today his witness to my failure is just disheartening.

"Looks like burgers again tonight." I give a half-hearted laugh.

"You'll get it, sweetie. Just keep trying."

I nod at him, grateful for him. When his wife passed away a couple of years ago, he sold their house and moved into this new complex, about the same time I did. My first kitchen snafu in this apartment was the first time I met him. I barely heard the pounding on my front door over the fire alarm. Neighbor Bob was quick to shuffle inside, assess the situation, then turn off the alarm and help me air out my apartment. That evening he invited me to share the dinner he had already prepared. He stepped right in as a father figure when I was having a hard time being on my own. Even though my family only lives a few towns away, I'm trying to prove I can be independent. I haven't let myself visit them too frequently while I pursue what I believe is right for me, unhindered by family expectations. Well, by family, I mean mainly my mom.

Neighbor Bob let me bemoan to him and even fed me homemade dinners. Yes, he is a better cook than me. For fifty-two years, he and his wife cooked alongside each other as part of their nightly routine.

I'd love to have someone to cook with someday. Yet another reason why I need to learn how to cook. I just wish I liked it. *Please, God.*

CHAPTER 4
I NEED SOME BEAUTY

CANDACE

The temperature is unusually warm for seven in the morning as I walk toward my home away from home. The windowed walls of my office building reflect green trees, blossoming flowers, and glistening morning light. The handle of the glass door is cool against my palm and pushes open easily. Already unlocked. Mr. Jacobs must have started his day early.

I buzz down the darkened hallway and peek inside the room with the light casting a stripe across the tile floor. "Good morning."

"Oh, Miss Carlson! You're here early. Anxious to get to your observations? Or couldn't sleep, knowing you'll be taking over the education section?" The fatherly voice of Mr. Jacobs coaxes a calm breath in and out of my lungs, and my shoulders let go of the tension I didn't know pinned them to my earlobes.

"Both, I guess. I'm curious to see if any of the educational blue morpho have emerged from their chrysalides. I could use some beauty to start my day."

My lips pull down at the corners. I don't mean to frown, but I woke up dreaming of that encampment I passed on the way to the library. The dream sent storm clouds across my mind.

"You okay? You don't seem your usual, cheerful self." My boss's furrowed brow reminds me of my dad. I miss him. Should at least call home to say hi. I don't want to disconnect myself from my family completely.

"I'll be okay. It's just…" I shake my head, then point over my shoulder. "You know the area near the railroad tracks?"

Mr. Jacobs lets out a huff. "You mean where the unsheltered hang out during the day?"

"Mm-hmm." I pinch my lips, how do I politely share what's on my mind? Then I give up and just blurt them out. "It bothers me. We live in such a beautiful county, but that corner is cluttered with garbage heaps, and the people who hang out there don't seem to care. I know I must sound uncompassionate, but the whole thing just makes me sad. Even depressed, if I let myself think about it too much. I don't get it."

I drop my head. "It seems like I can't stop my thoughts from going there. I need some beauty to counter what my soul is feeling. Does that sound ridiculous?" *Oh Candace, this is not something to dump on your boss.*

"It isn't ridiculous. I understand. The county's homeless situation needs to be addressed. It doesn't seem we've learned how to effectively change much. I can't say I haven't felt the same way as you and turned to work for relief. We are privileged to be surrounded by so many magnificent specimens." He folds his hands on the edge of his desk. The signature move indicates it's time to let him get back to his work.

"Thanks for listening. I didn't mean to bother you. I'll go see if those butterflies can cheer me up." I knock my knuckles on the wooden door frame and amble down the hall, toward the lab where we keep our observation habitats. Cool air hits my face as I enter the lab and meander to the glass case where strings of a hundred chrysalides, at various stages of metamorphosis, zigzag from side to side like switchbacks climbing a mountain.

A gasp escapes as I see a flutter of shimmering blue. One butterfly emerged sometime during the night. Movement and swishes of color inside other chrysalides indicate more beauties will be free from the confines of their little cocoons. Soon they'll live a life their caterpillar minds didn't dare dream of. Freedom to fly!

In a few days, I'll take these specimens to share with second graders. Describe the life cycle of butterflies and why they are so important to our world. As pollinators, for one thing. Also as gifts of beauty. I believe we all desperately need to counter the despair that can sometimes consume us. *Why such a philosophical mood today, Can-Can? Shake yourself out of it.*

I open the case, gently pinch the emerged butterfly's wings near its body, and transfer it to a larger habitat. It will be happier, free to fly and munch on the fruit slices I've set out. I watch the creature flit and land on a brown banana, then lift in flight to explore its new world. The wave of metallic bright blue on the upper surface of the wings and the brown eyespot on the underside mesmerize me as the butterfly floats through the air and then lands.

"Thank you." I gently tap the clear glass and make my way to my desk. Time to get to the work of work.

———

A golden hue makes the landscape outside my window gleam. The clock in my office says the workday is done. I shut down my computer, stretch my arms toward the ceiling, and twirl my wrists to loosen the stiffness from pounding out pages of facts on the keyboard.

I've thought about calling home all day. I should do it now, before I leave the office. Once I get home, it will be too easy to get caught up in my latest read and put off the call. *Quit avoiding it, Candace, and pick up the phone.*

I set the phone on speaker mode and wait to see who answers. *Please let it be Dad. I don't want to deal with Mom's scrutiny.*

"Hello?"

"Hey, Mom." I let out a silent sigh.

"Candace! We haven't heard from you in a while. To what do we owe the pleasure?"

My forehead drops hard into my palm. "I just wanted to check in. See how everyone is doing. Is Dad around?"

"No, honey. He's not home from golf yet. The guys are having dinner at the club together, since I'm hosting my book club tonight."

"Oh, sorry. I should let you go so you can get ready."

"Nonsense. I've done all my prep work and only need to warm the hors d'oeuvres. Oh, I found some wonderful recipe books I could share with you. Maybe you could have a book club with your friends there." Mom stifles a giggle. "How's the cooking goal progressing?"

I slouch. I shouldn't have told her. Now she'll check up on me at every opportunity.

"In progress. I've checked out a couple of cookbooks from the library and am trying to make my way through them."

"Oh! Not *Mastering the Art of French Cooking,* I hope. I'm not sure you would be ready for that."

"No. I'm starting with books with the word *easy* in the title."

Her muffled giggle hits a nerve. "Good for you, Candace. I know this will be a useful pursuit."

"Yes. I hope so."

"How is that bug business of yours?"

My back straightens. I'm happy to talk about something I love. "We had a handful of blue morphos emerge from their chrysalides today. By the time I teach on the life cycle of bees and butterflies, we'll have more than a dozen butterflies I can show the students."

"You'll be teaching?" Mom almost sings.

"Yes. Mr. Jacobs asked me to take over the education program. Next week will be my first time to lead the lesson."

"I always thought you would be a good teacher. I'm not sure why you went into that bug business. Never seemed ladylike. But now..." Mom always exaggerates her pauses when she's about to say the equivalent of *I told you so.* "This will give you a taste of the joy of teaching."

"Yes." I count to four as I draw in a breath.

"Well, honey, I have to put the stuffed mushrooms in the oven. It was so nice to hear from you. Please come home soon. I'll cook a special family dinner. You can catch up with your sisters."

"I'll look at my schedule. Please tell Dad hi for me and that I love him."

"Of course, honey. I love you too."

"Yes. Love you, Mom. Goodbye."

"Goodbye, sweetheart."

The phone clicks on the other end. My mom insists on keeping the same old-school, olive-green rotary phone she had as a kid, with a curling cord that reaches down the hallway. We girls would hide in the walk-in linen closet and talk on the phone for hours as teenagers. That fun memory shakes off the weight on my shoulders. My mom means well. I don't think she is aware of how her words make me question myself. She has always been a good mom, supplied all our needs, made sure we had the best meals and clothes, and provided all kinds of opportunities.

An audible sigh escapes my mouth. I can't be like her. Her to-do lists are so particular. I never was good at keeping up with them. I'd barely get started and she'd point out where I was falling short, which may be why I've avoided cooking. My sisters were the pros in the kitchen, I just messed things up, so I'd escape outside and climb a tree. I wish I didn't let it get to me so much, but trying to meet expectations I think she has for me is too hard.

Plus, I don't *want* to be her. I want to be me. I love what I do. Yeah, I'd like to cook like her, in theory. But my personality has always been more like my dad, so not ladylike enough.

"Miss Carlson?" Mr. Jacobs knocks on my open door. "Here early and now staying late? You're young. You should go home and enjoy the rest of your evening elsewhere."

"How about you?" I volley back.

"Oh, the wife has some kind of ladies' get-together. I'm on my own for dinner. May stop by that new Greek restaurant, grab something to go, and read through the latest *Entomology Today*."

"Sounds delightful. Maybe I'll do the same."

His eyebrow rises, then relaxes toward a gentle smile. "Well, good evening, Miss Carlson."

"Please call me Candace."

He nods. "See you in the morning, Candace. Not too early I hope." He chuckles, knocks his knuckles on the door jamb like always, and leaves.

I click off the desk light, gather my bag, and make my way down

17

the hall, switching off more lights as I go. The deadbolt clicks as I lock the door behind me, to keep all our beautiful specimens safe.

A warm breeze ruffles my hair. I take in a deep breath of fresh air and close my eyes. The wisp of honeysuckle from our pollinator garden tickles my nose, my eyes take in the smattering of yellow, coral, and red blooms in front of my office. The afternoon sun sprinkles the atmosphere with kisses of gold.

Ahh, beauty. Such a healing force. *Thank you, God.*

CHAPTER 5
WHERE DOES HE SLEEP AT NIGHT?

HANK

E ven from inside the library, I hear Lyle sing out "Henry James" as he waltzes toward the entrance. I set aside my latest read, *No Limits*, smile from the other side of the glass, and make my way to unlock and push the door open.

"Lyle." I hold my breath, back up, and let him in. Lyle is always the first one in the library each morning, and he always offers a giant smile.

I admit I was judgy at first, before I knew him. His grungy jacket, too-big khaki pants, crazy hair, and messed-up teeth put me off, not to mention the sometimes overwhelming odor of his unwashed body—a smell like aged sweat and vinegar. Members of a local nonprofit offer a mobile shower once a week, at a nearby church parking lot and hand out bagged lunches at the same time. The odor has somewhat improved since I hooked Lyle up with them. They also got him some new shoes and the right size in pants. They even give haircuts occasionally. But I still don't have the guts to ask Lyle where or how he lives. I figure he'd tell me if he wanted me to know.

"Seen that pretty girl from the other day? The one that made your face turn all red?" He chuckles.

I laugh. "You'd know. You're here as much as I am."

"I don't know where you go outside a' here."

"No, I haven't seen her yet." I guess he's right. I haven't thought about him not knowing much about me outside these hallowed walls.

"Gotta be soon. Been a week."

"There were enough recipes in those books to last her a month."

"You let her check out too many books." He shakes his head slowly.

I grimace to inform him he can stop the harassment. "I'll let you know when the coffee is ready."

"Fair enough." He nods and moves to his favorite cushioned chair in one of the back corners. He'll probably sleep half the day. Makes me wonder if he has to stay awake through the night. Where does he sleep at night? I don't want to think about it. I already feel down. I'm not sure I can take on the woes of the world on top of mine.

My woe? It's dumb. But Lyle hit the nail on the head. I can't stop thinking about Girl Who Boils Water. I laugh to myself at the name I decided to give her. My coworker Nancy, and Lyle, are the only ones I've talked to about her. No girl has sparked my interest in quite a while, but this quirky stranger intrigues me. She was cute, in a nerdy sort of way. I've been told I'm cute in a nerdy sort of way too. A couple of girls described me that way. I'll take it.

"Hey Lover Boy, how's the coffee coming?"

Lyle gives me a serious expression. I glance at the clock, shocked. Fifteen minutes lost in a daydream.

"Sorry. I was distracted."

Lyle snickers at me. "Somebody's lovesick." He spreads his arms like he's presenting that detail to an audience. Thank goodness he's the only one in the library. Nancy doesn't come in for another forty-five minutes. I offered to open on Saturdays so she could have breakfast with her husband before he heads off to work. He's an attending physician at the hospital and works weird hours. Saturday mornings are the only mornings they have time together. It's easy enough for me to cover for my coworker.

I move to the flimsy card table in a corner near the kids' section, a little sitting area with a coffeepot where parents can rest while their little ones explore the kids' area or listen to the weekly story time. The only rules: use a lid and no drinks in the aisles. Our library tries to be user-friendly, tries to "keep the dream alive." The library in the neighboring town lost funding and shut down. I'm not sure how much time we have left, but for now, lightening up and offering coffee has kept people coming. Including Lyle. I pour him a cup and take it to where he lounges in the orange and brown scratchy plaid chair that, believe it or not, is one of the most comfortable in the place.

"Thank you very much, sir," he says, easing the cup out of my hands with his thumb and pointer finger. His other fingers splay as if lifting the cup into flight. I paint on a smile and return to my island of book returns. What have people been reading? It always interests me to see. I've gotten some pretty good recommendations that way.

The library door opens and blonde hair catches my eye. My head drops as what has to be a crazy smile overtakes my face. I try to gain composure and look up with what I hope is a relaxed smile.

"How's the cooking going?"

Girl Who Boils Water drops cookbooks in a pile on the counter in front of me and drums her hands on top. "I'm doomed."

I try to offer a sympathetic look. "But you can still boil water."

"No, no, I can't. I have officially been demoted."

"How so?"

"I killed my pasta pot." She pushes her turquoise frames up the bridge of her nose and lifts her hands in what I guess is dismay. "A watched pot doesn't boil, right?" She shakes her head and wags a finger at me. "I walk away for just a second for my latest read and *Boom!*" She flashes her hands like an explosion. "I boil the water beyond evaporation and cook my pot to oblivion. The smoke alarm goes off and my apartment still has a funky burnt-metal smell. Like I said, I'm doomed."

"You walked away to read? I assume something other than the cookbook."

"Yes." She looks at me like it should be obvious. "I love to read. Okay, so maybe it was more than a few seconds."

"Maybe."

She glares at me. I pinch my lips together, so I won't laugh or say anything else stupid. Her nostrils flare, but it's kind of cute.

21

"It's been nice knowing you." She turns to walk out.

"Wait. Let me help." That sounded a little too beggy, if I do say so myself.

Her blonde hair bounces ever so slightly as she turns around in slow motion. "How? You want to cook for me?"

I wouldn't mind. "Did any of these books help at all?"

"Well, about that amateur one?" She air quotes. "It's not amateur."

I could have told you that.

"And I tried the other two, but since the burning-water incident happened, I've lost hope." Her hand pounds on *Cooking for Amateurs.* "I need something with, I don't know, less than five ingredients. Something really, really, basic. But at the same time..."

Her eyes droop and her lips get pouty. *Oh no, don't notice her lips!*

"I need something to make cooking fun. I want to want to cook, but —" She nods her head to emphasize each word. "It's...just...not... happening."

"You want to want to cook? Why? You got a boyfriend you want to impress?" Oh wow, that came out before I could stop it. *Try to look cool, Hank.*

She gives me a funny look and shakes her head. "I don't have a boyfriend. I told you last time, I don't want to kill my friends. And now I'm even more worried since I've single-handedly become a water murderer." She smacks her hands to her thighs with a thud and hangs her head.

Oh man, I know I shouldn't think this, but she's adorable. "Let me show you the fun section."

Her head pops up, and like sunrise, a smile dawns across her face. I push through the swinging half door and gesture for her to join me as we walk under the Reading Rainbow banner hanging over the broad entrance.

"The kids' section?" She moans.

"Trust me." I look down at the sparkling blue eyes her turquoise glasses emphasize. "It is one of my favorite sections."

She walks with me, so I think she's buying in. We find the kids' cookbooks and I pull out my favorite one. It's got all kinds of other information to make food seem more interesting, including sly ways to teach nutrition. All the recipes are made with brightly colored food, arranged in visually appealing ways.

"You want me to make celery and peanut butter logs?" she says after leafing through the pages. "With raisins posing as ants?"

"There's a whole lot more within those pages," I say. "But making 'cookless' meals might be the way to start. Then get back on the horse and boil some water. We can build from there." I raise a finger. "And every recipe in that book has five or less ingredients. Thus the name."

"*Cooking for Kids with Five Ingredients or Less.* Sounds right up my alley." She looks at me, and her drab expression turns into amusement.

"So?" I feel my eyebrows rise a little too high.

"You seem awfully excited about this find."

"What?"

"The look on your face. You're pleased with yourself. You've saved the damsel in distress." She leers and raises an eyebrow at me.

"Wait. What? I was trying to be helpful." I rake my fingers through my hair and readjust my glasses. "It's my job. I—"

"You're patronizing me."

"No." Aw man, is that what she thinks?

Something pounds on my back, and a familiar smell passes my nose.

"Oh no, honey. He's got a crush on you. That's what the stupid look is all about."

My eyeballs nearly fall out of their sockets. "Really, Lyle?"

"Just helpin' out." He pats my chest like we are old chums. "He's been waiting for you to show. Watching for you every day."

"Not every day."

Lyle huffs a laugh, then nods at the girl who now *murders* water. "He's a good guy. He means well. I can vouch for him." He looks at me, winks, then mutters to himself as he walks away.

I close my eyes. "Sorry. Lyle is…"

"Your friend?"

"He comes to the library every day. I met him the day I started working here. He can be—" I try to choose my words carefully. "Full of stories."

"Like the rest of this place." The sound of her sweet giggle draws my attention from the brown nubby carpet to an amused smile and rounded pink cheeks.

"Yeah." I let out a sigh. "Like the rest of this place."

"Okay, library man, I will give this book a try. If it helps me, I'll be pleased. If not, I may need to resort to drastic measures."

"Drastic measures?"

She shakes her head and walks to the checkout counter. "You were the one who offered to help."

CHAPTER 6
WHAT'S BRINGING THIS ON?

CANDACE

W hat in the world was I thinking? I practically asked Library Guy out. I sure gave him permission to ask me out. He didn't seem to catch on, so I guess I'm okay.

But why didn't he catch on? Is it true he'd been waiting for me to show up, like his friend said? My stomach flutters almost to nausea. *Stop it, Candace. Focus on the task at hand.*

Celery, peanut butter, and raisins. Yeah, a simple start. I've successfully warmed up soup and such, but back to basics it is. I'm going to make every single recipe in this cookbook for kids. If kids can succeed with this book, I can. I used to be a kid. Hey, I still feel like one.

My teeth crunch down on the cold green veggie. The soft peanut butter makes my mouth water, and there's a spark of sweetness from the raisins. Okay, this is sad, but I think I just found my new favorite snack. I'll make this again. I giggle, then turn the page.

Cucumber and tomato with a slather of cream cheese and a sprinkle of dry dill. Sounds good to me, but would a typical kid like this? I'll have to make it for Jillian's kids next time they come to use the pool.

My hope rises after I munch on a half-dozen three-inch ant-covered logs, I sit down with a notepad and write out every ingredient needed for the entire cookbook. Diligence. Accuracy. Attentiveness. I will apply every skill needed to conquer cooking, follow every recipe to the T, just like the girl in *Julie and Julia*.

I meander to my bookshelf and wince at the title of the book that inspired the movie. Oh dear, is the title a warning? *My Year of Cooking Dangerously*. I'd love to curl up with the book and note every caution it has for me, but I need quick inspiration. I'll find the movie and watch it tonight.

Cooking my way through *Cooking with Kids* will build my confidence for greater things, right? I'll make an awesome holiday feast. I'll feed my friends with no demise and shock their pants off. Candace can-can cook!

———

My dearest friend in all creation sits across from me at the small bistro table. Her bright green eyes penetrate into my very soul. Sometimes I think she understands me more than I do. My emotions are close to the surface. A storm is brewing, but Jillian knows how to walk on water. I hope she can help me not sink my own boat.

Matthew's offer to take their kids to the park so Jillian and I could have girl time is just what I've come to expect from the sweetest guy I ever met. He must've seen a frantic look on my face when we were all talking after church this morning. Since we went to high school and college together, I can't hide much from either of them. They noticed each other for more than just someone to hang out with, before senior year at university. It made our threesome a little uncomfortable for a while, and jerked me into the role of third wheel. But now that I get to be auntie to the cutest kids ever, I can't complain.

"You're avoiding my question." Jillian raises an eyebrow at me. Her wavy strawberry-blonde hair is the perfect crown. She pulls off the persona of spicy Scottish woman like no one I know. Cute as a button, with a touch of blazing fireball underneath, she is funny and a blast to spend time with. And oh, do we have stories. She liked to climb trees and play in the dirt as much as me. We hit it off from day one.

"So you're interested?" she asks again.

"I don't know. I guess."

"You *are* interested!" She points a skinny finger at me and grins like the Cheshire cat. "Let's double-date."

"I haven't even gone out with him. I don't know if he's interested. Or if I've scared him away." I push my glasses into place. "I'm sure I've already given him reason for concern."

"How?"

"I told him I murdered water."

Jillian breaks into a roll of laughter. I can practically see the waves hit the shore as her giggles subside and then crash with new exuberance. "See!" Her voice gets caught on a chuckle. "That's why I love you."

"Because I kill water?"

"No!" She grabs her stomach. "Because that's how you explain it."

She washes a hand down her face and suddenly gets serious. "If he's worth his salt, he'll find you amusing and endearing. Just like Matthew and I do."

"Yeah, that's why I get asked out so much." I glower at her unintentionally. A soft spot has been poked.

Her hand drops on mine. "Oh Can-Can, all those other guys are just stupid. You need someone who can keep up with your vigor, your humor, your…"

"Lack of ability."

She squishes her face, and draws back as if I've hit her.

"What are you talking about? You are one of the smartest, most talented people I know."

"I just can't cook. Or get anyone to ask me out."

"What's bringing this on?"

I shake my head. What *is* bringing this on? I search the dark corners of my heart.

The truth? I'm jealous of my friends who are getting married, having kids, finding "the one" while I can't even get a date. Lately, it seems like my datelessness is being crammed in my face, and for whatever reason, I care more than I ever have. I've noticed how lonely I feel. Which is crazy because I have amazing friends who include me as much as they can in their lives. We get together consistently. But coming home each night to an empty apartment...

Maybe I need a cat.

Ugh! I'm allergic to cats.

"Okay. I've given you a sufficient amount of time and those wheels are a'turning. Let it out." With both eyebrows raised, Jillian looks like my third-grade teacher trying to coax information out of me.

I verbally barf all my ugly thoughts over the red-and-white checkered tablecloth. She listens, keeps eye contact, and doesn't say a word. So I blabber on. I hear myself say things I didn't even know about myself. Wow. I really got hurt by Pablo, and the wound I thought had healed apparently has not. I think maybe I've been sabotaging opportunities with my snark because I'm scared to get hurt. Or scared to be loved. Or, now that I'm a certain age, scared that love won't be what I hoped. Like I won't get the happy ending the way I think others do. *What am I saying?*

"Wow." Jillian sits up straight.

I contort my face. "That sounded ugly."

"No. It sounded honest."

"I'm an independent, successful woman. I'm not supposed to care about these things."

"Who says?"

I look at her, and wonder: who *does* say? All I know is that it feels like it's been pounded into my generation that you don't need a man, that you can have it all without one. And yes, I could. If that's what I wanted.

But you know what? I want to be married. I want to build a family of my own with the man of my dreams. And I don't think I'm unrealistic. I don't expect someone perfect. I just want to find someone I like to be around daily, someone who sparks my interest and loves me. Yeah, the whole love and be loved thing. I'll put up with his humanness and he'll put up with mine, and we'll teamwork through this life together.

Yeah. Lord, I really do want that. Is it in your plan?

My bold friend reaches across the table, holds my hand, and bows her head. Here she goes. My face flushes and my heart pounds as she prays. And yes, she prays out loud for not just God but the world around us to hear.

"Lord, you know what is going on in Candy's heart and mind. I can see the struggle, so you must really know. I don't think we have desires for no reason. Please be her comfort and help her as she waits. And if it is your will she meet someone and someday be married, then your will be done. And he better be the best guy on the face of the planet. Amen."

My head pops up and I draw my hand into my lap while I scan the restaurant to see if anyone is looking. Thankfully, it doesn't seem like anyone noticed our praying. "The best guy on the planet?"

"Why not?" She shrugs her shoulders. "Well, I have the best guy. I meant the best guy on the planet for *you*. God knows what I meant."

My sweet, bold friend. She can completely freak me out sometimes. But I love her. I admire her chutzpah and wish I could be like her, but praying in public feels forced and uncomfortable for me. I berate myself for feeling embarrassed about sharing my faith or being so bold in public. *God, I love you. You know that, right?*

CHAPTER 7
GET ON THE STARTING BLOCK

HANK

Every time I get on the starting block, I'm self-conscious. At least I'm not the only beanpole in a Speedo waiting to dive into the water. The announcer sets us, and the gun fires. I lunge my arms forward and kick off. For a second, I'm flying. I glide into the cool blue. As soon as my body slows a millisecond, I kick my legs and circle my arms. I've won against these guys before. I'm not ready to give up my title. Even amateurs like to be good at something.

Swimming serves my vow to stay in shape for the rest of my life, my goal for my older self is to thank my younger self for being disciplined. It all starts now. I will not allow the midlife paunch to overtake my lean, mean, string-bean machine.

At the flip turn, I assess my position with peripheral vision. Neck and neck with the Michael Phelps of the group, I still have some gas and streamline every last ounce of energy into the final lap. My hand hits the edge and I pop up to check my time. Not bad. Yup, I still got it. I congratulate the guys in neighboring lanes with the traditional handshake with pull in for a shoulder pat, then I hop out, dash to the locker room, and thank God for hot showers.

Typical talk breaks out as steam fogs the space. Rather than join in, I keep to myself. Yeah, I like girls, but the way some guys tout conquest and concentrate on body parts is not my jam. I thought we'd all move on from that kind of thing after college. I guess some guys don't grow out of it. Anyway, I'm here to swim and not to hang out.

Am I an old fogie? I guess I'm deciding who I want to be, and locker-room chatter doesn't match my goals. Old Fogies Club it is, then. Sign me up for the OFC! Except I hope I keep my sense of humor like some of the old guys I admire.

For now, I'll go home to my quiet little apartment, cuddle my cat, and read a recommended book from one of the OFC, *The Wingmen*. Man, you can tell I grew up with only sisters. That doesn't mean I don't know how to be manly. I can fix things. I'm responsible. And I can cook. My mom always says men should know how to cook and feed themselves, and it doesn't hurt to have that skill up your sleeve to impress someone sometimes.

Because a certain someone has been inspiring me lately, I think I'll make chicken cacciatore tonight. It's a shame I don't have someone to share it with. Who knows? One of these days, maybe that'll change. I might just get up the gumption to see if Girl Who Murders Water wants to cook together. I could help her learn. Huh, would she be interested?

My wheels turn on the drive home, my shirt bounces off my chest to its own beat because all I can think about is the girl with turquoise glasses. I really like this girl. I know I don't know much about her, but she's intriguing. And oddly honest. She doesn't put on some kind of "I got it all together" attitude. I'm not sure if she's interested in me, but visions of her pushing her glasses up the bridge of her nose to frame those sparkling blue eyes have cut into my thoughts at the strangest times. How much longer can I point her to cookbooks when all I want to do is ask if I can teach her myself?

Tomorrow is Saturday, so my hopes are up. Maybe she'll come into the library for another cookbook and be ready to move from the kids' section to cook with the adults. With *this* adult. She was pretty cute when she went on and on about her niece and nephew's excitement about the ants on the log. I can imagine her surrounded by kids smearing peanut butter on celery and throwing raisins at each other before planting them in place.

Aw man, I gotta stop this. My imagination is going wild. *Back to reality, Hank. If you like the girl, just ask her out, will ya?*

———

A familiar knock draws me away from the simmering pot on the stove. I open the door to a sullen face. Brown eyes shaped like mine shimmer with a transparent glaze, ready to overflow with tears.

"You okay, sis?" I back up, and welcome Megan inside. She bends to pick up Cat, makes her way to the couch, and plops down. "Guess not," I mumble and sit on the coffee table in front of her.

Here we go again. Like clockwork, my sister shows up to talk through the worry and pain she's been feeling for the last year. Shoot, I think I finished the ice cream off last night. "So?"

"Mom would kill you if she saw you sitting on the table she gave you in good faith."

"Meg, don't stall. What's up?" We've been close since we were little. While our three older sisters were off at cheerleading practice, hanging out at the mall with friends, or dating their most recent "love" interests, Megan and I played hide-and-seek or skateboarded around the neighborhood.

"I miss him." She nuzzles her face into Cat's fur, probably to hide tears.

"Only one more year."

She lets out a choked laugh. "That's if he decides not to stay longer. And even if he comes home in a year, then what? He's changing. I'm changing. What if… ?"

"You can't predict the future. You're gonna have to take it as it comes." That did not sound compassionate. I can tell she thinks it didn't by how high her eyebrows rise.

"Sorry. I don't know what to say." A sputter sounds from the kitchen. "Oh shoot!" I run to the stove and turn off the flame, and try to rescue dinner. "You hungry?" I look over the peninsula to where Megan sits on my old plaid couch. Man, even my home is reminiscent of the library.

Megan sets Cat down and comes into the kitchen to survey the nearly overcooked chicken. "I could eat."

After I bless our food, I silently pray to be prepared for whatever Megan needs to get off her chest. She takes a couple of bites before setting down her fork.

"I got a letter today. It was sweet. You know how Mike is. Just the basics—what he's up to, all the ways the corps is helping the community he's in, how he loves it. But not a word of how he loves..." She shakes her head and straightens. "Well, it's not like he has ever said *that*. Her fingers make air quotes and her voice deepens. "We'll see where we're headed. I'll write you every day." She lets out a *ha*. "Every week is more like it."

"What do you want him to say?"

"That he loves me and misses me and can't wait to hold me in his arms again."

Whoa, she is in rare form. She usually holds these cards closer to her chest. "You're telling *me* this? Have you told *him*?"

"I can't. It makes me sound uncompassionate. I feel guilty because I want his attention, his time and energy, whatever he gives to the people he serves. How off is that? Am I horrible?"

"You knew what you were in for when Mike signed up for the Peace Corps. You had that discussion, remember? That's why he didn't make any promises. He didn't want you to put your life on hold for him. That's what you told me." I shrug my shoulders. "You could date other guys if you want."

She glowers at me. "He's not just any guy. And I'm not the type to date *just* because I'm lonely." She looks at Cat meowing at her feet. "Maybe I need a cat."

I laugh. "I guess I could loan you Cat for a while."

Megan's eyebrows dance up and down while she laughs. "Then *you'd* be lonely."

She huffs a breath and becomes still. Her face sobers. Then her eyes light up the way they did when we were kids and she wanted to pry something out of me. "Wait! Why don't you look like my lonely little brother?" She circles a pointer finger at me like she's casting a spell. "You met someone."

"I thought tonight's conversation was about you."

"I'll get over it. I always do. I just needed to cry and vent. So tell me." She smacks her hands on the table. "Who's the lucky girl? I know you met someone." She wiggles all her fingers at me. "See. It's written all over your face."

I shake my head. "Nothing's happened. There's just this girl who's been coming into the library. She's cute and funny and spunky. I wouldn't mind getting to know her."

"So ask her out."

"That's what I keep telling myself. But—"

"Oh Hanky-poo, get over your awkward self. Ask her out. You're a great guy, she'd be blind not to notice you're worth getting to know."

"Says my unbiased sister."

"Ahh, no. Truth is truth." She circles a finger at me again like she knows some kind of secret. "You're blushing. You have a crush on her." She nods. "I bet she'd say yes if you asked her out."

Wouldn't it be nice if I could get the nerve to ask?

Megan stands. "Well, I've sufficiently been cheered. I have to get going." She takes her plate to the sink, rinses it, and stuffs it in the dishwasher. Then she taps my shoulder. "Walk me to the door and tell me you love me."

"Really?" I groan. "There is such a thing as too much PDA."

"Giving your sister a hug and telling her you love her is not a public display of affection. Besides, I need to hear it." She corrects me then shifts to sing cheerfully, "I'll always love you."

"I love you, sis." My monotone is grumpy but obedient.

Before we reach the door, we sing "always and forever" in unison and laugh. Our parents reprimand us to this day for cracking up during our cousins' wedding when they sang the Heatwave song to each other.

CHAPTER 8
MR. LIBRARY

CANDACE

Dang it! My heart is already racing, and I haven't even made it out of my car. *Lord, help me.* This is now a Saturday tradition. I don't need to be here. I haven't made every recipe in the books I have, but I think I want to graduate to something more. That is the excuse I use so I can see the cute librarian.

I push through the filmy glass door and see a smile on his face. My gaze drops to my hand on the door handle. My cheeks must be red, I can feel the heat in my eyeballs. *You have to look up, Can-Can. Act casual.*

"Hi," he says, his brown eyes sparkle behind his studious rims.

"Hello." I try to keep my smile small.

"No returns?"

I look down at my empty hands. "I can keep them for three weeks, right?"

"Yeah, I-I just uh…" He's even cuter when he stutters. "What can I help you with today?"

"I want to graduate. I still want to complete every recipe in the kids' book for good measure. But I can't have a dinner party of ants on a log and cucumber stacks."

"Hors d'oeuvres?"

We both laugh. He looks around, and I follow his gaze. A handful of kids and moms are in the juvenile section, a newspaper blocks a guy's face in the reference section, and the back corner's resident is in his usual place. I turn back to see Mr. Library's eyes fixed on me. I'm not sure what the expression on his face means, but if I were to guess, it looks like, well, adoration. Yikes! What am I thinking?

"Looks like I'm free at the moment. What is your goal in coming to the library today?"

To get you to ask me out. I stifle a snicker. "Well, could you direct me to a simple but more grown-up cookbook?"

He glides out from behind the counter and waves his hand. "Follow me."

We both know where he's going, but I follow one step behind, willing my heart rate toward a normal pace. I don't want him to hear the nervous jitters pounding in my throat.

"Here we are." He faces the books as if they are a gold mine. His hands wave over the titles like he's performing magic, then he hooks a finger over the top of a book and presents it to me like a treasure.

Simple Meals in 30 Minutes or Less. The picture on the cover makes my mouth water, reminding me I forgot to eat this morning. I look at him cheerfully. "Perfect."

His lips curve up. I wonder what he looks like without his glasses. I mean, they work for him, but they cover his cheekbones and mask his eyebrows. I bet his hair is soft. It has a silky look to it.

"Did you want something more?"

"Oh. Um, no. This looks great!" I grab the book out of his hands and swiftly trot to the checkout desk. *What's the rush, Can-Can? He has to check you out, you know.*

I feel stupid as I stand like a statue and watch him move behind the counter. His hip hits a corner where the Formica is chipped off. He grunts as he slaps a hand over his injury.

"I keep doing that!" He looks up to the ceiling, and I notice how his hair waves back as if a gentle breeze is wisping through it.

I sigh, then slap my hand over my mouth. "I-I'm sorry. Does it hurt?"

Half his face squishes up as he gazes at me. "I'll survive."

"Good." I try to give him a compassionate smile.

"This will do it?" He pulls the book back into his hands and shows it to me.

No. I want to linger here and stare at you all afternoon. "I guess so. Thanks."

"Okay." He looks disappointed as he opens the book to reveal the scan code. I study the counter.

"Hope you have good success with the cooking, Candace."

"What?" My face pops up. "How do you know my name?"

"Your library card kinda tells me who you are."

There's heat in my cheeks again. *Cover your stupidity with humor, Candace.* "So you can hunt me down if you want to?" I ask, feigning alarm.

"I swore, by oath, to protect library patrons. I may hunt down books, but not you. Scout's honor." He lifts two fingers and a corner of his lips.

His pupils are large but still show the full-bodied chocolate brown in his eyes. He has decent eyelashes too. Why do guys have some of the best eyelashes? I'd have to use triple coats of mascara to get mine that full.

"Candace?"

My hand nervously fingers the bee charm dangling from the chain around my neck. I never wear necklaces. Why'd I put this one on today? I clear my throat. "You know my name, Mr. Library. But I don't know yours."

"I kind of like you calling me Mr. Library."

I smirk. "No really. What's your name."

"Nothing glamorous, I'm afraid." He tilts his head like he doesn't like his own name. "Henry, officially. But my friends call me Hank."

"That's my grandpa's name. It's a good solid name." My heart warms.

"Well, Hank, it's nice to officially meet you." I offer my hand over the counter. "Even though we've already met." I shake my head and inwardly roll my eyes at myself. Our hands dance up and down a couple of times, he gently squeezes mine, then quickly lets go and wipes his hand against his pants.

"Sweaty palms," he says with a jittery chuckle.

I step forward and bump into the edge of the counter. *What are you doing, Can-Can?*

"Do you… ?" I straighten and rethink what almost escaped my lips. "Do you know how to cook?" *Great cover. Not what you wanted to say, but good save.*

He offers a confused look. "Yeah. I've cooked every recipe in every book in our cooking section."

"Seriously?" Now I'm intrigued.

"Research. So I know how to direct patrons like you." He gives a coy smile. "Why do you ask?"

Oh, here the rubber meets the road. "Well, maybe you could give me a few tips."

"I thought that was what I was doing. Directing you to appropriate cookbooks." He raises an eyebrow and volleys the conversation back to me.

My arms drop to my side as I let out a too-loud huff. "Okay, I was thinking of help that's more…" I fumble my hands in front of me.

"Hands-on?"

Oh, he is enjoying my awkwardness way too much. I give him a stink eye. He lets out a low chuckle.

"Yes, do you think we could talk or something?" I scan the library. "Maybe somewhere else? I've been reprimanded on multiple occasions for making too much noise in this establishment."

The corner of his lip rises. "What do you have in mind?"

I can't believe I'm doing this. My hand rubs my forehead. Can I wash this idea out of my mind? Can I save myself from rejection and embarrassment?

"Will you help me cook one of these recipes?" I reach for my checked book and wave it at him. And yep! I have officially made a fool of myself. What in the world has gotten into me?

CHAPTER 9
WHAT DO I DO?

HANK

I s it my imagination, or did she just ask me out? I'm not sure how to answer. "Okay."

"Does that mean you will?" She has a look that could be interpreted as fear.

"Sure. It'll be fun." I try to make light of the idea, to set her at ease. "When do you want to make this meal?"

Her big blue eyes bat at me. "I don't know. When do you want to?"

Now. "I don't have anything on the calendar tonight?" *Oooo, too desperate? Well, too late.*

"Really?" Her face lights up. "Me either. What time do you get off?"

I feel my face make the Richie Cunningham smile I used to get teased for. "Library closes at five. It doesn't take long to clean up the joint. I could get out of here by five thirty."

"So, how does this work?" Her face shifts to freak-out mode.

"How 'bout we pretend I just asked you out?" Oh man, that sounded patronizing. *Dumb move, Hank.* "Sorry. That came out before I thought through how it might sound."

"I'm okay passing the baton to you. I've never—I don't—"

"Tell you what." I think for a second. "Why don't you meet me here at five thirty. We can choose the recipe then, or you can figure it out ahead of time. We could walk across the parking lot to Lucky's grocery and get the ingredients, then it's up to you if you want to cook at my house or yours."

She has a sweet smile. One of those smiles that lets you know she truly cares for others. Kind, gentle, nice. Nice doesn't seem to be as popular anymore. But I like nice!

"I like your idea, and I think I'd be more comfortable at my apartment." She squints her face, looking apologetic.

"Totally fine."

"Great." She picks up her book and hugs it to her chest. "See you at five thirty, then."

"Five thirty," I say to the back of her head, and watch her long tresses bounce with each step until the dingy glass door blurs my view of her.

"I saw the whole transaction. Got a date with Blondie, I see." Lyle chuckles under his breath as he leans against the counter.

"I think she asked me out before I could get up the gumption to ask her out."

"Lucky guy." He raises an eyebrow at me.

"Well, I'm not sure it can be considered a date. She asked me to help her cook one of the recipes in the book."

"Yeah, it's a date." Lyle hits the counter with his grubby hand.

I give him a forlorn look.

"Buddy, it's a good thing."

"I know."

"Then why the look?"

It's suddenly real. "Out of practice. Bad experiences. Don't want to get my hopes up."

His hair waves in chunks as he shakes his head at me. "You only live once."

"You only live once?" I raise an eyebrow at him.

"Oh, don't get all judgy on me. You haven't heard the whole story."

"Enough to know your life could be different. Maybe better?" I think the guy has more potential than he will acknowledge.

"Currently I like my life. I do what I want when I want. No one bosses me around."

"You barely survive." I try to see into him. I just don't get it. I've tried to put myself in his position, based on the little that I know. But I just try to come up with a plan to find him a home, a job. He doesn't seem to care to make a change.

Wow, Hank, you are judgy. "Okay. One of these days, Lyle, I want you to tell me the whole story. I want to understand, because honestly, right now, I don't. You're a great guy. Quirky, yeah, but aren't we all? I don't know if I could be okay living like you do."

He frowns at me. "Like I said, you don't know the whole story."

"Tell me."

"Tomorrow." He walks out the door with his multiple plastic bags, leaving unusually early. I offended him. *Lord, I'm sorry. I don't know what to think, what to say. I'm trying.*

———

For someone who has experienced one of the best things to happen to him in a long time, I've spent the rest of my shift in a strange funk, going through the motions. I feel the life drained out of me. The Lyle thing haunts me. If I were at home, I'd cocoon in my bedroom and pray until hope returned. Instead, here I am staring at a snotty-nosed kid who wants a half-dozen Dr. Suess books. Even the bright colors and whimsical characters on the covers don't cheer me up.

Once the last patron pushes through the exit. I slouch toward the door and lock it. Blah! I gotta get in a better mood before Candace gets here. I don't want her to think I'm a dud. I slide a dustrag over the counters and go to the closet to pull out the vacuum.

Vacuuming the library every night not only keeps the place clean, but relieves my allergies. When I first started here, I would go home sick from an overload of funky, musty dust. Massive headaches, itchy eyes, runny nose. Once I deduced why, I started to vacuum at the end of every shift. The difference is amazing.

Nowadays, the library puts the money toward more books, instead of outside cleaners. I'm not sure what the cleaners did. Clean the bathrooms maybe? So yeah, I do that too. As I dust every bookcase and display, I get the chance to scan the shelves and read the titles. It connects me to the place, the books, the words. Some may consider me a dork because of that. Maybe I am.

The dwindling glimmer of light from outside is cut off as I close the last shade. Once every light switch is off, the library gets an eerie stillness. The scuff of my shoes on the nubby carpet accompanies me to the entry door. I peer out but don't see a silver Corolla. My wristwatch says I closed in record time, so I sit in the plaid seventies-style chair, where I can see the front door.

I've waited for silence all day. I realistically have ten minutes of it. So...

Lord, I'm sorry I put my foot in my mouth with Lyle. You know what's really going on there. You know the things I've asked you about him. Help him to be okay. Help his needs to be met. And help me to care for him the way you want me to. I just don't know what to do. What do I do?

In the quiet, I wait and listen. Will anything new stir in my heart?

A warm melancholy swirls in my gut. Peace and comfort bubble up, soothing yet aching. I'll never understand how those two sensations go together, but my grandma called it hurting for the world. She said it was a good thing. *"It means you care. It means you're still listening to the voice of love."* Thank God for Gran! I miss her.

My elbows are on my knees, my hands are in my hair, and my eyes are squeezed shut when I hear a rat-a-tat-tat on the door.

CHAPTER 10
COOKING TOGETHER

HANK

y head pops up to a beautiful smile on the other side of the window. Warmth floats through me, and heats every corner of my being. I beeline to the door, turn the deadbolt, and push it open.

"Hi," I say softly, as if there are still patrons inside.

"Hi," Candace whispers back.

"I guess it's a habit to talk quietly, but we don't have to." I try to laugh, but a weird cough comes out, so I point to the cookbook in her hand. "You wanna look at the book and choose a recipe here?" I sweep my hand in a grand gesture for her to come in.

"Sure." She breezes past, a wisp of lilac follows her. I breathe in a moment of simple pleasure.

I lock the door and join her at the open table she's claimed and sit across from her. She sets the book in front of her and raises an eyebrow at me.

"Can you see from there?"

"Upside down." I don't want to be too forward.

"Here." She pats the chair next to her with a smile and doesn't have to ask twice. "Since you've cooked through all the cookbooks, I thought you might have a good suggestion on where to start in this one."

From the seat beside her, I look into her eyes. I've never been this close to her before. My temperature rises and my heart dances inside my chest.

Her button nose squishes up, and her hands drum on the book cover. She raises both eyebrows and her glasses slip down her nose. The way she pushes her glasses back in place and giggles is so cute. "So?"

"Oh. Well— " I reach for the book, move it in front of me, and scan the table of contents. I turn to page thirty-two and scoot it back in front of her. "What do you think?"

"That's the one I killed water trying to make."

"I'll be with you this time. No murders on my watch."

Thankfully, Candace laughs.

———

Thirty minutes later, I roll our cart of ingredients up to Lucky's magazine-infested checkout and cram a debit card in the machine before Candace can. She gripes at me, but I insist, so she gives up. I carry the full brown paper bag to her car.

"Shall I follow you?"

She nods.

"Can I have your address, in case you're a speed demon?"

She gives me an annoyed look.

"Or in case a light turns red on me?" I plaster an appeasing smile across my face.

"Good thing you're cute," she says as she scribbles her address on an old receipt and hands it to me.

Heat rises to my face. I wonder if she knows what she said. She thinks I'm cute. Score me!

"There's a guest spot next to my parking space. I'll see you there." She closes her car door.

After scrambling to my car at the back of the lot, I look in my rearview mirror and comb my fingers through my hair. Then I grin as I follow Candace into Saturday-evening traffic.

I feel like a cop trailing someone on their best behavior. Her driving is impeccable. She even stops when the light turns yellow, so she won't lose me. Which would be hard at this point. I pull into the parking space of a clean, well-manicured complex. There's no apartment number written on the receipt. I turn it over and notice it's from a hardware store and records a strange purchase. Ladybugs?

A tap rattles my window. I look up, and Candace waves me out.

"Nothing fancy. But I like it here and it's safe."

"I don't need fancy. Safe is preferred." I keep in step alongside her and pull the bag out of her hands.

"Chivalry isn't dead." She winks at me.

We travel a sequence of concrete walkways surrounded by patches of grass and juniper hedges. The pungent evergreen smell prickles my nose. An older gentleman waters plants on his front porch liberally splashing water on the ground as he looks up and offers a friendly smile.

"I see you have company." His eyes graze from me to Candace.

"Neighbor Bob, this is Hank. Hank, this is my good neighbor Bob."

I put out a hand, which he pumps up and down. "You wouldn't be Mr. Library, would you? You look the part."

She mentioned me? I look at the red spreading across her face and then at him, not sure if I should let my exuberance show. "That's me."

He winks and ducks his head as if to tell me a secret. "I know her cooking woes. Had to save her a few times myself."

"Bob!" Candace exclaims.

He chuckles and aims his waterspout at a terra-cotta pot with green and white moss on the outside. "You two have fun."

Candace unlocks her door and walks in. I follow into a place bright with natural light and a feminine touch. Cheerful yellows and blues accent the ecru couch. A fuzzy tasseled blanket is thrown neatly over the back of a navy wing chair. A simple coffee table supports three canister candles in the center and a pile of books. I chuckle and nod my head to the book on top. "The culprit?"

She laughs. "Oh, Percy's always getting in sticky situations."

The combination of orange blossom, lemon, and basil diffuses through the air as we drift toward a white-tiled peninsula.

"My kitchen," she announces.

"Oh." I point to the blackened fan hood above the stove.

"Yeah. Evidence of the crime scene." She huffs and claps her hands against the side of her legs.

I look around for something to help change the subject, and notice a large bowl of oranges and lemons on the counter. "You eat that much fruit?"

She blushes, then shakes her head. "What I can't eat I send down the disposal to take care of the sink stink. Plus, they are pretty to look at." She pats the squeaky-clean countertop. "You can set the groceries here."

I set the bag down. "Nice place."

"Oh, don't be fooled. Once I knew you'd be coming here, I spent the rest of the day cleaning." She raises her eyebrows and leans in. "Found things I didn't even know existed."

"You didn't need to go to the trouble for me."

"Trust me, I did." Her nose squishes up. "Sink stink."

"Okay. Well, I can't fault you for lack of honesty."

She opens her hands. "This is me. You get what you see. I figure you already know my greatest weakness. Why try to hide under a cloak of fake perfection?"

"Oh good. Just so you know. I'm not perfect either." I feel more at ease than I expected. "Great way to begin a, um, friendship."

A twinge flashes in her eyes, then she smiles and nods. "I agree."

After she unloads the groceries, I fold the bag, and she points to the cabinet under the kitchen sink. There I find another paper bag filled with various other bags. She's a recycler. Nice.

Water hisses out of the faucet as she fills a saucepan, which she puts on to boil.

"I do know this part," she snarks at me. I must have a questioning look on my face.

"Anything larger to cook with?"

"No. Remember? I killed the pasta pot. And it was my grandma's, one of her favorites. She gave it to me as a graduation present, knowing I was going to move out on my own. My mom will kill me if she finds out I abused my grandma's offering for my independence."

If this goes well, I can help the situation. I have pots galore. Is that sad, a single man enjoys good cookware?

I open the cookbook to page thirty-two. She doesn't have to know I know the recipe by heart. I point to the next steps and read them to her. We fumble around each other, then I step back, so she can wash her hands before I wash the vegetables.

She pulls out two chopping boards and two sad, dull knives. I begin to julienne the carrots and zucchini the way I like as she hesitantly peels off the outer layer of an onion. Shame rushes over me. I should have thought to grab the onion before she could. I open my hand to her, and she looks down at it with an alarmed look.

"The onion."

"Oh," she says in what must be relief. Did she think I was asking to hold her hand? I snicker.

"What?"

"Nothing." I shake my head. Would it be so bad to hold my hand?

"You obviously know what you're doing. I'd still be washing the vegetables, not practically done chopping them." She pops a quarter-inch strip of zucchini in her mouth, chomps a few times, and grins.

Her expression makes me laugh. "We are kind of cheating here with the rotisserie chicken, but it's how you get the meal done in less than thirty minutes. I can take the meat off the bones while you get one of your larger pans."

"I haven't killed my fry pan yet." She opens a cabinet. Clangs and bangs fill the air, then she produces a copper-colored wok. "Voilà!"

"That'll work. Why don't you heat about two tablespoons of olive oil in the pan? Then we can sauté the veggies." I scoop up the onion pieces with a sniff. "Thank God for glasses. This onion is potent."

She laughs and approaches the pot steaming on the stove. Her glasses fog up. She has no idea how cute she looks as she reaches out like a zombie and giggles. "I can't see. I can't see."

Just what I needed, lightheartedness and laughter. Whatever weighed me down earlier is vanquished by the space she's taking up in my brain. *Lord, thank you.*

The noodles are ready. While the primavera bubbles—red, green, and orange vegetables dance in the sauce—I ask for the biggest bowl she has. She presents a beautiful hand-painted pasta bowl made in Italy.

"Another of my grandma's gifts."

"It looks like it's seen some amazing meals. Tonight's will be another. And you made it!"

"With your help."

"Team effort."

She seems to like the comment, from the way she sways forward and back, toes to heels. The table is set, so I place the bowl of steaming fettuccini on it, next to the grated parmesan, green salad, and fresh sourdough. Warm savory smells make my mouth water. We sit to eat, and I wait for my next cue.

"Um, I usually do a little thing." She holds her palms against each other. "Do you mind?"

"Not at all."

"I know you helped make the food, so we are probably safe. But…" She points to the ceiling. "Divine intervention is always a good way to go. Especially in this house."

I stifle a laugh, fold my hands in my lap, bow my head, and whisper "Go for it."

She clears her throat, obviously nervous to expose this part of who she is, but I'm grateful. "Dear Lord, thank you for this day, for this food, and for this company. Please don't let any of it make us sick." Her voice travels to a higher pitch as she says "Thanks so much," then it drops down to a soft "Amen."

Head raised, I scan her face. "Thank you. I have even greater confidence we will survive dinner."

She laughs effortlessly, as if laughter is her native language, and raises her plate to me. I serve her with two big forks as best I can. When some noodles flop onto the table, she grabs them with her fingers and pops them in her mouth.

Her eyes brighten. "Wow, so good."

Conversation flows easily. She asks about Lyle, and I tell her what little I know. Then she lights up as she talks about bugs, and how she advocates for them. Mainly, she advocates for honeybees.

"Save the honeybees, save the people. That's my motto. I believe in saving the bees." She glows as she shares about her passion—the research she's done and how many times she's been stung, which seems like a crazy amount, but she says it's minimal compared to some of her peers.

We talk about our hobbies. Mine? "Swimming mostly. You know, typical high school athlete, drama club, choir."

"Typical?"

I give her a sheepish grin. "Okay, I just wanted to see your reaction. Swim team, yes. But I can't act and I'm not so great at singing either. I love a good movie or concert, though."

"Well, that we can agree on. I'm not much of a swimmer. I do love to lounge around and float on the water on a hot day, but the sun doesn't really like me." She raises one arm and points out all the cute little freckles in various configurations.

I point to the spattering on my face. "Irish."

She nods and pulls at her hair. "Scandinavian."

"Both Northern European. Maybe we're related."

"I hope not!" She grabs her mouth, then waves her hand at me. "Not that you aren't decent. I just..." Her face flushes as she pushes food around on her plate.

A crazy grin threatens to take over my face. "You don't have to finish."

"Oh, but the food's good. And I'm a member of the clean-plate club."

I laugh. "Not what I was talking about, but okay."

We clear our plates and drop them into sudsy water in the sink. She covers the pasta bowl, salad bowl, and leftover bread with foil. I must have a funny look, because she stumbles over her words to explain her actions.

"I don't want to take too much time cleaning when I have company. Believe me, there's plenty of space in my fridge."

I hand her the last dried plate and suddenly feel paralyzed. What now? I'm not sure what she wants. Maybe I should go. "Well, thanks for the meal and the company. I guess I should be going."

Her eyes grow large. "Oh, okay." She doesn't move. "Well, thanks for your help. I think I learned a valuable lesson tonight."

"And what's that?"

"Maybe the key is to stay in the kitchen when cooking."

Stay. I tilt my head. I'd like to stay. *Calm your nerves, Hank.*

"I usually sit and read a little." She points across the kitchen peninsula to the wing chair in the living room. "Maybe it's not the best setup for success."

I nod. "Maybe not when you have something on the stove." She looks at the apartment door, so I look at the door. "Well, I'm happy to help." Maybe we could do this again, I want to say, but I'm not sure where this is going.

An awkward thought invades my mind. Do I kiss her goodnight? I look at her. She sways from left to right and pushes her glasses into place. I mimic her accidentally. I just don't know what to do with my hands.

Her phone rings and we both jump. She points over her shoulder, retrieves her phone from the counter, and looks at the screen.

"Oh, it's my friend." She sets her finger ready to answer.

Her friend? One of those friend calls designated for such-and-such a time to get rid of the guy? I've had that happen before. My hope deflates. "Okay, I'll get out of your hair. Well, thanks!" I stride to the door and open it.

There's shuffling behind me, but I'm not sure if I should look back or keep going. I fumble at my car door and throw myself into my seat. She waves at me from her apartment with, I don't know, maybe a smile. I can't tell from here. I wave and start the car. It was fun while it lasted.

CHAPTER 11
THE ONE EVERYONE COMPARES TO

CANDACE

M y overstuffed chair lets out a *pff* as I plop into it, pull my knees to my chest, and groan into my phone.

"I guess I blew it."

"Why do you say that?" Jillian asks as kids scream in the background.

"He left. I thought we were having a nice time. He's easy to talk to. And wow! I've never been party to cooking such a good meal."

"Maybe you didn't blow it," she says before resorting to screams herself. "Kids, cut it out! I'm talking to Auntie Can-Can." Children's voices descend into the phone.

"Hi, Auntie!"

"When are you coming over?"

Stories of their mischief overtake the line. I guess this is what I needed, to know some people adore me.

Jillian comes back on the phone. "I'm so sorry, Can-Can. I've gotta get these kids situated. They have way too much energy, and we have to go to the early service tomorrow. That's why I called. I can't do Sunday lunch. We have to go see Matt's folks. Mom's not doing well. She's apprehensive about the possibility of cancer and her surgery. Dad thought the kids would cheer her up."

"I understand. Another time."

"Thanks, friend. I'll check in when we get back." She hums to announce a song is on the way, and I expect the line that always makes me smile. "Every little thing is gonna be alright." A picture of her dressed as a pink and purple cat comes to mind. She sang the line to me on Halloween last year after Pablo and I broke up. That night we devoured a carton of mint chocolate chip ice cream and watched old comedy shows on youtube. We found The Carol Burnett Show, her guest was Phyllis Diller. When I looked at Jillian, her face paint had smeared into high eyebrows like Phyllis Diller's. We laughed so hard we decided then and there the following Halloween we'd dress up as Carol and Phyllis.

"Thanks."

"Love you."

"Me too."

I hang up and stare at the ocean waves on my phone's wallpaper, a sensation like seasickness threatens. *Don't let negative feelings overtake you. You had a lovely time. Focus on that. Maybe Hank was just nervous, like you.* I throw my phone on the couch and decide to go for a long walk before it gets too dark.

———

On Sunday morning, I go to the late church service. Have faith the size of a mustard seed is the theme. I guess a little faith is all I need. *Okay, Lord, what now?*

There is no logical reason for me to feel lost, but I do. I wander out of the sanctuary and past multiple groups of people. Friendly hellos and nice-to-see-you's are aimed at me, and I'm grateful, but I keep moving. I walk the long sidewalk to the section where my car is parked and get in. The leaves on the trees in the planter across from me are a pretty crimson at the edges. The season is changing, and a breeze rustles through the trees, whispering "Get ready." For what, I'm not sure.

I start the car and drive to see where the road takes me. Twenty minutes later, I find myself in the library parking lot. I don't know why. It's noon and Lyle is seated in a heap on the ground, his back against the concrete wall. I get out and wander over to him.

"Hey, Blondie! What are you doing here?"

"I don't know. Guess I didn't have anything else to do."

"Lover Boy doesn't work on Sundays."

I smirk at him. "I came here on a whim. Maybe I came here to see you." The sarcasm flew out my mouth, and the thought startles me, but maybe I did come here to get to know Lyle. He comes to mind often. As I mentioned to Hank last night, I'm not sure why.

"Me?" Lyle holds his hand against his chest in mock surprise.

"Why not?"

"This place is usually open by now. I haven't even had my morning coffee."

An opportunity presents itself. I look down the road, then wave a hand for him to join me. He hides all but one of his plastic bags in the planter behind a big fern, and tucks one inside his jacket. We move through the next-door mall's car-infested parking lot to the McDonald's at the end of the strip.

"Not the healthiest restaurant."

"You don't hear any complaints from me."

Lyle orders first. I tell him to get anything he wants, my treat in exchange for some of his fascinating stories Hank mentioned to me. Lyle's game and orders a chicken sandwich, a quarter pounder, fries, and an apple pie, along with a large coffee. I order a McMuffin and a coffee. When our orders are up, we gather them and move to a corner table where we can talk.

"So. What do ya wanna know?" Lyle asks.

"You're getting right into it, aren't you?"

He huffs and looks down. "Look, I have people do this a lot. Help the local tramp, give him food, act like ya care, then move on. I guess I should just be grateful. It's a meal I wouldn't get otherwise. But it'd be nice to keep a few friends."

Hmm. I tilt my head and ponder the comment until he continues.

"Meeting Hank has been the closest thing to a friend I've had in a while. He listens. Asks me questions on a daily. Every time I'm at the library, at least one of his breaks is spent talking exclusively to me. He's even stayed late to hear the end of one of my stories."

I nod, and remember the one thing Hank mentioned last night that he hasn't asked Lyle. "Where do you live?"

Lyle laughs, throws his head back, and sweeps a hand toward the window. "Out there."

"Where?"

"You want to come visit?"

"I have no idea. I just want to understand."

"Understand what? Why a thirty-something-year-old man lives alone on the streets, spends his days stinking up the library, merely to survive?"

"Is that how you define your life?"

He stares at me and doesn't say anything. We each take a bite of sandwich and a swig of coffee. The clap of both our cups hitting the table breaks the silence.

"Okay, I'll tell ya, Lady."

"Oh, now I'm 'Lady'?"

"Ya like Blondie better?"

"Not really. My name would be fine. Candace."

"Pretty name. Can't say you look like a Candace. I would've thought Bridget."

Okay, why? I blink at him in confusion but he doesn't notice my reaction. He starts his story.

"I went to college and, like most students, played around with drugs and alcohol. Thought what I was up to was normal, ya know, just like the other kids. But..." He smiles and shows me his decayed teeth and grayed gums. "Meth. Dropped out of school, lost my job, family had enough with me, and here I am years later."

"You've been living on the streets for years?"

"Family took me in for a while. When they kicked me out, people with the same addictions let me hang with them until they didn't. I guess I was farther down the rabbit hole than them."

Lyle focuses on his fries until the last one is gone, then continues. "I ultimately ended up at the gospel mission. They offered help with addiction. I tried. Got clean, fell back into drugs, got clean, fell back into it. Broke the rules too many times, so on the street I went. The city I was living in offered to bus me and others on the streets up here. So…"

He spreads his hands. "This place is a little friendlier to the homeless than where I was before. Now I rotate around to different camps until I'm kicked to the next one. I try to stay within walking distance of the library. It's been the one consistent thing makin' it worth staying alive."

"Wow. I don't know what to say."

"Yeah, most don't." He runs his wrinkled, scabbed hand through his greasy hair.

"Do you want this to be your life?"

He laughs. "Everyone asks me that, including your lover boy."

"He's not my lover boy. He's just helping me learn to cook."

Lyle's face goes dark as his eyes stare out the window. "I could tell you about the year I learned to cook." He jerks his head like he's been shaken back to reality and looks at me. "You wouldn't mind more between you and Hank, would you?"

My lips pinch tight. I've gotten all up into his life, so I guess it's fair if he does the same.

"He seems like a nice guy. I wouldn't mind getting to know him better."

Lyle nods. "He *is* a nice guy. Wish I could be like him."

"What would that take?"

"That's ripe." He gives me a crazy-looking grin. "Like I haven't heard it before."

"Do you have an answer?"

"Be somebody else," he says. "Almost anyone other than me."

My heart pounds. His firm response devastates me. I'd swear I'm supposed to have some kind of miraculous response that lifts him out of poverty and into a simple, self-sufficient life.

"Blondie, my choices put me here, and my choices keep me here. But for the grace of God… Well, you know the saying. I'm the one everyone compares to."

"You don't think grace is offered to you?"

"Maybe it is. I'm just too deep in for any help." He closes his eyes. "I'm tired. I'm done with the interrogation."

We must've reached all the truth I can take too. My already depleted soul is incredibly drained. "Library?"

He opens his eyes and nods. We walk back to the still-closed library and sit on the concrete retaining wall, watching people go to the window and cup their hands to look inside. A crowd has formed, with shared complaints that the library opens at noon but it's already one thirty.

"Sorry, everyone!" a voice shouts from the parking lot.

A flurry of brown hair flops across Hank's glasses as he jogs toward the library. The rattle of his keys quiets the swarm of people. His eyes catch mine, and a smile breezes across his face before the crowd parts to let him through.

Lyle stands up. "It's your lucky day, Blondie. Lover Boy never works on Sundays."

CHAPTER 12
YOU WANTED TO SEE ME?

HANK

My entire day has been off. I woke up late, so the late service was my only option for church. Unfamiliar faces surrounded me, but the message was good. Love one another. We can never hear that enough. God knows we could all use a little more love in this world these days.

I scoot out the back door and weave through boisterous conversations toward the parking lot, where I toss my bulletin on the passenger seat of my car and open the glove box. I make a point not to take my phone into the sanctuary. My skin crawls when a ring interrupts the flow right as the pastor gets to a crucial point.

Man, I must still be cranky about last night. I blew it. What's new? I got antsy and nervous, so I dodged out of Candace's place even though I really didn't want to leave. Her phone's ringtone sent an uncomfortable pain through my chest. I have more than one bad memory of a girl ditching me after a phone call, so I bolted.

I gotta get rid of this pent up angst, so I'll head to the gym and swim enough intervals to work out all this emotion. The release of endorphins always puts me in a better mental state. I toss my phone back in the glove box and drive.

After speed training in the pool and a hot shower I make my way back to my car. My workout and the sunshine has somewhat lifted my mood. My car door screeches as I get in. I pull my phone out of the glove box and find several missed calls, but none from Candace. A text from my coworker Libby catches my attention. *My car broke down. I can't get a hold of anyone. Can you open the library?*

I look at my watch. Great, it's already late. I punch in Libby's number.

Her hello is shaky. "No, no one else has called. I'm so sorry, Hank, but I'm stuck here for who knows how long. Do you mind taking my shift?"

I put my car in reverse and head to my home away from home. What do I have planned anyway? Cleaning out my fridge?

A dozen people hover outside the library's front door. I race out of my car, slam the door, and run to my stone castle.

"Sorry, everyone!" I shake the keys as I dodge my way around the people. My eyes scan the crowd. Lyle is seated on the edge of the planter with a silly grin on his face. Next to him sits Candace! My cheeks heat. I hope I don't look stupid. I focus on unlocking the front door and letting everyone in, apologizing profusely to each patron.

With the flood of people, uncharacteristic noise enters the building. Lyle holds the door open as Candace breezes in. Her floral pink dress matches her lipstick. Great, she has a date and is here to rub it in my face. Man, she looks pretty.

She stops in front of me and irons her skirt with her hands. "I came here from church. I didn't even go home."

"It's nice to see you."

"Lyle and I just had a chat over brunch."

She had a date with Lyle?

Lyle pats my forearm. "She bought me coffee at McDonalds."

Candace stumbles over words and settles on "It was educational."

"Yeah." Lyle grunts. "Thanks for lunch, Blondie." He makes his getaway to his corner of the library, and leaves Candace and me facing each other.

"So, you had lunch with Lyle."

"I asked him your question."

"My question?"

"Where he lives."

Wow, she dove right in. How long have I known him and stayed away from that conversation like my life depended on it? "Did he answer?"

"Kinda. Not really." Her brow furrows as she focuses on something on the ground. "One of these days I may just follow him and find out."

My hand instinctively rests on her shoulder. "Not by yourself."

Her face pops up, and her eyebrows do too. "I guess you're right. Maybe I'll get to know him better and then find a friend to join me."

I could be that friend. What is happening here? *God, what are you doing?* I thought getting to know this girl was about maybe finding romance, but is this about Lyle?

"I'm sorry." She lifts her wrist to her nose. "Do I smell bad?"

She smells like vanilla, melted butter, and brown sugar. "No, why do you ask?"

"The look on your face."

I shake my head. "Sorry, I guess the whole Lyle thing…"

A strange hacking sounds behind me. A mom and her son wait at the counter, ready to check out. The kid glares and hacks again. I give Candace a nod and move to my position, eyeing the kid. "You sure you want to check out all these Harry Potter books? You only have them for a month. Someone else might want to check one of these out."

"I want to read them all," the kid says, and wipes his palm up his nose.

As I scan the seventh three-inch-thick book, a woman with a bright pink scarf rushes over and points a pink manicured fingernail at the books I'm checking. "Sorry to interrupt. My son finished *Half-Blood Prince* and is desperate to read *Deathly Hallows*." She looks around me at the rolling cart. "Are there any copies in the return pile?"

I glance over, I already know the answer. "I'm sorry. All our Harry Potter books appear to be checked out."

"Oh bubber-snot." The mom huffs, then gives me a gracious smile. "Thank you for your help."

The kid with the indignant face appears unchanged by the conversation, but his mom has a hand over her mouth. She reaches for *Deathly Hallows* and pushes it toward me.

59

"I think we have more than enough reading material."

"Mommmmm!" The kid whines.

"Shush." She pushes his pile of books toward him. "This is enough. Let's go."

"It's your lucky day, ma'am," I say to the woman in pink. "Someone just turned this in."

She motions to a boy in a Henley with blue and green stripes. A smile spreads across his freckled face as I hand him the only book he checks out to take home.

I reach for the rolling cart and act like I'm busy working, but Candace holds my attention as she stands in my periphery where I left her. I don't know what to say but I can't ignore her. Would she be here if she wanted to get rid of me last night?

"Can I help you with anything, Candace?" *Candace.* Does that name mean laced with sugar? It suits her.

She smiles. "I don't know why I'm here today. I just got in my car and ended up here. Maybe I was supposed to feed Lyle. Or maybe, well, I didn't know if you'd be here, but I thought it would be worth a try."

"You wanted to see me?"

"Yeah, I guess. I just..." She looks up at me with puppy-dog eyes. "You left so abruptly last night. Did I do something wrong?" Her hand slaps across her mouth. "Oh no. I didn't poison you, did I?"

A laugh I can't hold back escapes and shushes echo through the library.

"No," I whisper. "I was one of the chefs, remember?" I smile. "I just didn't want to overstay my welcome."

"Oh." She looks at her watch and fumbles with it. "I guess I should go." She moves toward the door, then turns back, opens her purse, pulls out a wadded receipt, flattens it, and scribbles something. The wrinkled paper reveals a pleasant surprise as her hand lifts off of it. "Call me when you get off. If you want."

She scoots out the door so fast I don't have to worry about her seeing the stupid grin I'm sure is plastered on my face.

CHAPTER 13
I'M GOING TO NEED YOU

CANDACE

My mind is muddled. *Call me if you want?* Okay, I know I want one thing. I want Hank to call. I'd like him to help me cook dinner tonight, hang out and shoot the breeze, keep me company. All the things my heart hurts for when I think of him. Yikes! I didn't know how bad I had it.

Oh Lord, help me not make a fool of myself. Help me not lose myself in somebody else. Help me keep my heart safe.

A warm calm settles over me as I turn my car's ignition. Somehow, I already know I can trust Hank, and I don't think trusting him is foolish. But I do need to take things slow and not just throw my heart at him in hopes he'll catch it. Why do I want him to catch it?

At the exit of the parking lot, I scan right and left, then turn down the street in the opposite direction of my home. I guess I'm not done driving. The hum of the motor soothes my soul like bees' wings vibrating at a perfect pitch. I meander down a tree-lined street. A few vibrant red and yellow leaves flip and turn before me like spinning ballerinas. The entrance of the local park beckons me into the peace of a well-kept garden.

Minutes later, I set a blanket on the lawn and stare at waterfowl as they swim circles around each other. Water striders join in their own dance, carving paths on a gray-blue surface. A tall weeping willow across the pond reaches down and grazes its long limbs over the water's edge, ripples reverberate out from the tendrils. My lungs take in the cool fresh air, rejuvenated. Heaviness lifts from my soul momentarily, just enough for me to realize my conversation with Lyle weighs on me.

I'll take care of it, I sense God whisper to my heart. *But I'm going to need you.*

A laugh escapes my throat. What in the world am I thinking? I care. I do. I just don't know what *I* can do.

You can help just by being you.

My eyes scan the rolling lawn. The closest people sit at a picnic table over a hundred yards away. Where did that come from?

I pretend like I don't know, but I do. It's just been a while since I listened. Really listened. The sky fades from a pale blue above into soft yellow at the horizon. The sun will hide below the horizon soon. I guess it's time to move on.

———

The click of the light switch announces my arrival to my empty apartment. A shiver overtakes me. I give in and walk over to the thermostat to turn on the heat for the first time this season. Suddenly fall is chasing the warm days of summer toward winter. Not that we have extreme weather here, but I'm a wimp when it comes to the cold.

My cozy sweats and fluffy slippers call to me. I obey. Maybe my soul needs empathy from my flesh. Somehow it works. I flop on my comfy couch, grab my current read, and relax for about two minutes. Until my phone rings.

"Hi." I'm loving the sound of his voice. I bet he's a baritone if he can sing. For some reason I expect him to be able to sing even though he said he couldn't.

"Hi."

"It was nice to see you. A nice surprise, since I don't think either one of us anticipated a trip to the library." Hank's voice sounds a little jittery.

"Yeah." I sound just as nervous. "It was a nice coincidence."

He chuckles. "Yeah, coincidence."

"Really, I didn't plan on going to the library. And I know it's your day off. You told me that. I just didn't want to go home after church and, well, I ended up there. And then Lyle—"

He laughs. "Did I make you feel like I was accusing you?"

"No. I just..." I huff.

"What's up, Blondie?"

"What?"

"Sorry. Lyle's voice is stuck in my head. I was just talking to him before I left work. You made quite an impression on him today."

"Speaking of that, are you free? I mean, I'd like to talk to someone about Lyle, and I think you might be the best person to talk to. If you're okay with it."

"Sure. What's up?"

"Well, could we talk in person?" My stomach clenches. "I don't want to assume anything. Maybe you already have plans." Too late now. *Just bite the bullet, Can-Can.* "If you're free, would you like to come over?"

"You want me to help you make dinner?"

"No. Well, not unless you want to. But I would like to talk, and it is almost dinner time." I giggle nervously.

"Let me get cleaned up and I'll be over. Does that work for you?"

"Yes. Thank you."

He says goodbye and I hang up the phone. *Did I just ask him out again? What is with me?*

Wait. No. It's okay. We are friends, and friends get together and talk. No one has to know I think he's cute and probably one of the nicest, most decent guys I've ever met.

Oh Candy-girl, you've got it bad.

———

HANK

Here we go. I pound my fist against Candace's front door, and try not to sound too demanding. The door swings open to her cheerful face. She's wearing navy blue oversized sweats and fluffy slippers striped yellow and black like fat bumblebees. Her yellow sweatshirt has red USC lettering on the front.

I point to her shirt. "Did you go there?"

"No. My friend Jillian's husband did, to get his master's. He got the shirt for me as a joke. But it's warm and cozy, so joke's on him."

"And the joke is?" I ask as she ushers me in.

She points to herself. "Stanford."

"Ahhh," I say like I know what she means, then I change the subject and show her the brown paper bag in my hand. "I brought supplies for an easy dinner from the last cookbook you checked out. Teriyaki chicken rice bowls. Plus some prefab mixed fruit." I pull out the plastic container and shake the multicolored fruit inside then set it down on her counter.

"Sounds great, and healthier than anything I had in mind."

"Don't fool yourself. There's lots of sugar in the sauce. But also tons of vegetables."

We're still new to cooking together, but we seem to have a groove as we dance around each other. I can almost hear an epic soundtrack in the background.

"Dinner is served," she says as she sets the bowls on the table. We sit kitty-corner to each other, and she smiles big. "God bless the food and help us not get sick."

"Amen."

She tilts her head at me. "What do you believe? About God, I mean. That kind of stuff."

Wow, right to it. I'm not sure what she believes, but the moment of truth has hit. I know she prays over meals and went to church today.

"Well, I believe the Bible is true, and I try to live by it. God loves us and sent Jesus as proof. The whole John 3:16 thing." I lift my eyebrows. Does she know what I mean?

A broad smile stretches across her face. "For God so loved the world that he sent his only son." Her head wags. "Can't say I'm exactly on fire for him. A slow smolder is probably a more accurate description." She furrows her brow and her eyes get serious. "But something happened today that kind of woke me up." She taps her forehead.

"Your chat with Lyle?"

"Well, kinda. Not exactly. It's all connected, I think. I don't know." She takes off her glasses, spends several seconds swirling her napkin over the lenses, then repositions the frames and looks at me.

"When you're ready, I'm all ears." I push the tops of my ears forward so they stick out. Her laugh warms me more than the sweet hickory-smoked chicken I just put in my mouth.

She tells the story of her and Lyle's conversation between bites, then she gets to the point. "Later, I heard something. In my heart. Like a call." She looks at me expectantly. "Have you ever had that happen?"

I slowly blow out a mouthful of air and contemplate my answer. "Yes."

CHAPTER 14
ON A MISSION

CANDACE

"Can you tell me about it?" I watch as Hank shifts in his seat and stares at the table. "Because what happened to me today is kinda freaking me out."

The wheels spinning in his head are practically visible as his expression sobers and his lighthearted voice drops. "I pray when something happens like your conversation with Lyle. My grandma taught me to listen when my heart speaks."

Hank focuses back on me. "She called it listening to the Holy Spirit. I try to listen when he nudges at my heart. It's not like I hear an audible voice. I just get a kind of impression. Sometimes it's a thought that won't go away. Sometimes it's so loud I can't ignore it. Or it makes me so uncomfortable I have to do something about it. I try to listen and pray when that happens."

By the guarded look on Hank's face, he must expect me to think he's nuts. But I don't. Everything he says is something I've heard before. Just never from a man, especially one my own age.

"When it happens, you pray. Is that it? How often does it happen to you?"

He lets out a slow exhale. Seconds pass before he continues. "It happens frequently. Sometimes, all I do is pray, as if it's the only thing God wants me to do. Other times, I get more impressions. Kinda like instructions. Something to do. When that happens, I try to do it."

"You try to do it." I look down at my hands wringing each other. "What if it's unusual, not typical, or maybe even scary?"

"Like I said, I try to do it. I'm not the most courageous person in the world, but I try. I've talked myself out of it more times than I'd like to admit."

He rakes his hands through his hair, takes off his glasses, and pinches the bridge of his nose. "I'm not perfect. Not even close. Honestly, there's something that has dogged me for a while. But I'm hesitant to do it." His fist drops on the table, making the silverware jump.

My hand drops on his. "I get it. I'm there right now." My heart pounds out of my skin. I wish I knew the best way to express what's in my heart.

"What do you do when you run across a homeless, unsheltered, unhoused person?" I lift my shoulders. "Do you take time to get to know them? And if you do, then what? If you get connected, if they get into your heart, then you gotta do something, don't you? But what?" My hand releases his and grabs my neck, holding in some kind of pain that wants to escape.

We stare wide-eyed at each other. Weighted energy pulses between us. I wait for him to break the silence.

"Lyle."

"Yes. I think I'm supposed to do something. Help him somehow. But I have no clue how."

He nods, a huff escapes his flared nostrils. Then he zeroes in on me.

"Maybe we're supposed to do something together, Candace. What-ever is going on with him, whatever the connection is that placed him in my path and yours, is for a purpose. But honestly, my faith isn't anywhere close to a place where I believe I can do anything to help him. I listen to his stories. I try to treat him decently. But I'm— " He groans. "I'm concerned he'll end up another statistic. There's no easy fix, and I'm not qualified to help."

"So, what do we do?"

"Only thing I can think of for now is pray, keep doing what we're doing, see what opportunities present themselves. What we do has gotta be whatever God wants, because even the thought of trying to do anything drains the energy right out of me."

"Time to grow up." My head bobs up and down. "That's what my pastor talked about today. Not being a baby still needing milk, but growing up, serving others, that sort of thing." A glint of hope raises my finger into the air. "He who began a good work in us will complete it, right?"

The corner of his lip twitches to a half smile. "Ever prayed about this kind of thing before? I mean, with someone else?" He lifts a palm across the table to me, my heart skips into a sporadic rhythm. *Don't panic, Candace.*

Hank's determined expression softens. "I'll pray. You can just agree. If you agree." He waits for me to nod. "Okay, then."

His hand is strong and warm as it envelops mine. Brown bangs fall across his glasses when he bows his head. I join him and close my eyes as his baritone voice sends our request up to heaven.

"Father God, you've placed Lyle in our path and inspired us to do something. We don't know what, but you do. Show us what you want us to do. Please make it clear. And Lord, I know at least *I* need the courage to step up and obey."

I squeeze Hank's hand, and he squeezes back then continues.

"We ask that Lyle would become self-sufficient. That he would believe in you and what his life could be. That he would make the choices necessary to get off the streets. Help him develop healthy habits and receive the help he needs. Help the right people to cross his path. Give him a roof over his head, clean clothes, healthy food on his table, and the future and hope you have prepared for him. Thank you for your help. Amen."

I say amen and look up, but Hank's head is still bowed, like he's listening for a response or has gone to some other world. Quiet fills the room, but it isn't uncomfortable. It feels like the experience I had at the park earlier. As then, my heart is stirred.

"God has already started answering our prayers."

Hank slowly raises his head. "How so?"

"You and me."

"You and me?"

"Yeah, we've crossed Lyle's path. I think that tells us two things. One, we are some of the people God has placed in Lyle's life right now. Which means, two, we are supposed to do something to help. So now what?"

"Not just what. But what can we do that Lyle will accept?"

I lift my face toward the ceiling. "Hey God, help Lyle to accept the help we give." I clear my throat. "I mean, the help you want us to give."

"Amen." Hank stands up and starts to clear the table. "I think I need to chew on this for a while. Process all of this. Can we talk about something else? Play a game maybe?"

I nod as a rush of appreciation floods my soul. I'm so glad I just prayed with this guy. I've never done that before. I mean, outside of Jillian praying or listening in at church to someone else. Talk about the right people crossing paths. I think he's one of the ones that was supposed to cross mine. Wow.

When the dishes are clean, I pull out two decks of cards and we play Nertz. The competitive solitaire game is fast and great for distraction as we break out in bouts of laughter. Our moods are light when I walk him to the door.

"Thank you for coming over."

"Can I call you tomorrow?"

"Of course. We're on a mission."

He points to the sky. "We're on a mission from God," he says in a weird voice.

I give him a side eye. "Um, yeah. So?"

"You know, like in the *Blues Brothers*. The movie? It was supposed to be a joke, except it's not, but—"

"Never heard of it."

"It's a classic. My older cousins have the DVD. They quote that line all the time." He laughs and shrugs his shoulders. "Maybe we'll check it out together sometime."

"I'd like that."

After a smile and salute, he heads down the walkway to his car. I exhale, then let the night air fill my lungs as I watch red taillights drive away. I really like this guy.

CHAPTER 15
THE NEXT THING

HANK

E very evening, when I get home, I call her. Tonight's no different. She hasn't seemed to mind. We stay on the phone for hours each night, and fill each other in on our lives—family, background, school. We talk about our mission and try to figure out what to do, what will matter, what will last.

I've come to a conclusion. "I hope you don't mind me saying this, but unless we have at least one specific thing to pursue, it's better to trust God and wait. Not jump the gun."

She gets quiet for a minute. "Just so you know, Hank, you can say whatever you want with me. By now, we are at a point where we can do that, right?"

My cheeks warm and I pinch back a grin. This girl keeps saying things I didn't know I wanted to hear.

"Yeah, I think we're at that point. So, what do you think?"

"I think trusting God is key. But what's that poem? 'Do the Next Thing'?"

"What do you think the next thing is?"

"What we've been doing, I guess. Be Lyle's friend, talk to him, build a relationship, and see what opportunities come up in those interactions. Basically, just care. But I don't think it would go over well if Lyle knew we called him our 'mission.'"

"Just like being called 'Blondie' doesn't go over well with you?" I laugh.

"Ha ha. I don't like 'Blondie,' but it's better than 'Lady,' which Lyle resorted to when I offended him with interrogation."

"Yeah, he calls me 'Glasses' when I cross the line. Well, he calls me that most of the time."

We get off the phone, and my heart lifts because tomorrow I get to see her in person.

————

CANDACE

This is the first time I'll visit Hank's place. My heart is pounding, because this is not my favorite night of the year. Thank goodness he sent his cat to his sister's for the evening. She doesn't get trick-or-treaters, so Hank doesn't have to worry about his cat escaping out her door and trying to mingle with droves of kids. Plus, he said his sister likes the company. She'll be watching *Hocus Pocus* with his cat by her side.

So there's one less thing for me to be concerned about, one less weakness I have to admit to. I'm allergic to cats. How sad is that? But at least tonight, with my antihistamine as backup, I won't have to worry about being able to breathe. At least, not because of the cat.

I hope Hank doesn't think I look stupid in my costume. Everyone is dressed up tonight, right? This is not a big deal. It's okay. We're just handing out candy together. I take a deep breath and scan my surroundings before I knock on the door. This is a nice apartment complex with a well-trimmed landscape, its lawns golf-course green even on Halloween. A whoosh of air fans toward me as I turn with a raised fist and almost pound on Hank's chest.

"Oh sorry."

He laughs and gestures to my getup. "Phyllis Diller?"

"You know who she is?" I'm sure my face is lit up.

"My gran wrangled me into watching old Bob Hope and Carol Burnett Shows. Phyllis Diller was one of her favorites." He points to my crazy wig and raises an eyebrow. "So?"

"It's a long story, but at this time it is the only costume I will wear on this particular evening."

"Not sure what that means, but okay." The beanie and red-striped shirt perfect his costume. With his lanky frame, he looks like he inspired the *Where's Waldo?* puzzle books.

For tonight's homemade pizza, store-bought premade dough will save time, so we are ready to hand out candy to the kids in Hank's complex. I've learned it's harder to mess up food when you actually care. I want to be a good student for Hank, so I've been more attentive. And cooking with him is fun. We laugh and flirt and bump into each other. I think the contact is accidental, but it still sends a zing through my core.

Tonight, though, I need to channel my inner Phyllis Diller so I won't lose my cool or scare Hank off. Do not talk about Pablo. I won't think about Pablo. I won't compare Hank to Pablo. They are two completely different people. Shoot! I'm already doing it.

"What's going on?" Hank asks, setting his hands on my shoulders.

I raise my eyebrows like I don't know what he means. All he has to do is tilt his head and I know he doesn't buy it. Oh no, here it comes.

"Last year, on Halloween, my boyfriend of two years broke up with me out of nowhere. At least, I thought it was out of nowhere." I slap my hand across my mouth. I have just ruined the evening.

"Sorry." His look is spry. "I'm not him, Phyllis, and we have fun plans for tonight. Pizza's out in ten, and kids will start knocking on the door any second. Here's the rules."

"Rules?"

"Yeah. Every year, there are prizes for the best individual costumes and family costumes. First, second, and third place, broken down into age-groups—adults, teens, elementary age, and toddlers/babies." He hands me a small notepad and pen.

"This is official."

"Yep. At eight forty-five, porch lights are turned off and trick-or-treating stops so the neighborhood can deliberate. We have to turn in our scores at the clubhouse by nine, and prizes are awarded at nine thirty. They make it a big to-do, then it's lights-out at ten."

"Seriously?"

"Yeah, it's pretty cool. One reason I like living here is they do stuff like this for different occasions. It helps kids and families in the community and keeps people safe, plus we get to have peace and quiet by ten. This whole thing was a solution to vandalism that happened late at night. I'm not sure why it brought about change, but it did."

A ding rings in the air, and my salivary glands gush at the smells of basil, tomatoes, olive oil, and melted mozzarella billowing out when Hank opens the oven door. I stand next to him in the warmth emanating from the half-opened door. The oven warms my outside as much as being next to him warms my inside.

He lifts his palm to me, and I drop my hand in his. It's warm and solid and comforting. I close my eyes. He prays for the food and for every person who'll come to his door tonight. I whisper my amen, look up into his brown eyes, and smile. It's true. Hank is nothing like Pablo.

———

We've barely taken a bite when the doorbell rings. Numbers on the shoulders of each child, teen, and adult make them look like they're running a marathon. They *do* take this seriously. Hank and I hop back and forth from gulping down bites of pizza to handing out candy and marking down our favorite costumes by number. He told me to rank them, otherwise I'd get lost. He's right.

The costumes inspire and delight. I give high marks for the dad dressed as a shepherd carrying his baby covered in fluffy cotton balls and a lamb headdress. And of course I support the teen dressed as a mad scientist. By the end of the night, my favorite costume is the eight-year-old boy who had no problem dressed in a bright purple hippopotamus costume. His mom must be an amazing seamstress. He could have passed for a character on Sesame Street, and his confidence floored me. He stood with pride—straight back, confident smile surrounded by a hood sporting stuffed white felt teeth and bugged-out blue eyes with long eyelashes.

74

At eight-forty-five, without even a second of breathing room, Hank turns off his porch light, locks the door, and heads straight for the table to tally his scores.

"Got mine in order." He waves his pad at me. "You think you're ready?"

"I think so." I show him my top three.

"Yeah, that hippo was something." He stands up. "Shall we go? Grab your coat. It's cold out there." He is all business as I follow him out the door and into the star-studded night.

Bright lights and chatter greet us inside the clubhouse. All the characters we handed candy to earlier flank the walls as we approach a line of tables where a half-dozen people tally the scores. We add ours to the mix. A man accepts them, nods at Hank, and thanks us for participating. "They upped their game, didn't they?" he asks Hank. "Better every year. Halloween night is one of your best ideas, especially adding the teen category."

Hank nods as his face turns red. I follow him to an out of the way corner and point a finger at him when he turns around.

"You? This whole thing was your idea?"

He pinches his lips and grimaces. "It was born out of a community meeting."

"But it was your idea at said community meeting?" I can feel my mom's stern eyebrow raise taking over my face.

A half laugh escapes through his nose, then a high-pitched screech from the sound system startles everyone to attention. It's time to announce the winners. Hank is off the hook. For now.

I'm happy to see my top picks awarded. The shepherd and lamb win their category, and the eight-year-old hippo wins his, but the winner that stands out to me is the teen boy dressed like Einstein. He gathers his prize, then aims for our corner, his eyes narrowed in on Hank. He puts a hand out and they shake. A smile spreads across Hank's face. "You took me up on it, huh?"

The boy nods.

"Good to see you here. I owe you lunch, then. Where and when?"

"Sunday?" The boy taps his chin as if in deep contemplation. "Applebee's?"

"I said anywhere."

"Yeah, I know."

"Okay, but it has to be after twelve."

"Yeah, I know. Church." The boy rolls his eyes at Hank then sorta smiles. "See you then."

Hank echoes his goodbye, then leans back against the wall. My eyebrow twitches as I look at him. He shakes his head and pats his chest over his heart. "Just an idea. I guess it was a good one to follow." He grabs my hand. "Let's get out of here."

Five minutes later, we enter his apartment. The kitchen is a mess, dishes and leftover pizza clutter the table. I pick up a plate.

"Don't worry about it." Hank takes the plate out of my hand. "It's late, and I already don't like the idea of you driving home alone."

I laugh. "I do it all the time."

"Still. I can clean up." He rubs the back of his neck. "I hope you had fun tonight. I know it's a whirlwind, but I never liked Halloween until we started doing this. It's like I'm a secret agent with a hidden plan to rid the world of evil." He chuckles. "Sorry. That sounded stupid." He wipes his hands across the red and white stripes of his shirt. I never thought Waldo was particularly handsome, until now.

A smile spreads across my face as I try to slyly watch Hank walking next to me toward my car. He waves as I shift my car into reverse. I have to pull my eyes away so I can drive safely. After shifting into gear to move forward, I lift a hand and wave as I pull away from his place.

Thank you, God, for replacing one of my biggest hurts to date with a new, better memory. I don't think I'll forget this night for the rest of my life.

CHAPTER 16
A SAINT AND EINSTEIN

Guido's is hopping as usual. Families are scattered at the restaurant's various tables. Parents corral kids lined up at video games back to their seats to eat their dinner. Jillian and I have adopted the festive and chaotic atmosphere as one of our places to hide from our everyday worlds and catch up with each other. We settle at a table with our deep-dish pizza, puddles of orange grease shimmer between the pepperoni and black olives.

The moment of truth has come. I look up at my crazy, ever-faithful friend and feel found out. Jillian's green eyes penetrate my soul so easily. I'm not good at hiding what's in my heart from her. She sniffs it out like a bloodhound.

"He hasn't kissed you yet?"

"Our relationship isn't like that." I stare at my fumbling hands, thankful she can't see them due to the red-and-white checkered tablecloth.

"Yeah right." She looks amused. "Soon, I betcha." She puts her hand toward me over the table like we're gonna shake on it.

"No way!"

"Ha! You won't bet because you know it's gonna happen."

"I don't know anything." I take my glasses off and rub the bridge of my nose, then try to clean the lenses with the edge of my blouse, even though they don't need it.

"Can-Can, it's okay."

My emotions have roller coastered from excitement to totally freaking out, my anxiety growing since I woke up this morning. Why? It's not like Hank's putting any pressure on me.

"Maybe he's too good for me." I slump my shoulders.

"What in the world?" Jillian flinches her head back then bounces it forward, zeroing in on me.

"It's like he's a saint. He prays every time we eat together, prays when we have a serious question about something. He planned the whole save-the-neighborhood Halloween. And now we're working on helping Lyle."

"Lyle?"

"The homeless guy that frequents the library."

Jillian raises her eyebrows. "Can-Can, maybe Hank is just being who he was made to be." She grabs my hand from the table and squeezes it. "Maybe you are being exactly who you were made to be."

"Yeah, big difference I make in this world." My eyes roll despite my efforts to keep control of them. "I'm not saving future generations by teaching them 'foundations of life' like my mom or sisters."

She tilts her head at me with a look of exasperation. "You make a difference in this world every day, saving the planet one bee at a time."

"Pfft!"

"I'm serious. I don't know many people who care so much about bugs. I remember when you took your first bug class in college. You were so excited to study and save them. We need people like you, because most of us hate bugs. And who's to say the little things you do every day don't matter? You matter to our family, make our lives better in big and small ways. And what about Neighbor Bob? I don't think you realize how much your smiles and check-ins add to his life."

"Oh no!" My throat catches. "I haven't had dinner with Bob since I met Hank."

"Honey, I think Bob's okay. You can have him over this week. I think he can see what's happening between you and Hank, even if you can't."

My eye twitches.

"Anyway, my point is, we all have our own place in this world, and we all have something to give. It's not like those things rank in importance. They all matter. Remember when you gave me this pep talk when I struggled with 'only' being a mom?"

"Being a mom is crazy important." I pat the tabletop for emphasis.

"I know that now. At the time, I felt like I had given up who I thought I was meant to be. I love my kids dearly. You know that. But tabling some of my dreams was hard. You helped me see the season I'm in, that I'm supposed to focus on my kiddos. And now I love it. It wears me out, but I love it." Her light and airy laugh flits through the atmosphere, lifting my spirits.

We finish catching up and head our separate ways. Jillian has a family to attend to, and I have a neighbor to reconnect with. I guess it's okay if my purpose in life is to save the bugs and be nice to my neighbor. Oh, and I guess Lyle is on my list. That add scares me. *God, how in the world can I help a homeless man who doesn't seem to care he's homeless?*

HANK

The driveway circling the off-white wood-sided apartments jerks me alert as my car bounces out of a pothole. *Oh Lord, help that one not to have caused damage.* The kid on the sidewalk, cuffed jeans falling off his butt, hides his face under his black hoodie. Thank God it's a long hoodie and covers enough to leave his underwear of choice a mystery. I smile and wave as I stop in front of him. He doesn't respond, just opens the car door and plops in like he couldn't care less.

"How ya doin', Marcus?"

We're out of the parking lot and well down the street before he responds to my question.

"I'm hungry, ready for some hot wings." He huffs a laugh. "Who'd have thought you and me would ever go to lunch together."

"I had an inkling. That's why I offered the challenge."

"Yeah. Get the bad kid off the streets."

79

We're at a stoplight, so I turn my gaze toward his stoic profile.

"You're not a bad kid."

"Ha!"

"You've made some bad choices. You can choose to make better choices."

"Geez, you sound like every teacher I've ever had."

The light turns green, so I focus on the road. I don't want this conversation to escalate into Marcus getting defensive. This lunch is supposed to be a reward for stepping up and choosing to participate productively with his community.

"I thought your costume was great. Candace said it stood out to her."

"Your girlfriend?"

Oops. Candace does not need to be part of our conversation. I need to be as focused on this kid as I can handle. She's way too much of a distraction, even when she's not around.

"Just a friend."

"Awww, too bad."

"So why Einstein?" I ask.

He shifts in the seat next to me, blows out some air, and clears his throat. Maybe something else shifts too, because suddenly he starts to talk like a regular kid, not one who has to defend every breath he takes.

"I like Einstein. He looked like a crazy man but was super smart. When you said to dress up like someone who made a positive impact on society, he was the first person to come to mind. Well, the only one I could think of."

Marcus's hands shape some invisible structure in front of him. "I got this whole picture in my head for the costume. I knew my mom had a crazy wig and my sister had the white coat from when she was at the junior college."

"Your sister went to the junior college?"

"Yeah, but she dropped out. She missed too many days, got behind, and lost her scholarship. Anyway, I pictured math problems written all over the coat. So, I looked Einstein up at the library and wrote down the equation $E = mc^2$. I kept looking, and all these other equations showed up. It was interesting." His hands drop. "Crazy."

"So, you think Einstein is interesting."

"Yeah. I might check out more about him someday."

"Sounds like a great plan." My mind whirs. I had an idea where this relationship with Marcus could go but didn't want to think too far ahead. Just wait and see how lunch turns out. Just be patient. *God, you've got a plan for this kid. Show me my part.*

Lunch with Marcus zooms by. He's pretty talkative when given undivided attention. Not surprisingly, he's had some hard knocks along the way. Single mom who works multiple jobs, lost his dad before he was old enough to remember him, and his sister got pregnant so she quit school. They all live together in a two-bedroom apartment, so Marcus's bed is the couch. And he's too young to get a job—at least a "real one," as he puts it. He's gotten caught for petty theft. Been to juvie and hangs with a group of guys in the same boat.

"At least we have each other," he says.

"Is that what you want for your future?"

"Future?" He scoffs.

A flood of thoughts and Bible verses run through my head, but my gut says to shut up and listen. I haven't earned Marcus's trust. If I went all spiritual or overly positive on him, he'd just laugh or never listen to me again. And now I care even more about this kid.

What if I had grown up like him? Man, I'm so blessed. A mom and dad still together after thirty-plus years. Sisters who love me almost obnoxiously, always helped me with homework and still give decent advice. As a kid, I never thought about getting a job to buy necessities, let alone stealing for survival.

Here I am with what I see as a bright future. I've always had hope, always thought there were possibilities yet to be found. *"Through faith and patience inherit the promises"*—that's been my life verse. But this kid doesn't think God cares about him, let alone that God is on his side. So, I keep my mouth shut about the God stuff for now and just listen.

"You up for another challenge?" I ask.

"You have to tell me what it is first."

I tilt my head. "I love that you trust me." Guess I'm still earning it.

"Hey man, I barely know you. This has been a decent time, but how do I know you'll keep up your end of the deal?"

"Fair enough." The waiter drops our bill on the table. I pick it up, pull out my wallet, and set my card on the plastic tray. "Okay, here's the next challenge, should you choose to accept it. I will take you to lunch again, anywhere you want, if you do some research on Einstein and write a two-page paper on him. Whatever interests you, whatever you want to say. Two pages, typed, double-spaced, one-inch margins."

"Wow, that's specific."

"If you need help setting that up, we have computers at the library you can write it on."

"I gotta get home soon to watch my nephew, so my sister can go to work. When am I gonna do all this?"

"Do you have time to go to the library now? Check out some books to take home? Then some afternoon, *after school*, I'll get you set up on one of the computers." I count off the steps on three fingers. "Study at home, take some notes, write it up."

He looks at me suspiciously, then settles into what looks like a glint of possibility. "Okay. Let's go to the library."

CHAPTER 17
MOODY BLUES

CANDACE

Jillian is at her in-laws again this Sunday, since Matthew's mom is still recovering from surgery. I could go visit my family too, but I'm not ready. I still haven't figured out how to stop feeling defensive of who I am or the choices I've made. I didn't follow in my mother's footsteps. As a kid I squirmed and hid outside whenever she went into one of her *"foundations of life"* teaching modes she deemed so important, cooking being one of them. I guess that would have been helpful, but I had no interest at the time. My sisters soaked in every word she said. Eventually my mom gave up on me, although the sly comments continue to this day. I guess I've translated it into being not quite good enough and not quite fitting in.

I'm still not sure where these feelings come from. My parents, or some hypersensitive self-imposed impressions of their expectations, like my psych professor talked about?

Maybe it has to do with my mom's turned up nose every time I talk about my career. Or her every correction when I climbed trees or collected bugs. She wanted me to be a teacher. An honorable job, she'd say. And yes, it's honorable, but it was her dream, not mine. I like to teach kids to care for their environment, but that's only a fraction of what I get to do. I like to get my hands in the dirt, and explore outdoors. Not a ladylike activity, according to my mom, not an appropriate career. She hasn't come right out and said this, but it certainly is how she makes me feel. The rest of my family hasn't helped much. While they are okay with my career choice, none of them will admit it when my mom gets on one of her "Candace should…" rolls.

Whatever the case, I feel the need to stand on my own two feet. My distance helps my resolve to pursue *my* chosen interests.

Maybe I can go over for Thanksgiving. Like old times, only I'll be more secure in myself, not tossed by every whim I pick up in the emotional atmosphere. That's the plan, then. But what do I do for now? What *is* my life on my own two feet?

I stare out my front windshield as people weave in and out of small gatherings in front of the sanctuary. Like the murmuration of birds, a sacred dance of beauty fluctuates as people find friends and visit, then move to other friends they haven't seen in a while. Hugs and handshakes flutter all over the landscape in front of me. I'm blessed with this community, feel safe here, but service is over. I need to find something meaningful for the rest of this day.

Lyle's face crosses the screen of my mind. I wonder if he's at the library. Maybe I could go talk to him for a bit. Maybe we could catch lunch together, since Hank has a lunch date with Einstein. I laugh to myself remembering the crazy white wig perched on the head of a too-cool-for-school teenager.

"To the library," I say with a fist charge. I reach to turn the ignition and I'm off.

How much the library has become an integral part of my life in a short time amazes me. Like a home away from home. In a way, a family is developing. Hank and Lyle have bounced their way to the top of my relationship list. In different ways obviously, but my thoughts revolve around both.

The plaid worn-out chair in the back corner of the nubby-carpeted library is occupied. A handful of plastic bags filled with who-knows-what clutters the feet of the thirty-something-year-old who sits there. I approach and offer a smile. His head lifts slowly and a suspicious grin moves across his face.

"Hey, Blondie," he whispers. "Why are you blocking my light?"

"I thought your eyes were closed. You hungry?"

A half smile stretches his chapped lips. I should get him some lip balm. He stands, gathers his bags, and gestures to the door. We don't say a word the whole length of the library. He opens the door for me.

Without discussion, we turn toward McDonalds. I'd like to feed Lyle something better than Mickey D's, but I'm not ready to drive him somewhere in my car. Maybe I would if Hank were with me, but not by myself.

We order and carry the red trays to a corner where there is more space for Lyle's conglomeration of bags. I tell him about my job and how I got where I am, which leads to more conversation about who he used to be, his goals then, and where he is now. *Lord, give me the strength to take it all in without being completely depleted or judgmental.* Lyle doesn't catch any negative feedback from me, so he keeps going. Tells me more than he ever has, like his current living conditions.

"Wanna see where I live?"

My jaw drops so hard I expect to feel the impact against the tabletop.

He laughs. "I'll show you if you still want to know. We don't have to. I just feel generous at the moment."

I chew on the possibility. No, the opportunity. Is this what I've been praying for? Be careful what you pray for. You just might get it. I consider Hank's concern, but it's broad daylight and I may not get this chance again.

"O-okay."

"Let's go." He stands up, gathers his bags, and leads the way out the door and around the corner. "It's about a mile." Lyle tilts his head and raises an eyebrow.

I nod. I'm as ready as I'll ever be.

We walk silently down a back alley. Grayish water trickles in the gutter next to us, an empty wrapper floats to a partially clogged storm drain and escorts us into another world. A shiver sweeps through my body. The atmosphere turns colder, darker with each step, even though it's the middle of the day. Lyle stops where a path slopes to a ditch below. Several feet down are worn blue tarps in precarious configurations. I'm glad I wore my rain boots today.

85

Lyle holds his hand up to me. "It's slippery here." His weathered hand steadies me as I climb down. How does a young man have hands like an old cowboy? Worn and wrinkled, chafed and rough.

I hop off a protruding stone to a flattened area, and we turn down a well-worn path lined with tarp tents, cardboard forts, shopping carts filled with indistinguishable stuff, and an odd collection of bicycle parts. We pass people with coats pulled over their faces, arms wrapped around themselves, and feet extended. Lyle moves past like it's normal.

"Moody Blues!"

I startle at the high-pitched call.

"Yur never around this time a' day." A woman with blue and purple stripes in her stringy blonde hair raises her hands at Lyle. "And you brought a girl! Like that!"

I look at Lyle, eyebrows raised. "Moody Blues?"

"Oh honey, that's what we call him around here. He's moody and sad." The woman jabs Lyle in the arm.

His head bounces back and forward with a chuckle. "Mindy, this is my friend Candace. She wanted to know where I live."

"And you brought her? A girl like this?"

Mindy's sun-parched face can't be more than forty, but the scabs and bruises all over her forearms, and the way her skin hangs on her bones disturbs me. She's too young to look like she's pounding on death's door.

"Well, honey—" She spreads out her arms. "This is the world we live in. Don't worry 'bout me none. I've been around the block and I'm still kickin'. Invincible, that's me!"

I don't know what to say, so I don't say anything. I try to smile as Lyle and I walk past her to the next cardboard structure, which looks thought out and well-constructed. Two appliance boxes intertwined for extra strength support a blue tarp battened down with rope. Lyle opens the plastic curtain just enough for me to look inside. His shelter consists of a mat with a couple of folded blankets and provides enough room to sleep plus a space in the corner to store his handful of bags.

"Home." Lyle smiles, then drops the curtain and stares at me.

"You're comfortable here?" I ask.

"As comfortable as can be expected."

"You're safe?"

"We watch out for each other." He yells "Don't we?" down the row. Loud grunts respond in what I guess is agreement.

"You're warm enough? Get enough to eat?"

"Blondie, like Mindy says, this is the world we live in."

"Is it what you want?"

"There you go again." He rolls his eyes at me.

"Sorry. I'm done." I raise my hands in surrender.

"Had enough? Ready for the library?"

At a loss for words, I nod. What else can I do?

A hand pats my back and I startle. "Oh honey, it'll be alright," Mindy says. "We're used to this. We get food from the restaurant up the way. You'd be amazed at what's left at the end of the day."

Her touch is surprisingly comforting and soft. I fight to keep my tears at bay, and force a smile. But gravity draws the corners of my lips down as I look at Mindy. Traces of a previously young and vibrant woman peek out from her dulled irises. What brought her here? What brought any of these people here? I just don't understand.

"Moody, she's gotta go. She's melting as we speak."

"Yeah. I see it too." Lyle nudges at my elbow. "Let's go, Blondie. It's warmer at the library anyway. Who knows? Maybe Lover Boy will show up magically like last time."

My feet idle forward. I nod at Mindy and want to say something. A nice-to-meet-you, a pleasant goodbye. Nothing comes out.

"See ya around, honey," she says.

I fumble up the dirt ledge behind Lyle, I grab a tuft of long grass to pull myself the last stretch to the asphalt alley. He points up the road to a Chinese food place with chipped red molding around the back door and a large trash bin, the bags inside ripped open. "That's the restaurant Mindy was talking about. One of the perks of living here."

The smell of vinegar and sour food hangs in the air. "They give us to-go boxes at the end of the day. We just have to wait until they close. We have an agreement. They agree they hate to throw food away, and we agree we hate to not eat."

We walk in silence down the dingy backstreet and emerge into the world I know—cars honking in the street, people scurrying in and out of stores with shiny bags loaded with new purchases. Lyle still holds his wrinkled bags, which look like they are filled with wadded-up paper and ratty material.

"What's in your bags?" Oh boy. After all the times today when I couldn't get words out of my mouth, that's what comes out now?

He laughs. "Wouldn't you like to know?"

That's all he says until we get to the concrete planter outside the library. He plops down and sets his bags in a row in front of him, then looks at me with expectation.

"Are you gonna sit or what?" He points to the spot next to him.

Confused, I squint at him.

He shrugs. "You asked what was in my bags. I was gonna show you. Didn't think they'd approve of this inside."

"Oh." I sit as he pulls out his personal items.

From a couple of the bags, he produces a flashlight, batteries, a flannel shirt, a pair of dirty socks, a pair of brown shoes with the sole separating from one of them. Another bag holds two dingy t-shirts, a toothbrush with grayed bristles, a comb, and an empty lip balm container. The last bag, the one he keeps inside his jacket, is full of papers.

"This is a pencil."

He holds it up, and I glare at him for teasing me.

"The rest in there is personal papers."

"Personal?"

"I like to write and draw." He looks at me and hesitates, then rifles inside and pulls out a worn yellowed piece of paper folded in quarters. As he opens it up, his countenance drops. Serious sadness floods his face and swirls around him. It's palpable. He presents the paper to me like a fragile heirloom. "This is the last letter I got from my mom."

The paper, cool and stained from years of being read over and over again, almost feels wet to my touch from the evidence of tears darkening the surface like pocks. I read.

My precious son,

When I held you in my arms as an infant, I never would've imagined I'd be writing you a letter like this. You were so small, so fragile and helpless. I thought I would burst with the love I had for you. I still wonder if I might burst. All I wanted to do was protect you and keep you safe from all harm. I couldn't have known then how powerless I'd feel today. Powerless to protect you from your own decisions.

I can't continue to stand by and watch you throw your life away. I've tried, son. You know I've tried to stop you from continuing down this road. I've tried to walk with you to a healthier place. But you've resisted and fought against me. I can't continue. I must make an ultimatum. How I hate that word. But even more, I hate the power meth has over you. I'm watching you kill yourself. I can't take it anymore. It's killing me too.

I can't help you if I'm not healthy, and I didn't want to tell you this, but I have cancer. I can't help you fight your battle if I lose my own. I want you to be safe. I want you here with me. But I can't have you at home if you are influenced by drugs or any other unhealthy substance. Please, I beg you, get clean. No drugs inside you or on you if you are in my house. I hate having to say it. But I must if I am to have any hope of getting healthy again.

Please understand, my dear Lyle. I love you so much it's ripping my heart out. But neither of us will survive if we continue the way things are.

I believe you can break the chains of addiction that bind you. I believe there is hope. You know where to find it. I trust the help you need will appear and strengthen you to fight this battle. Please, please get help.

I hope I'm here when you recover. I hope I get to see you free from drugs so we can be a family again before it's too late. I'm so sorry I couldn't keep you safe from this. Please do what you need to so I can welcome you home.

Just know that I love you,

Mom

A cough and sputter escape as I read the words that catch me off guard. A sharp pain of emotion rises, threatening to explode from my soul, and erupt into a tidal wave of tears. My shoulders convulse and I lean my elbows on my knees, letting my hair hang around my face. There is nowhere to hide. How does my failure to hold in my emotion make Lyle feel?

Warmth and weight descend onto my shoulder. "Candace, it's not your fault. You have nothing to do with it."

Too late to be glamorous now. I suck in the snot ready to leak out of my nose and use my sleeve to wipe as much wetness off my face as I can. I'm a blubbering mess, like a kindergartener who doesn't know how to blow her own nose. Even my hair has gotten caught up in the flood and sticks to my face. I peek through the yellow strands and see compassion on the face of a man who is the master of snark. I straighten up.

"Lyle, I don't know what to say."

"You don't have to say anything." Suddenly he seems more sober than I have ever seen him. "I made choices. I'm sleeping in the bed I made." He folds the letter and looks back at me. "I don't want to forget. I see people forget or give up. I guess there must be a guy somewhere inside of me who still believes there's a different life ahead of me. A life worth living."

I wipe my hand on my slacks, pat his knee, and catch my breath. "I believe you have a life worth living." I hope my expression offers encouragement, but I've lost all control. Lyle doesn't seem to mind. Instead of anger at my self-righteous confusion, he has empathy. For me.

He looks out to the parking lot. "Oh look." He points, and I follow his gaze. "Today is a day of miracles."

"Oh my gosh." My hands scramble through my purse, and I quickly look into my compact to try and make my face more presentable.

CHAPTER 18
I CAN'T NOT

HANK

Today's my lucky day. Lunch with Marcus turned out to be a positive experience for both of us. I'm probably beaming as we walk up to the library. Then I notice Candace, distressed.

"Are you okay?" I rush up to her and see bloodshot eyes overpowering the typically crystal-blue irises. Powder from the compact in her hand covers her face but can't hide her distress.

"It's okay, Glasses. She's just been slapped with a dose of reality. Guess it hit home a little harder than expected." Lyle strokes Candace's shoulder like she's made of glass.

She wipes her eyes with the heels of her hands and straightens her glasses. "I'll be alright. I just..." She blows out a loud breath, then looks at Lyle, her eyes brim with tears.

"I appreciate it." Lyle smiles at her with an expression I've never seen his face carry before.

I hear a loud throat-clear. Marcus squirms, dances from one foot to the other.

"Candace, you remember Marcus."

"Einstein." She attempts to paint on a smile.

Marcus nods.

I look at Lyle. "Marcus won the costume contest last night. Now we're here for the next challenge."

"This guy loves to give homework." Marcus sounds less than pleased, although I think it's just a show. Why else would he agree to this? Candace and Lyle nod knowingly.

"Hey, I told ya I gotta get home. I have to babysit. My sister'll kill me if I'm late."

"Okay," I say as I hunt for signs of Candace recovering. "You want to get something to eat later?"

She shakes her head. "I'm not up for going out."

"I can bring dinner over." I hope I don't sound desperate. "It seems like maybe you might want to talk."

"Yeah, Lover Boy, she wants to talk. Get her something good. Don't make her cook tonight." Lyle's hand swirls in a circle like he's stirring a pot. "No homework."

"I'll cook for you," I tell Candace. "You don't have to do anything."

Marcus punches my arm. "Hank, I'm serious. My sister'll kill me."

I point to Candace. "Six?"

She nods.

Satisfied for now, I walk with Marcus into the library to choose research books for his project. Is homework so bad? He'll earn another free meal if he writes a good essay. Maybe I should do the same thing with Lyle. I laugh to myself as I lead the skinny, dark-haired teenager to the biography section.

———

While I'm still knocking, at six o'clock on the dot, Candace opens her door and I see a freshened face and curled hair. Girl-next-door beauty always appealed to me more than anything on those celebrity shows or in magazines. Candace's kindness and care shine from her face, and the dash of sass that periodically escapes puts a smile on mine. I like this girl. She must know. It's got to be written all over me.

"How you doin'?" I ask.

"How *you* doin'?" she says with her best impression of Joey from *Friends*. She backs up, and gestures me in. I set brown paper bags on the counter, unload the ingredients for fajitas, and make myself at home, grabbing pans and chopping vegetables while I make small talk. I don't want to ask why she was crying earlier until I can give her my undivided attention.

"I'm sure you want to know..." Her blue eyes beg my attention, and then she looks at my hands. "Maybe I should wait till you don't have a knife in your hand."

The knife drops out of my hand and hits the counter with a clang. "It's that bad?"

"I just want to get it off my chest and then we can move on." She huffs and blows a stray bang off her face, then fixes her gaze on me. "Lyle showed me where he lives. He showed me his belongings. All the stuff in those bags he takes everywhere. A letter from his mom." Her eyes become glassy and wet.

I have no idea what to say.

She straightens and sets her shoulders. "I don't get it. The guy was in college. He was self-sufficient. Then one bad party and..."

"One?"

"Well, no, I guess not. But that's how the downward spiral started. And now..." She wrings her hands, then pounds white-knuckled fists on the counter and glares at me. "I'm supposed to help him. I know it, clear as day." She pulls at her hair. "I don't even know how to help the guy, but I can't not. You know?"

I nod, conflicted by her passion and my thought that romance was in the air when we first started cooking. Have we really been brought together just to help Lyle? My heart sinks. *Lord, I'm sorry. I don't mean to be selfish, but I really like this girl.*

She must not notice the disappointment on my face, because she keeps firing words at me. Propelled by the cadence of her voice, I keep the rhythm and chop vegetables with purpose.

"You know how you help people?" she asks. "It's like it's automatic. You see people and respond. I've watched you. I don't even think you know when you do it. That doesn't come naturally to me, not with people. Well, not with people outside of my own little circle. My global vision is to help bugs. Gyah!"

Her eyes widen. "It was always okay with me. My simple purpose in life. Save the bees. I do still think it is vastly important." Each of her sentences is sealed by a drumbeat of her fist on the counter. "But suddenly all I can think about day and night is how I can help Lyle back to a life of self-sufficiency and safety and purpose. He said something about not even knowing if it was worth being alive."

She massages her temples. "That freaked me out. He's only five years older than me!" She flings her hands in the air. "Why is it like this? Why is he in that place?" Both her hands come down on the counter with a thump, making the cutting board dance.

Our eyes lock for several seconds. What other thoughts lurk behind those crystal blues? What is going on in her overactive mind?

"What's the next thing?" I ask.

"I don't know." Her countenance changes, her look now pleads. "Help me. Can we do this together?" It seems a light bulb goes off behind those eyes. "I could cook him dinner. Have him over." She sweeps her hand.

"No." My knee-jerk reaction startles her.

"Excuse me?"

"That's not a good idea. Not yet. You already went to his place without me. Thank God you were safe."

"I thought about safety, but it was broad daylight, and I didn't want to miss an opportunity."

My pulse drums in my ears, but I try to keep my voice calm. "If he comes over to anyone's house, it should be mine. I'm a guy. You don't want—"

"Because I'm a girl?" Her fists dig into her hips.

Oh boy, I just cracked open a hornet's nest. *Lord, help.* I take a breath, close my eyes, and carefully set down the knife.

"I'm not saying you aren't capable. It's just, he's a guy. I'm a guy. I want you to be safe, and the thought of him knowing where you live concerns me, at least until we know him better. I'm not hip on him knowing where I live either. Maybe we could ease into that idea. Try something else first? Maybe bring home-cooked food to him at the library."

Her eyes are like a vacuum pulling my words out of my brain. She churns them in her mind. "You have a point. I can get over excited about things sometimes." She drops her head. "Okay, let's make a date. Let's plan what to make and when to bring it to him and maybe he could share it with Mindy and the others."

"Mindy?"

"Yeah. His neighbor, I guess. They all live in the same encampment by the utility creek behind the Szechwan Diner."

Shame floods my soul. She knows where Lyle lives. She's known him a couple of months. I've known him for a year and never had the guts to find out. Some things scare me. Homelessness is one of them.

"I guess I just needed to have a plan," she says. "I can't do nothing. If we put something on the calendar, I think I can move on with life." Her look up at me is apologetic. "I would like to try to enjoy your company tonight."

She asks me to pray before we eat. I do and it goes longer than I planned. Sometimes that happens. I start with a simple "Hey God, could you help?" Then the words tumble out like a flood over a dam. Candace doesn't seem to mind. In fact, she thanks me. Says it made her feel better. *Thanks, God.*

The night ends with us sitting cross-legged on the floor, laughing and slamming cards on the coffee table between us. When I look at the clock, I'm floored.

"Sorry. I didn't mean to stay so late."

"Time flies." She smiles.

"Can I—can we—?" I swallow hard. "Can we go on a hike or something? For fun? Forget about the rest of life for a while and just get into nature?"

"I'd love that!" She walks alongside me to the door.

We figure out our next mutual day off. A week away. I don't know if I can stand the wait. I thank her at the door, and she jabs my arm.

"I should thank *you*, Hank. You listened to me yammer on and made me dinner and turned this sad girl happy again." She smiles, staring into my eyes. I'd like nothing more than to kiss her. But I can't. Like she said, she was sad. Her emotions have been all over the map today. I don't need to add any more twists to the mix.

"Well, I look forward to next Sunday. After church, right?"

She nods and looks at me expectantly. I drag my hand over my face and pinch my mouth into fish lips. "Well, I better go." I turn as fast as I can before my face falls into hers. *Be a gentleman, Hank. Be a gentleman.*

When I get to my car, I turn and wave. I know I can't see well, but she seems to have a confused look on her face. Yet again, I'm disappointed with myself. Maybe one day my timing will be right.

CHAPTER 19
DO WHAT YOU CAN

CANDACE

Hank has called every night this week. He is so easy to talk to. Sunday can't get here fast enough, but I have to do a little homework before then. I'm not sure I'm good enough for him. He's so...spiritual. I mean, he was raised in a Christian home, and his family, all of them, still go to church together even though they are all grown and on their own.

It's not that I don't appreciate my own family's faith. We were just the hit-or-miss type when it came to church, hopped around, never connected to one place. I hope to change that now that I'm on my own. And I've read some of the Bible and have my own level of prayer, I guess. But not like Hank. He prays like he's really having a conversation. Like he hears back and doesn't just yammer on and on about the things he wants. Sometimes, I think I can even hear God's response when Hank prays. I wish I could have that when I pray.

The new ringtone on my phone sings out "You're My Best Friend."

"Hey, Jillian."

"Ooh, I'm your best friend," she sings with her silly Kermit the Frog voice the ringtone she set on my phone. I make no argument. She is my best friend and always will be.

"What's up?"

"Just checking in. I haven't heard from you in a week, with Matthew's mom stuff and your new heartthrob."

"He's not my heartthrob."

"Oh." Her tone conjures up an image of her pouty face. "Trouble in paradise."

"No. He's great. It's just…We're friends."

"Ahhh. In the friend zone and your heart can't handle slowing the beat?"

"Ha! I guess. I mean, sometimes he gives me a look like he might kiss me, but then he doesn't and I'm confused. He says yes to every opportunity to see me. His eyes got all glazed over the other night when we said goodnight. He even started to lean in, but then he turned on a dime and beelined to his car."

"Maybe he's being extra cautious. Maybe he isn't confident in how you feel. Maybe he's—"

"Not interested?"

"I doubt that. I mean, look at you. You're fun, smart, great at climbing trees."

I laugh.

"And you have the best laugh I've ever heard. Not to mention, he must have noticed you're pretty dang cute."

"Said by my obviously biased best friend."

"Oh, Can-Can. It's true! If he hasn't noticed all of those things, something's wrong with him and there's someone else for you."

"Nothing's wrong with him," I pout.

"Wow."

"Okay." This conversation is circling. "Not to change the subject, Jilly, but I am. Do you ever wonder if there's more to the God thing than what we're doing? I mean, do you ever think he has a specific purpose for people. Not just super spiritual people, but us commoners?"

"No one is common. Maybe everyday life is more important than we give it credit for. Hey, didn't you say something like that to me not too long ago? It's true. I think you may be weighed down by the whole thing with the homeless guy."

"His name is Lyle."

"Sorry. I meant no disrespect."

"Yeah, this is about him. And Hank. And how somehow both of them have turned my whole take on life upside down. You know I'm passionate about my job. I'm saving not only the bees but future generations through the work I do. I feel good about that." A sigh escapes. "But now, with Lyle, I... I gotta do something. Ya know?"

"Can-Can, if you gotta do something, I'm sure you will figure it out. You've never been one to let anything get in your way once you know what you want."

"I don't know what I want. I mean, yeah, I want Lyle to not be homeless. I want him to be successful in his own way. To have his needs met and be self-sufficient. But it's not about what I want. It's gotta be about what he wants, right? How do I help him? What if he doesn't want help?"

"Good question, isn't it? Okay, not to get all spiritual, but didn't Jesus say we'd always have the poor among us? Why do you suppose that is?"

"Because some don't want help? Don't know how to receive help? Won't help themselves? Can't? I don't know." My free hand thuds on my leg. "I don't get it. I don't feel equipped to deal with this. But I have to. I just know it."

"Then, sweet friend, do what you can. Give your best and take the opportunities as they come. And don't get down on yourself if Lyle doesn't receive help."

"And if he does?"

"Then he does, and we can all celebrate." Jillian clears her throat. "I have to go deal with bath time, but I wanted to check in. When do you see your heartthrob again?"

"He's not my—" I groan. "We're going on a hike in a couple of days. After church. He wants to show me the view from Gunsight Rock."

"So, he is interested!"

"He likes nature, just like me."

"Okay, you can think what you want, and I'll think what I want. He's interested."

A familiar chorus of screams screech in the background.

"I gotta go, Can-Can, the natives are restless. Love you."

"Love you too. Bye."

My phone goes silent, and I stare at the graying light of my living room. One tabletop lamp spotlights its amber glow on my scratched wooden table, and my dusty Bible whispers to me. I wonder if there's comfort to help me feel better or wisdom to show me what to do. Anything. I move to my overstuffed chair and pick up the sacred book. *Lord, can you help me out? Please show me what to do.* I open the book, see where the pages fall, and read.

CHAPTER 20
OKAY, I'LL GO

HANK

This week just drags on. The weight of the encounter between Candace and Lyle churns so haphazardly in my mind I can't think straight. What I thought might become a sweet romance is now an intense mission. *Can I have both, Lord?*

Lyle shows up at the library like clockwork. Same as always, I hand him his coffee like a barista, and he makes his way to his favorite chair and plants for the day. He only rises for brief bathroom breaks and to fumble through a shelf of books. I have no idea what he's reading. Something in the political science or world history section. Sometimes he resorts to the latest *People* magazine, but he usually thumbs through quickly and practically throws it back with a huff. Maybe he doesn't like the direction the world is going. I don't know.

I've mostly avoided him for the last few days, even changed the subject on the phone every night when Candace starts to talk about Lyle. But something inside tells me I need to get into Lyle's business before Candace and I see each other again. I can't put it off any longer. It's not just Candace I've been redirecting. I've been pretending I don't hear what the Holy Spirit has been dogging me about.

I turn my face toward the ceiling and kink my neck. It must be a sign to visit the back corner of the library. Rubbing my strained muscle, I look down at the open book on Lyle's black, mud-stained Ben Davis pants. He must have gotten a new pair from one of the mobile charities. *The History of the Nazi Regime* burns disturbing photos into the back of my brain.

"You tryin' to get my attention, Glasses?"

I wake from my stupor and examine his face. Is he really only five years older than Candace? His skin is aged, his teeth and gums have a gray hue. But every once in a while, I see a glint of youth in his eyes.

"Glasses!" His whisper is stern.

"Yeah. Sorry." I shake my head, to get my brain to register. "You got lunch plans?"

He raises a suspicious eyebrow.

"We haven't talked much lately. I thought…Let's have lunch. Talk. We haven't done that in a while."

"Sure, Glasses." He acts like he's thumbing through a date calendar and points to his palm. "Looks like I do have an opening. It's your lucky day."

I'm not sure if I hear sarcasm or if I'm just on edge. "I have a break in a half hour. Let's get out of here for a bit."

"Great," he says as if accepting a business venture.

"Great." I return to my station behind the counter, where a line is starting to form. That's how it usually is. Quiet for an hour until the second I leave, then the rush begins. *Lord, help me snap out of this funk. Please.*

I know I will once I have done what I've been trying to ignore. I've made the first step. Let's see if I follow through at lunch.

———

"So, Glasses," Lyle starts in, "I can tell you have an agenda. You and that girlfriend of yours have been giving me the eye lately. Acting all tangled with emotion. I'm not your charity case."

I stare at my greasy quarter pounder with cheese, slowly uncrinkling the wrapper.

Lyle leans forward like he's on to something. "I'm right. That's why you've been acting all distant and weird."

The wrapper gets a final ironing, then I lay the sandwich on top. I don't have an appetite. Just looking at the burger grosses me out. Worry has my stomach in a whirl.

"Okay. We have... We are..." I throw my hands up. "Whatever it is you are interpreting it as is probably right. You've been on my radar since the day I started working at the library. We've talked and kinda built a relationship. Had conversations, some not so easy. And yeah, I feel a certain responsibility for you. You're my...friend." I look for any indication Lyle knows where I'm going with this or even sees my sincerity. I am sincere, aren't I?

"Self-righteous."

"Huh?"

"That's what this responsibility you say you feel could be interpreted as. You must know better, right?" His eyes glare at me. "What if I am exactly where I'm supposed to be, doing exactly what I'm supposed to be doing?"

My eyebrows furrow so much they force my glasses down my nose. I push them back in place. I want to see accurately. "So you think my caring for you, Candace's caring for you, is self-righteous? You are exactly where you're supposed to be. Is that what you're saying?"

"Sounds like you just repeated what I said."

"You really think that?" I rake my fingers through my hair as if I need to get it out of my eyes so I can see straight, even though it's not in my face. "Can't we care? Are we supposed to act like everything is normal? Like living near a creek in a cardboard box is normal?"

"It is for some."

"But does it have to be? Is that what you want? Is that the life you see for yourself indefinitely? Don't you get cold at night? Hungry? Don't you want something different?"

His face reddens and contorts. "I told ya, man, it is what it is. My choices got me here. I'm stuck now. Like they say, I'm sleeping in the bed I made." He cocks his head sideways. "Besides, how do you know what I live in?" A light bulb turns on. "Oh, Blondie told you."

"Well, yeah, Candace told me." I look down. "Which bothered me. I should have known. I should've spent more time with you, taken you up on the offer to show me way back when. But honestly, Lyle, your lifestyle scares me. Probably because, yeah, I think there's something wrong with it. I think your needs aren't met. I was taught that we're supposed to be self-sufficient individuals productively fending for ourselves, that sleeping on the streets or whatever isn't a healthy goal in life."

Man, am I really getting into it with him, like this?

"Weren't you in college?" I ask. "On the road to become some kind of—"

"Fathead?"

"No," I say more sternly than I mean to. "You said you wanted to be a…" I tap my forehead, to knock the memory out into the open.

"City planner. Had some lofty ideas of cleaning up deteriorated metropolitan areas. Beautification, family parks, hiking paths. Blah, blah, blah." He scowls at me. "I told you. I lost that guy. I can't conjure him up. He left with the first snort. I lost my brain. Binged for days, then woke up in another world as another guy. I can't even remember—"

"But you do. You've told me."

"Oh buddy-boy, you don't know. Not really."

"When's the last time you used?"

His head jerks back in a sardonic laugh. "Doesn't even matter now. Damage is done."

"Recovery is possible. Come to church and…"

"Yeah, yeah, heard that before. But church folk don't like this mess in their pristine little chapels."

"You're being awfully prejudiced."

He bobs his head. "I'm prejudiced? Wow. Me? Prejudice?" He leans back in his seat and looks around like he's scanning a jury's reaction.

I'm not sure why he doesn't storm out. It's not because he wants to finish his meal. He hasn't even taken a bite. Neither have I. *Lord, help!*

"Okay, buddy-boy, tell you what. I'll go with you. To that church you're so fond of. The one that you say doesn't have a problem with people like me coming inside. Let's see which one of us is right."

"Fine." That's not exactly how I envisioned this, but inviting him to church is the one thing that keeps coming up when I pray for this guy. And I didn't even have to ask him. He invited himself.

"Fine." He reaches for his burger and rips a big bite out of it. "We're done with this conversation," he says around a mouthful of food. "We aren't gonna talk about it again until after that shiny Sunday service."

"Okay." I nod and decide I better take a bite, since my head is spinning and I have to get back to work in ten minutes.

———

"I have a family dinner on Saturday night," I say apologetically into the receiver. "So I won't be able to help you cook."

"Okay. I didn't know we had planned on cooking on Saturday." Candace's voice sounds on edge.

"Oh. I guess not." Aw man, I've assumed too much. "Candace, I actually wanted to tell you about my day. It's kinda throwing me off, so I'm sorry if I sound like my mind is jumbled. It is."

"We're still on for Sunday, right?" Her voice rises with each word.

"Yeah, of course. That's why my family wanted to get together Saturday. I told them I couldn't on Sunday. But I wanted to talk to you about Sunday too."

"Oh. Okay?"

Get the cat out of the bag before she freaks out anymore, will ya, Hank? "I took Lyle to lunch today. On my break. We talked, and it got kinda heated. Uncomfortable. But he agreed to go to church with me."

"That's great." Her voice chirps.

"Well, he wants to prove he won't be accepted. Which may be right. I know we're supposed to love everyone, and the church teaches love and acceptance, grace and compassion. But I do know some will turn their nose up when they see him. Man, I probably act like that myself sometimes. Self-righteous—that's what he called me. Maybe he's right. I don't know. I'm not sure we always see how others perceive us."

"We can only do the best we can. Besides, I know Lyle knows you truly care about him."

"Hmmm. I wonder sometimes. Anyway, I just wanted you to know. Maybe you could pray for me and him when you think about it. I'm feeling the pressure."

"Hank, you are the one who has been teaching me about trusting

God. We've prayed together about this. Which is crazy, because it's something I would have never done before with anyone besides Jillian and my family."

She gets silent. I want to hear more about what she thinks, but I don't even hear her breathe on the other end.

"You still there?"

"Yeah. I, um, I'll pray as best I know how. But what does Sunday look like now?"

"The same for us." Is that why she sounds so nervous? "I'll take Lyle home after church, maybe go through a drive-through so he has lunch. Then I'll pick you up by noon. We can hike to the top of Hood Mountain and have a picnic up there. The view is incredible. Bring your phone. You'll want pictures."

I hold in a laugh. I'll want pictures. I've wanted a picture of her since I met her. Maybe I'll get a picture of the two of us together on Sunday. A smile stretches across my face. "So, I'll see you at noon?"

"Yeah. I'm looking forward to it."

"Me too."

We get off the phone and I sit on the edge of my bed, and debrief with the only one who I know gets my situation completely—even more than I do. As faithful as the sunrise, he calms the churning waves that have washed over me and tells me to leave my worries in his hands. I lie back and pull on the covers. Cat jumps on the bed and circles on my chest until she finds her sweet spot. Her purr and the heat of her body warm my soul.

CHAPTER 21
THE SUN'LL COME OUT

CANDACE

S ince Matthew is spending quality time with his mom, I promised Jillian I'd hang out with her and the kids this Saturday night. Matthew is probably sleeping next to his mom's bedside in the hospital. After her chemo, it will take a while to recover.

I'm supposed to be the one calming everyone's nerves in this time of crisis, but I'm a bundle of frenetic mess. Emotions churn my insides in a chaotic whirl. The good—Hank. The scary—Matthew's mom's situation. The confusing—again Hank, but also Lyle. What is going on there?

God, I need your help. I end my prayer like Hank always ends his. *I leave it all in your hands.* Then I take a deep breath before I knock on my best friend's front door.

Giggles and screams rise in volume as little feet drum their way to the door. It swings open, and Hilary and James plow into me.

"Auntie!" they shriek in unison.

Arms are everywhere, I try to hold…I don't know what, but I maneuver to stop one of them from thudding to the ground.

James thuds anyway but bounces up. "Mama says you're teaching us to cook."

I raise an eyebrow at my deliriously gorgeous friend as she walks toward our jumble of flesh. By dressing to the nines, Jillian is "dealing," as she puts it—making herself as physically presentable as possible to mask whatever difficulties she's facing, her strategy for surviving the season her family is in. She does this for herself and to help the kids feel more grounded. She wants them to see their mom dressed and ready for anything, including a hot date, which is the look she's got going. Skinny jeans, a magenta sweater hanging off one shoulder, lipstick to match. I scan her up and down and give her a look the kids won't be able to decipher.

She stretches her hands out. "Don't you like it? It's my favorite color. It helps me feel happy and calm." She primps her hair. "Fancied my hair up too. Just for you."

"Or you." I paste on as good a smile as I can muster. She lets out a sucked-in breath.

"Yeah, for me." She pats my forearm as I set Hilary down feet first on the floor.

We share an understanding look meant to be unnoticed by the little eyes below.

"So, what am I teaching all of you to cook?"

"Cookies!" the rug rats sing.

I bite my lip and give Jillian as alarmed a look as I can.

"From what you've told me," she says, "you have success if you slow down, follow the directions, and stay engaged. You are one of the smartest people I know. You don't need some man to tell you that you can cook." She gives me an evil laugh.

"Not some man," I murmur.

"Besides, afterward you can wrap some up for your picnic tomorrow and impress said man." She gives me wiggly eyebrows and jabs me in the ribs as Hilary and James each grab one of my hands and drag me to the kitchen.

"What'll it be?" I ask the kids as I tie on the apron laid out for me. We all look the part of a prestigious cooking show. Tidy little matching aprons in a squeaky-clean kitchen. I halfway expect a camera to be set up somewhere. A white and blue flour sack holds center stage, with every ingredient in the supporting cast arranged in order.

"Chocolate chip!" James yells as he squeezes a package of butter.

Jillian must have set that out early to soften, because it is mush in his four-year-old hand. I let out a loud breath. This is just what I need. From the look on Jillian's face, it's what she needs too.

We all laugh as butter is scraped off the waxed paper and into the mixing bowl. The mixer buzzes as cups and teaspoons are leveled with a knife for perfect measurements. Jillian even has cookie scoops to make perfect dough balls and, with a pinch of the handle, drop onto the cookie sheet with ease.

"Who would believe I could have such a great time baking?" I say to her once the cookies are in the oven.

"Maybe it all comes down to the company you keep."

A smile stretches across my face as I remember the last time I shared a cooking experience.

She pokes me in the ribs. "You're glowing. Thinking of a certain someone?"

My face heats up.

"You excited about tomorrow?"

"What's tomorrow?" Hilary asks.

"Your auntie has a hot date with her librarian." Jillian wiggles her shoulders.

Hilary runs to me and holds my hand in both of hers. "Do you have a new boyfriend, Auntie? Is he nice?"

I smile. "Yes, he is very nice. But he's not exactly my boyfriend."

"Yet," Jillian adds, tickling Hilary's side. "But we have hope."

"Have you met him, Mama?"

"No. But I can tell he's a good one. I've never seen your auntie like this." She squats down and whispers loud enough in Hilary's ear for the whole room to hear. "She told me he is cute, and every time she talks about him she turns red."

"I do not."

"You're red right now, Auntie." Hilary points at my face, and my hand automatically rushes to my cheek to try and wipe it away. But I know it's too late. Jillian's right. Something is different this time. Hank is different. I'm just not sure if he feels the same way. Butterflies rise out of nowhere and take over my insides. *Oh Lord, help me handle tomorrow well.*

The cookies look and smell amazing.

"The moment of truth guys." I hand a warm cookie to each participant of our pretend cooking show. Hilary and James gobble theirs down, leaving melted chocolate smeared all over their faces and hands. Jillian grins at me and nods. I take my first bite of our creation.

"We did it!" I shout. "We made chocolate chip cookies like champion cooks." The four of us join hands and jump up and down and dance in a circle. I cry "Victory!" and we all throw our hands in the air, then the kids break out in waves of giggles and screams.

I can't wait to share some of the cookies with Hank tomorrow. I wonder what he'll think or say.

Those thoughts take a back burner as we clean the kitchen with clanks and water spraying everywhere. Jillian insists the kids clean up after themselves, even though it leaves a bigger mess for her in the end. When I question her tactics, she raises a finger at me. "Someday it will all pay off."

After the kids are tucked in bed, Jillian walks me to the door, and I voice my earlier concern about Hank's response to the cookies.

"Hold your horses, banshee!" Jillian sets a hand on my shoulder as we stand in her entry. "Everything will be wonderful. Believe the best for your day together. And don't bring up Lyle. Just let yourself... Let the two of you have some time to be just the two of you. Free and easy."

She ruffles my hair, then gives me her grateful smile. "Hey, thanks for the fun distraction. I needed a little vacay from Matthew's mama drama. Don't you dare tell him I called it that. I'm just emotionally tired. Mom's sickness, her surgery, my emotional husband, the need to put on brave for the kids. It wears me out sometimes. But this helped." She lets out a long sigh. "It really did."

My arms embrace my sweet friend and sway her back and forth. "I needed this too. I'm so grateful you're my friend. Tell the kids bye for me and give Matthew a hug when he comes home tomorrow."

A soft sliver of light disappears as Jillian closes the door behind me. I take in the night sky, sprinkled with diamond light. Time always flies when I'm with Jillian. Our friendship is magic like that. Easy breezy lemon squeezy.

I look at my watch to check the damage to my sleep schedule. It's past midnight. Fatigue threatens as I climb in my car and roll down the dark road spattered with an occasional streetlight. But my heart is lighter than before, my mind clear, and my hope reinforced. I sing a little tune the rest of the drive home. "The sun'll come out..."

CHAPTER 22
TODAY

HANK

Today's the day!

I tumble out of bed and catch myself before I accidentally step on Cat.

"Sorry, Cat."

She squeals at me in reprimand. My long-haired white cat was my parents' solution to help teenage me keep my mind on other things besides girls. I got one phone call from a girl and somehow that set off an alarm. I roll my eyes. I believe in being wholesome, in being honorable and respectful in romantic relationships. But sometimes it's a bit much—the "You gotta be good" mantra said in a way expecting one to be bad.

Yeah, I know temptation. But I also know me. I want the good stuff, so I choose to wait. I have waited. Not like a monk, but like a... I don't know. Not like a nice Christian boy. Just like a decent human being.

The reflection in the mirror makes me realize this internal rant comes from a place of hurt. Of being mistrusted before I even had a chance. But it doesn't matter anymore. I'm grown and taking things on my terms. Solid terms I've determined from personal study, research, observation. And prayer. God's my friend. Always has been. And I don't think he's a bit offended that I think every single one of us will be surprised in some way when we find out what he really thinks about things.

Cool scoops of water splash on my face as I try to wash away my heated thoughts. Crystal-clear droplets drizzle down my nose. I gotta have coffee and some quiet time before I conquer this day. I can't walk out my front door with guns a' blazin'.

This morning's rant is finally washed away by a hot-as-I-can-stand shower, a power bar, and minty toothpaste. The drive to the library helps too. Lyle decided on our meeting place. This'll be the first time I drive him anywhere. And this isn't just anywhere.

Lord, please don't let my church community prove me wrong. Sadly, my own mistrust lurks in the shadows.

Lyle stands stalwart on the sidewalk, in front of the concrete establishment that serves as home away from home for both of us. I wave as I pull up next to him.

"You look spiffy." My car door squeaks its own greeting.

"WD-40," he says, shaking his hand at the hinge. He sits and jerks the door closed with a grunt.

"It'll be okay," I say.

"Yeah, just oil it on the top and bottom of the hinge and..." He mumbles on incoherently, and wrings his hands.

"Okay." He doesn't want my sympathy, empathy, whatever. He acts unconcerned, points at every uninteresting thing out the window. I don't blame him. I'm nervous too.

The rest of the way to church is silent except for the hum of the engine. I give Lyle kudos for effort. He must've found a mobile shower somewhere and gotten a free haircut and new clothes. But the slight wild in his eyes hasn't been washed away.

"Here we are," I say, pulling into the driveway.

"Oh. You go to one of the big places."

"Big places?"

"Yeah. Lots of people. Big building. I was kinda hopin' for a little podunk chapel with only a few people scattered about, miles away from each other on wooden benches. You know, like you see pictures of in magazines." He looks at me with those feral eyes. I think I see fear, but he's come this far.

"Well, this is it." Neither of us move to get out. "No time like the present."

"Humph. We'll see." He clambers out the screeching door.

A few of my buddies come over and introduce themselves, with cool but friendly faces. Yeah, I warned them. My sisters are less discrete.

"Oh, you must be Lyle." Megan pats Lyle's shoulder. "Hanky-poo has told us all about you." All my sisters bustle around to shake Lyle's hand and tell him their names—exactly what I told them not to do last night at dinner. Do they listen? No. I'm just the little brother, who knows nothing. Clearing my throat brings them to a standstill.

"We're glad you're here, Lyle." Nina, my oldest sister, forces a toned-down smile. "We'll go find our seats now." She gathers my other sisters like a hen with chicks underwing and guides them into the building.

"Four sisters?"

"Yeah, and me," I say.

"And us." A familiar weight lands on my shoulder.

"Hey, Dad. Mom." The two are dressed old-school, as is their habit. The rest of the church world has gone blue-jean casual, but my parents still dress up. Navy suit and tie for dad and a dress with heels for mom. Nylons even. They look great, like they have a fancy wedding to attend.

"This is my friend Lyle." I motion to Lyle, then back to them. "Lyle, these are my folks, Gloria and Daniel."

"Ma'am." Lyle nods to Mom, then to Dad. "Sir."

"I hope you find today's service of value," Dad says, in true form. Then he reaches for Lyle's hand and shakes it. "It's nice to meet you. We'll be going inside now."

Lyle and I watch them move to the front doors.

"No time like the present. Isn't that what you said?" Lyle moves forward, which helps my own legs unstick. Here we go.

———

As I pull my car away from in front of the concrete building, somehow it seems darkened, like some random cloud doesn't believe the library deserves direct sunlight. "Drop me at the library" were Lyle's only words from the time we walked out of the sanctuary. I didn't want to push, so I didn't break the silence as he stared out his side window the whole way. He got out, didn't say a word, didn't look back. Just went straight inside the glass doors.

Well, Lord, I did what I knew to do. The rest is up to you. For now, can I please let it go and enjoy my time with Candace? I purposefully close the door to the events of this morning. The nubby radio dial reminds me how old my car is, but it works. And by the mercy of God, Mercy Me's "Happy Dance" plays on the radio and takes me to a different, light-hearted world.

A quick change and backpack grab and I'm out the door of my apartment and onward to my new hiking buddy's house. Today Candace is not Girl Who Murders Water or even Blondie. She's my hiking buddy.

I knock on my noggin to remind myself to let go of any expectations and simply enjoy the scenery, the exercise, and the company. "Let it be, let it be," I sing, knowing full well my hopes are set high.

CHAPTER 23
BETTER KEEP UP

HANK

*C*ontain your enthusiasm, Hank.* I restrain myself from skipping up Candace's walkway. Before I can even knock on the door, it opens.

"Hi, Hank!" Her smile is so sweet and cheerful I could turn into a puddle. "I'm so looking forward to this!" she says. "I haven't been on a hike like this in a while. Not for fun anyway." A freckled hand sweeps to the sky. "And look, what a beautiful day!"

The day pales in comparison to her. Oh yeah, my hopes are set high. *Cool your jets, Hank.* I fight my face's compulsion to explode with too big of a smile. Saying "You're in a good mood" seems safe. "You ready?"

"Yeah, let me get my pack." She turns away for a split second, then steps on my foot and into me as she pulls her door shut. "Whoops! Sorry!" She lifts her shoulders. "Guess I wasn't paying attention."

Man, did she throw glitter on herself today? She's beaming.

"No problem. I shoulda backed up." I'm not at all upset about being stepped on.

The passenger door lets out its usual screech as I open it so she can climb in.

"Wow, I had a car just like this." She sits in the gray bucket seat and pats the door handle like she's greeting a friend.

"You had a 2010 Corolla?"

"No." She looks at me apologetically. "One that screeched every time I opened the door." Her giggle is so cute I can't take offense. I dance around the back of the car. Let's face it. Today, she can't do anything wrong.

I slide into my seat, get the motor running, and we're off. The radio plays softly as she tells me about her morning church service spent sitting with her best friend's family, her godkids climbing all over her to their mother's fake dismay. She loves Jillian and her family. That's a good sign.

We pull into the dirt parking lot, strap on our backpacks, and approach the trailhead. Redwoods and scrub brush paint the edges of the red-brown dirt packed by countless hiking feet. Candace latches her thumbs under the straps of her green canvas pack and strides up the trail.

"You better keep up," she yells. "I'm on a mission."

I laugh and stumble into a trot behind her. Conversation volleys back and forth as we wind our way through groves of pine needles and dropped cones. Sun splatters through gaps in the branches, beckoning us up the trail. Until we hit our first obstacle. Serrated bark covers the broad circumference of a tree blocking the path.

"No biggie." Candace grins. "I love climbing." She hops on a stump and braces her hands to pull herself up. Feeling chivalrous, I hop around her. Being tall has its advantages. I offer her a hand up. She grimaces but decides to take my hand anyway.

My pull's a little too ambitious, and she bounces off me like a ricochet. I sweep my free arm around the back of her waist to catch her before she falls. She slams into me. My heart jerks through my chest, and sends a zing down my arms. I hold her tight. I can't help it. Her shoes slip down the silky bark. I didn't leave her any room to stand. I back up, taking her with me until she's solid, her feet set on the tree and her hands pressed against my chest.

"I got it." She pats my flannel shirt, then lifts her hands up. "I'm good. You can let go."

The warmth from her back radiates into my palms. I don't want to let go.

"Sorry. I didn't leave you room to get your bearings." I step away, maneuver the straight path the trunk makes, then jump down where it narrows.

I hear her thump down behind me, and I take a step before turning to see if I've made her completely uncomfortable. She's busy pulling her water bottle out of her backpack's side pocket. Alrighty then. Didn't faze her. Not like it did me.

As we travel up the trail, she names every insect and bird she sees, her eyes wide like a kid in a candy shop. She stops suddenly, kneels, and waves me over, gesturing to walk slowly.

"Look," she whispers. She points to a green stick-like creature, then rests her hand gently next to it, coaxing it onto her finger. "A praying mantis." Her eyes sparkle as she shows me her find. "They are great to have in a garden. Isn't he the coolest creature you've ever seen?"

She sets the insect back on a low-lying plant. She's in her element, telling me about her latest project at work—saving humanity by teaching others the importance of bugs. Hands-on research will take her to various locations as she tracks the census and migration of butterflies. The way she describes it makes the job sound fun, although she says she'll spend the approaching winter months mainly mulling over research papers and historic patterns. I didn't know she goes to classrooms as a guest speaker to teach elementary kids the importance of pollinators—captivating her audience, I'm sure.

"What's the elevation here?" she asks, as she stomps uphill. "How much higher does this path go? My chest is tight, and I thought I was in decent shape."

"A couple more turns and we're there. We can take a break at the next plateau."

"Nope. I gotta keep going with the momentum. If I stop, I might not want to keep pushing on."

"Ah. Like not wanting to follow a recipe when there are too many steps?"

"Ha ha. I've gotten a lot better, even *you* have to admit that. I'd even venture to say water is safe in my hands."

My laugh echoes as we trudge the last ascent toward the top of the summit. Trees thin at the last bend of the path. Open, clear blue sky welcomes us to our destination.

"We're here!" I stretch my arms out to the view. Stair steps of rounded green and gold hills flow down into the valley, then point, like an arrow, to the city below.

"Wow." Candace pants, then plops on a perfectly placed bench. "What a view."

I sit next to her and drop my backpack onto the soft dusty ground by my feet. My hands rest next to me on the worn wood plank of the bench as I take in the scenery. Something tickles the back of my hand. I look down as one rogue feminine pinkie brushes over my skin, sending a prickly sensation up my arm. My gaze hovers for a second on the warm flesh capturing my attention. I look up and see Candace staring straight into me.

It only takes a second for something primal to take over. My free hand sails to her cheek, drawing her face toward me. Then my lips fall into hers, and the rest of the world disappears behind my closed eyes. Warmth like honey pours over my head, down into my soul. I'm not sure how long our lips have been entwined by the time I slowly draw back. Her eyes are still closed, her lips parted and full. I engrave this image in my mind. I want to keep it forever. Some say you internalize what you feel when you close your eyes. I believe them.

Her eyes open like the first colors of sunrise, and a slight smile washes across her face. I pinch the corner of my lips tight and raise an eyebrow. A peachy blush brushes over her cheeks as her smile grows. I'm pretty sure she feels what I am. This is gonna be good.

"How do you start a conversation after that?" she finally says.

I point to my backpack and chuckle. "I guess like this. You hungry?"

I throw a small blanket out on the grassy area a short way down from the summit and set out sandwiches, oranges, and handy-dandy sanitizer wipes.

"Hand wipes even? You do this often?"

"Megan thought they would be a funny gag gift. Joke's on her. I use these all the time." Quiet laughter escapes as I think about my quirky

119

sister. Then I take a deep breath as I refocus on the expansive valley below.

"This is one of my go-to spots when I need to recoup from all the pain of the world."

"Pain of the world?"

"You know. When I need a break. When life gets sad or overwhelming. Or just when I need some time to myself. This is a great quiet place to think." Or pray.

Candace looks at me sideways, then nods. "I had my own special place when I was a kid. In the top of a catalpa tree in my backyard. It grew higher than our rooftop. There was this one place where the branches were positioned perfectly to create a seat. The bark was scratchy, but I didn't care. I'd throw my current read into my backpack, climb up, and stay there for hours. Nothing could touch me up there."

"Sounds like a cool place. It's not hard to picture you reading for hours in a tree."

She nods as she stares out over the landscape. We finish our meal as we talk about our hiding places as kids and even adults. She laughs when I describe being an adult as feeling like wearing clothes that don't quite fit. "Too big and loose and awkward. Like clomping around in your dad's shoes."

"Like how Lyle's clothes fit him," Candace says.

My heart sinks. I should've known better than to expect to get away from the topic of Lyle. I like the guy. I do. He's part of my life. I just can't let his story consume mine, right?

"Sorry to bring him up," Candace whispers.

I look up to a sweet but concerned face and shake my head. "I just didn't want to talk about Lyle. Not today." Wow, that sounds uncaring.

"I get it. Lyle's story is hard to swallow. You saw me break down the other day." She shakes her head like a windshield wiper swishing away excess water. "We can pick that up another time." She spreads her hands up to the softened sunlight. "Today is about this."

She flings her backpack into her lap, lifts the flap, and pulls out a container. "I have something for you." Setting aside the container's red plastic lid, she shows me the treasure inside.

"Cookies?" I smile and reach for one.

"Take a bite. Tell me what you think."

"Wait a minute. Did you make these?"

Her face lights up like a million candles.

"Jillian's kids and I made them last night." She pats her own shoulder. "I followed the recipe to a *T*. I couldn't wait to share them with you."

I don't even try to hide my grin. "You wanted to share them with me? Is this your way of saying you don't need my help cooking anymore?"

Her jaw drops along with her hands, which slam on her lap. "No! I just wanted to show you I could do it. I still want you to help me learn to cook. And now since we..." She covers her lips with three fingers and my heart starts pounding.

My face is tight from the smile I can't wipe off. "You're blushing."

"I am not." She rubs her cheeks, then stands up and walks to the edge of the mountain. "I want a 360-degree video to prove I made it all the way up here." She whips out her phone and slowly twirls in a circle, capturing me in the picture as she sweeps around.

"Now for one of us," she plops down next to me. "You have to take the picture. Your arms are longer."

She hands me the camera and leans into me, her closeness makes me fumble the phone before I finally snatch it in my grasp. I try to act cool as I lean toward her and smile at our reflections on the face of the phone. After a few clicks, I hand it to her.

"Will you send me the pictures?"

She nods and starts packing up. "We better head back down the mountain. Before it gets dark."

CHAPTER 24
NEIGHBOR BOB

HANK

The whole world can probably hear my heart pound as I walk Candace to her apartment. Anticipation is killing me. She'll let me kiss her goodbye, right?

"Hi, Neighbor Bob," she sings as we pass by her neighbor.

He looks up from the pot of flowers he's watering and grins.

"You remember my friend Hank." She gestures to me.

He gives a little wave with the hose and splashes water on the cement. "You two have a nice hike?"

"It was beautiful up there! We could see the whole valley. Even found the apartment complex." Candace scrunches her face. "I think."

"Nice. Nice." Her neighbor drawls out slowly giving me a suspicious glare.

I turn toward Candace, "I had a great time," She smiles expectantly, and I turn toward Bob the neighbor. He eyes me. I shift my feet and swallow hard. "Call you tomorrow? After work?"

I look back at her neighbor. He doesn't budge. I turn back toward Candace; her eyes light up and she nods. I glance from her to Bob. He's overwatering that pot and staring at me, lips pressed in a tight line. I can't kiss her in front of him.

"Well, okay. Um." I reach for Candace's hand and shake it. "See you soon." I turn and trudge down the walk.

What was I supposed to do? Kiss her with Neighbor Bob close enough to squirt me with the hose? I hear her faint "'Kay, bye." Yep. I did it again—let both of us down.

———

CANDACE

As Hank walks away, I turn around and see Bob's glare. I slam my fists onto my hips like my mother did when I got in trouble.

"Neighbor Bob!"

"What? I'm watching out for you."

"Some things are not your business."

"He was gonna kiss you. Or try to." He points two fingers in the direction Hank took and then at his own eyes. "I could see it. I know the look."

I harumph at him.

He rocks back on his heels and turns off his hose. "This was your first date."

"We've been seeing each other for a couple of months."

"That doesn't count. He helps you cook. Not—" He drops his hose to the ground and sways and bear-hugs himself.

I let out an aggressive huff. "Next time, kindly go inside your apartment and give us some privacy." I turn on my heels and fight to get my key into the lock. The whole key ring clatters onto the ground in complaint. I can't even make a dramatic scene. I just flub it all up.

"Sorry." Bob's gentle voice cracks.

I look into his glistening grandfatherly eyes. "No, I'm sorry. My attitude was uncalled for. I just…"

"Wanted a goodbye kiss?" The corner of his mouth lifts.

Not wanting to admit it, I pinch my lips and drop my head.

"Then I won't get in the way next time," he says gently. "Hey, how 'bout dinner tonight?"

My head pops up. "Give me a half hour, then come on over. There's a recipe I've been wanting to try."

———

My wet hair slaps my face, so I braid it down my back, wash my hands, then fumble through the kitchen drawer, to find the treasure I hope will cheer Neighbor Bob. Receipts and yellowed loose papers have overtaken the drawer. I shuffle them around until I find the vintage recipe card with a blue checkered border and yellow daisies in the corner.

The handwriting on the card is impeccable. "My Bob's Favorite Casserole." He forgot the card when he cooked dinner for me after my last breakup. When I told him I found it, he said to keep it. Said maybe it could be my favorite casserole too.

He's a sweet man. I sense his loneliness sometimes, although he is good at hiding it. I can't imagine being married to someone for fifty-plus years, losing them, and still somehow going on with living. But he has and does, and still finds purpose in each day. I guess I'm part of his purpose. He watches out for me. I'd love to find a love like he and his Margaret had.

A scuffle reverberates against my front door, then the familiar "shave-and-a-haircut" knock. Like the end of a joke. I open the door to a bouquet of Bob's best roses blocking my view of his face. He pushes them toward me.

"Bawwwb, you didn't have to do that." I draw the bouquet to my face, and take in the luxurious rosy fragrance.

"Please accept these as my humble apology." He grins as I gesture for him to come inside.

We sit across from each other at the table, the air fills with savory aromas of chicken, buttery white sauce, and parmesan. I tell him about the day's hike. The beauty, the trees, the view. Everything except the parts I keep hidden, safe in my heart. Moments only meant for me and Hank. But I think Bob already suspects.

He ventures into his own reminiscence of his life and love with Margaret. I've seen pictures of the two of them, eyes beaming at each other, their adoration seeming to color the black-and-white photos. I let him talk about her as much as he wants, even though I've heard the same stories over and over. He never tires of the memories. It's as if he lives them all over again. I'm happy to journey back with him.

We finish eating and sit on the couch with hot herbal tea. After *Jeopardy* and *Wheel of Fortune*, he stands up, stretches his arms to his sides, and waits a heartbeat before he takes his cup to the sink. He washes the cup by hand, swirls the dish towel to dry it, and returns it to the cupboard where it belongs.

Sweet Neighbor Bob—I love him so much. How could Hank be intimidated by him? Maybe Hank didn't even want to kiss me again.

———

After talking over second graders as a guest speaker all day, my voice is hoarse, my energy depleted. I hope I inspired them to care for their planet and the insects that keep it buzzing, but I can't wait to kick off my shoes and throw on my comfy sweats. An uncharacteristic creak screeches from my car door as I half-heartedly slam it shut. I drop my head on the car's roof and take in the brisk evening air.

Dang! I really don't want to cook, and I didn't think to stop at a drive-through on the way home. The second graders have rendered my mind useless. Pure mush.

I flail my hands in the air and stomp my feet toward my apartment. This is my tizzy fit before I enter my front door and put on my big-girl self. As I round the last curve of my walk, I see Neighbor Bob's arms circling toward my front stoop in grand conversation. Heat spreads from my center up into my face. I keep my head down to contain the sudden change in my internal atmosphere.

"Hi," Hank says. His hair is wet and slicked back as he sits on the ground, his back against my door with a full brown grocery bag between his lanky bent knees.

"Hi," I whisper.

"Hank here has been telling me all about how you have improved by leaps and bounds with your cooking." Neighbor Bob glows. "And I told him how great a job you did last night with my Margaret's casserole."

"Thanks, Neighbor Bob." Heat I feel no need to hide warms my cheeks.

"I'll leave you two to your cooking," Bob says. "I've got something in the oven myself and am sure it's time to pull it out. Have a nice evening." Unlike the other night, Bob promptly exits into his apartment.

Hank hasn't moved since I walked up. He gives me a cautious look.

"Sorry, just finished a swim." He runs a hand through his damp hair. "I brought groceries. Thought I'd surprise you and cook. You said today might be challenging."

"Yeah. Definitely."

He rises and bounces the groceries up into his arms. "So, you okay if I cook you dinner? Maybe hang out for a while?"

More than okay. But I shrug, not wanting to seem too excited. "Sure." Once inside, I kick off my shoes, and they fly across the floor.

Hank laughs. "Feel better?"

My hair flops in my face as I nod, then free-fall onto my couch. "Can I just take a minute before I help you?" Even with endorphins bursting at his presence, my legs and brain are still mush.

"Take as long as you want. No cooking homework for you tonight."

"Thank you." He's adorable as he buzzes around my kitchen like he owns the place, then floats like a butterfly from the sink to the spice cabinet to the stove. I guess we've cooked enough together for him to know where everything is. Somehow, he doesn't clang pans and bang into things the way I do. In almost no time, the food smells amazing. "What are you making?"

His eyes widen from across the room. Man, is he getting cuter? It shouldn't be possible, but every day he is more attractive, his eyes a richer brown. And oh, I love his smile.

"Chicken parmigiana," he announces with an awful Italian accent.

"Sounds heavenly." I yawn and let my heavy eyelids close, for just a second.

"Hey Candace..." A velvety whisper nudges me out of a deep haze. "Dinner's ready if you're hungry."

I throw off the unintended blanket of sleep, stand too fast and wobble. Stars circle in my head as strong hands grab my elbows to steady me. I clench the solid forearms to keep from falling. "Stood up too fast," I say as my vision clears to Hank's sweet, concerned face.

"Maybe I should have just let you come home and sleep."

"No. I wanted to see you." That admission flew out faster than I expected. Can't take it back now. Forget acting coy.

He chuckles as his grin broadens. "I'm glad to hear it." He bows and gestures toward the beautifully set table.

"Wow, I didn't notice those flowers before."

He pulls out my chair. "I see I wasn't the only one with the idea." He has a weird tone in his voice as he points to the bouquet on the counter.

"Neighbor Bob," I say. "A peace offering."

Hank gives me a questioning look.

I shrug my shoulders, not wanting to admit the reason. Maybe Hank wasn't even going to kiss me goodbye. I'm still not sure if yesterday's kiss was a fluke or intentional. But man, I can't stop thinking about it. The. Best. Kiss. Ever.

Hank sits across from me, folds his hands, and bows his head. I stare at the silky brown mop of hair falling over his dark glasses. His head draws up just enough that I can see his eyes peek over the rims. "You want to pray? Or do you want me to?"

I nod toward him.

"Lord, thank you for this day and this time that I get to spend with Candace. Thank you for your provision and the nourishment it provides. Please help Candace to recuperate from her busy day, and let this evening be a blessing to all of us. In your name, amen."

His head pops up. "May I serve you?"

I smile and lift my plate. "Blessing to *all* of us? Expound."

He chuckles under his breath as he lifts steaming layers of eggplant and breaded chicken breast onto my plate. "'All of us' meaning you, me, and God. I like to think he hangs out with us and can be blessed by our company as well."

The tender chicken is like slicing through butter. Each bite tastes as good as Hank looks eating it.

"What do you think?" He points to my plate with his knife.

"So good." So amazingly good. "Can you cook for me forever?" Aw man, there I go again.

Hank's head drops down toward his plate, and a touch of red flashes across his cheeks. "Might be able to arrange it."

Maybe he does like me.

CHAPTER 25
A THING

HANK

We sit next to each other on the couch, with leftover cookies from yesterday and hot chocolate. The evening has floated along without a hitch. Watching Candace sleep while I put dinner together felt comfortable, peaceful, like I was home.

She must feel the same way to be able to fall asleep, or else she was incredibly exhausted. Maybe both. While we ate, she perked up and the conversation took off. She debriefed her day spent with second graders. We cleaned the dishes together like an old married couple. Man, I gotta stop letting my thoughts get away from me.

"So—" There's an exclamation point in her voice. "You going to tell me about yesterday?"

My stomach clenches. I'm not sure what she means. Is she calling me out for kissing her? Maybe I blew it. Except tonight she said she wanted to see me.

"How'd it go with Lyle?"

Oh. I run my hand over my head, and brush my unruly hair out of my face. "Well, I picked him up at the library, and he went to church with me."

"And?"

"He walked out as soon as the service was over, and he didn't want to talk the whole way back to the library. Today was my day off, so I haven't seen him since."

"Could you read what he was thinking at all? What happened before the service?"

I tilt my head. "He seemed uncomfortable. Like he didn't want to be there. He met my parents and sisters. They acted normally, I guess."

She frowns but waits for me to continue.

"Honestly, I'm a little discouraged. I've been inviting him to church for months. I quit asking after a while, but when you and I prayed the other night, I got the impression I was supposed to ask again. I'm not sure why he agreed this time or what I'm supposed to do now. Knowing me, I'm gonna act all awkward about it next time I see him."

My head hits the back of the couch, and I stare at an old water stain on the popcorn ceiling.

Candace sighs. "My roof leaked last fall. Someone from maintenance painted over it, but it didn't work."

I lower my gaze and see her look of compassion, her eyes pools of turquoise caring.

She sighs again. "I don't know what all Lyle deals with or how he thinks about things. But with every day that goes by, the gotta-do-something volcano billows more steam."

She's funny. "Yeah, I know what you mean."

"So— " She squares on the couch, faces me and waves her hands back and forth between us. "I think we, if you're up for it, are supposed to do a little something each week to help Lyle. "

I nod for her to go on.

"Number one, I think we're supposed to really get to know him. And number two, I think I'm supposed to find out what it would take to get him into some kind of shelter. Not a 'shelter' shelter, but a place of his own that isn't next to a creek under a cardboard roof. There are services set up to help. Let's figure that out with him and see what we can do." She looks at the stain on the ceiling. "I know I can't solve the homeless crisis, but I— " Her eyes home in on mine. "*We* can help one person. Can't we?"

"You sure you want to be stuck with me for however long that might take."

She giggles and drops her head. If my eyes aren't deceiving me in the dim lamplight, she's blushing.

"I think I can handle it." Her head pops up with a look of resolve as she places both hands on either side of my face and plants her lips hard against mine. I can't breathe, but who cares. She pulls back and wakes me from a daze.

My glasses are fogged. I take them off and wipe them with the hem of my shirt.

"Sorry." She draws her hand over her mouth. "I was too bold."

Nope, I would not say that. I loved every second of it. "Don't be sorry. It was nice."

She giggles. Her pink cheeks come into clearer view as I put my glasses back on.

"You have a nice face," she says. "You look good with glasses, but I like seeing your face without them." She swirls her hands around her eyes. "I can see your eyes better."

"I wish I could see with my eyes better without my glasses too." *Corny, Hank.* I fumble, trying to find better words.

She reaches for my hand and holds it between hers. "It was a weird move to pull when we were talking about Lyle. . .. But then…" She fumbles too.

"Candace?"

The expectant way she looks at me gives me courage. "Do you think we can admit maybe we like each other?"

A wide grin spreads across her face as she lets out a laugh. "Oh good! Yes! I just… After yesterday, I thought you were going to kiss me goodbye. But Neighbor Bob… And then you didn't." She lets go of my hand and flings hers in the air. "So, are you saying you like me? Besides the cooking, I mean?"

"Yes. I like you, and it has nothing to do with cooking."

She giggles. "I like you too. Nothing to do with cooking." She squishes her face up and lifts her fingers to a pinch. "Well, maybe a little about cooking. Tonight's amazing dinner is probably enough to entrance me for life. But you get a like from me on your own merit, for the kind of guy you are."

Wow. I think that's the best compliment I've ever gotten from a girl. And she's not just any girl.

"So, are we a thing?" she asks.

"Yeah. I think we're a thing."

———

CANDACE

"I full-on kissed him," I announce to Jillian over the phone.

"Candy-girl, what were you thinking?"

"Jillian, you of all people can't criticize. You thought I was draggin' my feet."

"I haven't gotten to meet him yet. I have to approve."

"Really?"

"Nawww, I'm happy for you." She laughs, and I hear muffled yells in the background. "But you do need to have Matt and me over to meet this guy. I've been dying to get to know Mr. Library."

"And—" I pause for effect. "He agreed we're a thing! Jilly, he is the most upstanding guy I've ever met. I mean, I think he's cute, but more than that, he is just a super good guy. And it's so easy to be with him. I even fell asleep while he made dinner in my kitchen. What a bad hostess! But he was okay with it—let me sleep and made me dinner and woke me up so sweetly. And we talked and talked and...you know."

"Made out!" Her cackle pierces my ear through the phone, then I hear Matthew in the background. "Who made out?"

Although I know she'll tell him every detail later, I hear her tell him it's none of his business. She knows I don't mind if he knows. That's how they are. No secrets. Ah, to have a relationship like that. Sharing everything and still crazy mad for each other.

After we get off the phone, I sit in the quiet of my little apartment. It feels homier than ever simply because Hank's presence lingers between these walls.

CHAPTER 26
A SECOND CHANCE

HANK

A grizzled slump washes past my peripheral vision as I check in the books left in the return drop after hours. Straightening up, I try to make eye contact, but Lyle's reluctance to acknowledge me is almost tangible. My scanner beeps repeatedly, letting me know the computer has gathered the information it needs and I can return the books to their homes on the shelves. Will Lyle be able to ignore me when I'm standing inches away, putting books in their place?

The cart drags on the carpet like a disobedient kid sticking in his heels, but I muscle it forward. I could start in the kids' section, but I head straight toward Lyle's favorite, history, where he has claimed the plaid chair as his second home. I'd venture to say it is softer and warmer than the layered mat of cardboard and blankets Candace described.

Moment of truth. "Lyle, you didn't get your coffee this morning. Can I bring you some?"

He grunts and shakes his head without looking up. As he angles his body away from me, his shoulder masks his expression.

"I'll leave the cart here and be right back with a cup." I move quickly, but he calls out behind me.

"Already had coffee. Someone wanted to help the homeless guy and bought me a cup. I don't need anymore."

I turn and see anger, frustration, maybe even hate in his eyes. But I don't think his glare is directed entirely at me.

"You just gonna stand there lookin' stupid?" he asks.

Shushes characteristic of the OFC come from various directions.

My feet unstick and I take long strides toward my friend, then I crouch on a knee in front of him. "Are we going to talk about this?"

"What?"

"Your reaction Sunday and this attitude that permeates the place."

He huffs a laugh. "You want me to say what's wrong? Make you feel better?" His voice is rising.

"Shhh."

Lyle turns toward the nearby shusher and snarls.

Mrs. Jones scurries to my side and hovers over me. "Hank, I'm sorry, but your friend is going to have to leave if he keeps disturbing the rest of the patrons."

I shake my head at my supervisor. "He'll be fine. I'll take care of this." Mrs. Jones has been on edge lately. She's mentioned some recent issues at home, but didn't go into detail.

Lyle clears his throat and I turn to see his expression, his face is tilted up in an odd look, like he's challenging me to a duel. I don't break eye contact. "We can work this out. I just want to talk. Figure out what I did wrong so I can fix it."

"You want to fix something with me?" He scoffs at the idea.

"Yeah Lyle, I do. I want to be your friend. I thought we *were* friends. I have to do my job now. But can we talk during my break, maybe outside the library? Please?"

His gruff hand rakes back and forth through his sticky-looking hair. "I guess I'll give you a second chance."

A second chance? Great! "Thanks, Lyle. My break is in a couple of hours. I'll come over then and we'll go out on the back patio."

Silent prayer is all I can do. I want to howl to God but have to settle for the quietness of my heart and beg for guidance on what to say, for Lyle to be receptive, to not let me put my foot in my mouth, and for a miraculous breakthrough of some kind—I don't even know what.

Whatever Lyle needs, whatever I need. I wish I could scream for help, but pinching my lips and grumbling in my heart is the best I got.

Two hours later, I pour two cups of sludge from the percolator sitting on the flimsy table at the entry and walk back to where Lyle sits. He watches me walk toward him the whole way, isn't going to make this easy by meeting me halfway. I guess I should be happy he is meeting me at all. Two feet in front of him, I kneel and hand him the cup. "Peace offering."

"Burnt mud." He turns up his nose. "Your boss's coffee doesn't come close to yours."

"Want me to make a new pot?"

"You got what, fifteen minutes before you have to be back at it?" His expression softens.

"What'll it be? Fresh coffee or a quick chat?"

He stands up, giving me his answer. Silently, we walk side by side out the back sliding door, into the fenced courtyard the library uses in the summer for a kids' camp. A combination of mismatched dusty metal and green plastic chairs clutter the courtyard. We set our coffee cups on a metal table, once black but now grayed from being out in the elements.

"Just like home." Lyle laughs, slapping the plastic armrest as he sits in the chair.

I try to laugh, but nothing comes out. Instead, my eyes fix on him. There is a human like me behind the messy hair blocking the full view of his face. "What happened? What's going on?" It's all I can think to say.

"Nothin'."

"Yeah, that explains not talking Sunday and the attitude today."

Wrinkled hands grab at his head, his youth cloaked by the hard life he's lived. For how long? Ten years? I don't know. He shifts and squirms and readjusts again, then finally looks at me straight.

"You don't have time for the whole story, and I can't condense it in the next five minutes, so 'Nothing' is a better answer."

"I don't buy that. What's it gonna take for you to tell me the whole story?"

"Hours. Hours and hours. If you really want to know, Glasses, you're gonna to have to give me your undivided attention. And not here at your place of business. If we are friends, this has to happen out there." He points over the fence. "If you want a change, you've got to do something different."

I echo his movement. "We *were* out there. On Sunday. That was doing something different."

His stare pierces into me. "On Sunday. At your church. That hasn't been my world for a very long time."

A light bulb goes off in my mind. "You have a church background."

"Great deduction, Einstein."

A knock clacks against the glass door behind me. Mrs. Jones points to her watch and motions me to get back in the library. I nod at her and turn back to Lyle. "Lunch? Please?"

"Fine."

I lean against the table as I get up, and a horrendous screech sounds from the metal chair as it skids against the concrete. I love the library and don't begrudge returning to duty, but all I can think of is how to make the time go by without driving myself crazy for the next two hours.

———

"Sorry, but with only forty-five minutes, we had to eat close by."

"Mickey-D's is my other home away from home." He places his order and steps back, letting me take it from there.

Within minutes, we carry our red plastic trays to our usual, corner table.

"I can tell you one thing right now, Glasses. Even with all the conversations we've had, you aren't going to get a good grip of my story at this piddly lunch."

"So...dinner?"

"What do you mean?"

"Tonight. I'll cook for you. You can come to my house. We can talk longer. I'll take you home afterward."

"You sure you can handle all that?"

I can't stop my head from tilting. He squints.

This is where the rubber meets the road. I've been trying to protect my own life from Lyle, my privacy. Have I been worried he might take advantage and bring me down with him? Something like that, I guess. There may be some wisdom in discrimination, but after knowing the guy this long and listening to the compelling voice in my heart, I know I'm meant to take him up on this opportunity.

"Yeah, I've known you for a year. I've said we are friends. Obviously, it hasn't been a typical friendship."

"No. It's been acquaintances. It's been limited. I've been your mercy case, and I don't expect that to change. But I want to see if you mean what you say when it gets personal." He eyes me questioningly.

"You're coming home with me tonight," I say. Then my stomach clenches as I remember I was supposed to go to Candace's. "You okay if Candace joins us, or should I cancel the plans she and I made."

"You were going to cook with Blondie?"

I nod.

He huffs. "If she's okay with it, I'm okay with it. Heck, she already knows where I live, so she's one up on you anyway." He jeers at me.

Yep, she had more courage than me and sooner. But I have to let that disappointment in myself go. "I'll call her. Either way, it's you and me for dinner tonight." And that is that.

———

Mid-afternoon, Marcus stands in front of me and places a handful of papers filled with words scribbled on them. He slaps a hand on them. "I did it."

"You did it?"

"Yeah, read books, took notes," he pats the papers again. "These are them. Can you hook me up with a computer?"

"Of course, follow me." I lead the way to one of the work desks thanking God for the boost of confidence. Marcus sits at the desk and starts tapping the keyboard like a pro. I guess he's listened at school more than I've given him credit for.

An hour later I hear the whir of one of our printers. Then Marcus marches to the check-out and hands me a two-page, double-spaced essay titled, "Einstein, A Lot Like Me." The first couple of lines catch my attention, "Einstein and I have something in common. He didn't like school and neither do I." I chuckle to myself and expect the rest of the essay to offer more insight into the inner life of the teen with the sly grin standing in front of me.

"You did it. Good job." I nod. "So where and when?"

"There's a new steakhouse."

"Ah, upping the ante."

"You said anywhere." I've never noticed how white his teeth are, or maybe I've never seen him smile so big.

"Yes I did. I wouldn't mind checkin' the place out either."

Marcus almost laughs and heads toward the door. "Sunday, same as last time."

"You got it." I can hang out with Candace afterward. She's gung-ho about encouraging "Einstein." Says every kid could use a good mentor. I guess she'd consider me a good mentor. I wonder if he would.

CHAPTER 27
CAT

CANDACE

Shuffling a turtle's pace to the front door, I pray I don't have an adverse reaction. I took my allergy med, and Hank said he'd keep his cat in the bedroom, but sometimes even that isn't enough and I start sneezing or breaking out in hives. I *would* fall for a guy who loves cats. Actually, I love cats too. I just can't touch them or breathe very well around them.

Moment of truth. My knuckles beat out Neighbor Bob's knock rhythm on Hank's front door. It opens quickly to a man with wet hair and a wide grin.

Lyle is wearing Hank's Red Socks t-shirt and jeans with the legs rolled up. He's closer to my height than Hank, so our eyes are almost level. "Come on in, Blondie." He steps backward and swoops his arm to welcome me. "Hank's got dinner going already. He couldn't get away from the stove, so you get me."

Hank's Sierra cologne tickles my nose as I breeze past Lyle. The smell of a rich tomato base with Italian herbs fills my senses next. I follow the aroma around the corner and see Hank facing the stove, pinching spices over a big pot with one hand and holding a wooden spoon in the other. I move next to him and bump my hip against his.

His head tilts so sweetly as he looks down at me with a half smile. I think it's a look of apology and gratitude, so I smile back hoping he understands everything is okay.

"Hi," I whisper.

"Hey."

"It's what we both want. Remember?"

His shoulders noticeably drop as he closes his eyes and takes a breath. A moment later, he looks back at me. "Thanks."

Lyle rummages through cabinets, grabs dishes, silverware, and glasses and sets the table. He carefully folds our napkins into neat envelopes and lays the utensils inside. "Had a part-time wait job in college," he responds to my questioning look, then he grumbles something I can't quite make out.

I sit across from Lyle, Hank is the hinge between us at the square table. And so it begins.

"Guess you're wondering why I've monkeyed with your date, Blondie. Hank here wants to be my friend. Evidently, there is an urgency to it."

Hank tries not to roll his eyes, but both Lyle and I see it.

"I'm right," Lyle says.

I stare at Lyle over the rims of my glasses to convey I want to be serious. "Okay, I'm not letting this continue in this direction. Let me tell you what Hank and I have talked about concerning you."

"Concerning me?" he says, thumbing his chest with an innocent look.

"Lyle, you expect us to understand you, and I expect the same in return." I huff a breath. "We can't help wanting you to not be homeless. I can't stand the thought of the changing weather and you being cold and wet and uncomfortable. Not when I can see so much potential in you."

"Potential." Lyle lifts his hand to stop me. "Yeah, I've heard that before. Potential hasn't gotten me anywhere since I fell into this ditch. It's too deep, Blondie. No one's gonna give me a second chance—or more like a quadrillionth chance. No one's gonna give the homeless guy anything but a crappy cup of coffee for a story. I need a real job, but I can't even get a job at McDonald's at this point."

"Hold on. I don't believe that. I want to make you a proposition."

Lyle laughs, then looks at Hank. "Do you know about this proposition?"

Hank's face contorts, then relaxes. "I don't know exactly what she's going to say, but I'm in. We've talked enough about this. I'll help with whatever you need."

"Whatever I need?" Lyle throws his head back. "Okay, here's what I need. I need to go back to 2013 and tell myself not to take that first snort, not to hang with those stupid a-holes who said it wasn't a big deal. You can't help me with that, Glasses. Nobody can. I dug my grave that day. I'm just doing time till my body gives out on me altogether."

"Lyle..." I summon a calming voice. "You're right. No one can go back and change the past. But I know we can start here and change the future."

"Give me a future and a hope, huh? Yeah, believe it or not, I paid attention on Sunday. Do this, do that, and you'll be blessed. I heard all the qualifications the pastor gave out. Even believed all that before. But I bet'cha nobody there has a clue how hard it is to dig yourself out of the hole. That lady behind us wouldn't even shake my hand. Looked down her nose at me." He wags a finger. "I know I've lived a dead-end life for the past ten years. I've tried to get out, multiple times. I kept falling back into just wanting to feel good. Using, then clean, using, then clean. A human seesaw."

He pats his chest. "I've seen friends die. Scared me enough to somehow stay clean this round. Mainly by hiding in the library during the day, away from that life, away from my community." Shaking his head, he drops his hand on the table. "Unless they need me. See, I know how hard it is. I'll be there for people like Mindy, when their body's shakin' so hard they don't know if it's gonna give out. I've been there to hold her hand till she comes down, and I'll be there next time if she needs me."

His skin is rough and scratchy under my palm. He stares down at my hand on his. "You touch me today because Hank let me take a shower and borrow clean clothes, but next week—"

"I'll hold your hand and walk alongside you into whatever we all determine is the next step."

He looks up. "Alongside me? Whatever we determine? You don't get it. It's not that easy. You don't want me bringing you down." He shakes my hand off his and stretches one arm toward Hank and the other toward me.

"You two got something cool happening here. New love, maybe the forever kind. Maybe you'll get married and have babies and watch them graduate high school and college, then do the same with grandbabies. You two made it through the stupid years. I didn't. You don't have to pay my price. I got myself here, and I'll get myself out, or I won't. It's none of your concern."

"Too late!" I pound my fist on the table, making the silverware jump. "I can't not care. Trying to help every unsheltered person I see is overwhelming to think about. But you? God put you in my path. He put you and Hank in my path. I could've gone to any library. Could've decided I didn't need to cook and order takeout for the rest of my life. But here I am. I know you. I can't unknow you. You are my starfish."

My heart pounds, I glare at Lyle, and all the words I just spewed out start to register. Did I say the right things?

I gulp in air. "Do you know that starfish poem, Lyle? The one where the little boy tries to save as many starfish stuck on the beach as he can? He knows he may not be able to save every starfish, but he might save one. Just like him, I may not be able to help *every* unsheltered person, but I can try to help you. I'm sorry if being my starfish offends you. But you are more stupid than I think if—" I struggle to get words out from under the growing sensation of an elephant stepping on my chest.

"If you don't take us up on—" I try to pull in air, each breath becoming shorter and tighter. "On this." Pricks of light circle in front of me as a curtain of gray colors my vision.

"Candace?"

Pounding slaps against my hand.

"Candace, are you okay?"

A coughing fit overtakes me and color returns to view. "My purse." I jerk my arm in its direction. "My inhaler."

There are bangs and clatters, then Hank's hand pounds my inhaler into my palm. I crank my wrist up and down to shake the contents, blow out as best I can, and stick the mouthpiece in place. Depressing the plunger, I draw in a deep puff.

"You have asthma?" Hank asks.

I shake my head and let out a quick breath. "The cat."

CHAPTER 28
CAT FINDS A HOME

HANK

During my lunch break, Lyle is out like a light, sprawled over the edge of his worn-out plaid throne. I escape to the library patio and phone Megan. She's accommodating. Cats aren't her favorite, but she'll put up with Cat.

"Think of it as payment for the monthly emotional vent I throw at you," she says. "Plus my contribution to help Lyle. It takes a village, right? Besides, I want to meet this allergic girl. Something is different when you talk about her."

"First of all, you're my sister, and I get how difficult it must be with Mike halfway around the world. You did mention maybe needing a cat." I let a chuckle escape. "And second, yeah, something is different about her." My voice trails off to a visual of Candace laughing over something said at dinner last night, then later suddenly turning into a weird combination of red and blue before my eyes.

"Hanky-poo, what is going on with you?"

"You know I hate when you call me that."

Megan cackles. "It is my privilege, as your older sister, to razz you for the rest of your life. Someone has to keep you in your place."

I grumble but know she loves me. Of my four sisters, she was always the least patronizing—maybe out of empathy, maybe out of shared experience, since she and I were kind of our parents' second batch. My parents' original plan, so they say, was three kids, all two years apart. When Megan came along by surprise five years after those three, they rolled the dice one more time. After me, they were done.

"No more," my mom says, waving her arms across her chest every time she tells the story. She said chasing me around reminded her of her age too much and she was planning on staying young forever. I guess she didn't want another reminder.

"Hank, I gotta go and figure you do too. But I seriously need to meet this girl. Bring her by my place—before Cat comes over, so we can visit for a while." Megan's voice is pensive, I know her well enough to hear her wheels spinning. She's up to something. "Make a date with her to come over here *this week*. Don't tell everyone else. I want to meet her first. Pretty, pretty please?"

"Okay," I mumble. "I'll see what I can do. Bye."

Honestly, this plan is probably the best way to introduce Candace to my family without being overwhelmed. Megan has always been in my court. If she thinks Candace is a winner, she'll do her best to not scare her away. The rest of my family? They mean well, but they would razz me and, by extension, Candace. She just might be the type to laugh about it, but I don't want to push her. Not now. Not with where I hope things will end up.

I scan the perimeter of the library courtyard. My own private sanctuary, where I go during breaks to take in the quiet and hear myself think. Despite the low volume of my job, it isn't quiet. The books shout at me all day long. "Read me! Read me!" So many books, so little time. There've been times when I've had to remind myself life isn't all about books, that there are real people and a real world out there to experience. I used to have to talk myself back to reality more often, but since Candace and Lyle entered my life…Well, more than books inspire me these days.

———

"I had no idea it was that bad," I tell Candace, shaking my head even though we're talking on the phone. "I shut the cat in my bedroom and opened all the windows. I didn't have time to do much cleaning, since Lyle was with me."

"Hank, stop apologizing." Her voice is calm. "I took my allergy med ahead of time. It should've gotten me through the evening. I think I was just worked up. It happens. I'm sorry you're losing your cat. You didn't have to do that for me."

She's just funny. Can she not tell how looped I am for her? I'd move to Timbuktu if she asked me to. "Did you see Lyle perk up when I said he could adopt Cat once he moved into his own place? That incentive might make things happen faster. My sister is fine fostering until then."

"So you named your cat 'Cat'?"

"Yeah. Like in *Breakfast at Tiffany*'s with Audrey Hepburn."

Her giggle rings over the phone. "Yeah, I know." Her voice rises an octave. "Cat! Caaat!" She whimpers, then snorts. "I'm afraid that's my best impression. I do have dripping-wet hair like Audrey in that scene. I had to wash beeswax and honey out of it. Had a little snafu at work, but it was fun." If a sound could lighten a room, her laugh is that sound.

"Seriously, Hank, we need to do our homework. I hear getting someone off the streets is like pushing a boulder up a mountain. We don't want to end up like what's-his-name, the guy the boulder rolls back on."

"Sisyphus."

"Huh?"

"The guy with the boulder. Hades punished him with having to push the boulder up a mountain, only to have it keep rolling back down." I scratch my head. "Yeah, I don't want that either. But the three of us together should be able to get the boulder up and over the mountain, right?"

"The three of us?"

"You, me, and Lyle."

"And?"

Embarrassment silences me. Where has my mind gone? Where is my focus? Oh yeah, all I can think about is Candace.

"Maybe we need to pray before homework," she says. "I think it's past my turn." Her throat clears. "Father God, you can do anything. We want to help Lyle. You said if we ask anything according to your will, you hear us. I have to believe it is your will for Lyle to be safe and sheltered. Show us how to get him his own place and his own means to support himself. Bring him to the place you meant for him to be all along. And help Hank and me support him and be his friends, the kind he needs right now. Thanks."

The line falls quiet while I swirl in shame soup. Which doesn't help anything and just proves once again I'm stuck on myself. *Get over yourself, Hank.*

"Thanks, Candace. I guess I got sidetracked. Let me correct myself. The four of us."

Her sweet giggle lifts the shame off my shoulders. *Oh Lord, I've never felt this good with someone. She's good for me.* I drag my hand over my face and pinch my lips together. Man, where *is* this thing going?

"Oh, hey, I almost forgot. My sister Megan, the one fostering Cat, invited you over for dinner this week, before Cat moves in with her. She doesn't want a repeat performance of last night, so time is of the essence. What do you think?"

"Me, meet your family?" Candace sounds alarmed. Uh-oh, did I push the envelope too far?

"Just Megan, at her place. She didn't want to share you with the rest of the family yet." *I don't want to share you with the rest of my family yet.*

Candace's hum lilts over the line. "Well, it's a chance to get the skinny on you. Investigate your background. Who you associate with." She chortles. "Sounds fun. I'd like that."

We set the arrangements. As we get off the phone, my stomach starts doing loop-de-loops. Anticipation trickles from my mind to my throat, nausea waving at me from the background. Nope. I will not let worries about this dinner dog me. It'll all turn out fine. If this girl is the one, I have nothing to worry about. Right?

CHAPTER 29
WORTH MY TIME

CANDACE

A yellow glow covers the landscape outside my window as I tap away on my desktop keyboard. Reports are not my favorite part of my job, but I lucked out with this view from my office. The picture window smack-dab in front of my desk looks out on the huge field where we gather much of our information, now brilliant with the autumn hues of yellow, ocher, and burnt umber.

If ever I doubt God's goodness, this window view and my job wash away all uncertainty. And now there's Hank. When I think of him, I feel like a kid going to Disneyland. Possibility bubbles in my heart. The best guy I've ever met is interested in me. Interested in accomplishing goals together—that's a first. And when it comes to caring for the people around him, he's not just a sounding gong. He's doing it. Caring for Lyle and Marcus and me.

My cell phone declares 4:45 p.m. I have fifteen minutes to button up this report. My stomach lurches. Tonight's the night. Dinner at Hank's sister's place. He said it'll be low-key, but that doesn't matter. I'm worried I'll feel like one of my bees, put under a microscope to see what I'm made of. Will I be good enough for Megan's little brother? *Lord, I hope so.*

"Hey Candace, how's the report coming along?" My boss's traditional knock and aged voice breaks my musings.

I swivel my chair around to face him. "Almost there. A couple statistics to verify, a closing sentence, and I'll be done."

"Great. I appreciate your efforts. We'll save the bees yet." He chuckles, but it doesn't hide the concern in his eyes. "Wish we had more hands on deck, but we just can't afford to pay more staff. Not what they're worth anyway." One weathered hand pulls the glasses from his face while the other pinches his nose where they've left an indentation. His comment stirs up an idea.

"Mr. Jacobs, have you ever thought of utilizing volunteers? Maybe like an internship? People interested in pursuing a job in the field could gain skills and experience. You'd get more hands, with no extra cost."

"Free isn't free. It costs money to train. There may be liability insurance." He rubs the back of his neck. "Still, it may be worth it. Especially for obtaining some of the counts we need. And it never hurts to build awareness. Besides, there is always the need for *tzedakah* and *tikkun olam*."

"Excuse me?"

Mr. Jacobs washes a hand across his forehead, "Oh, charity and repairing the world, something I was taught growing up." He smiles and nods for me to go on.

I lift a finger. "I have a friend. He's struggling. Well, he's unsheltered—you know, homeless. I've been trying to figure out how to help him. Would you consider letting him help me with my counts? He could be my assistant. I'd be more effective in my work, and he'd gain some work experience to put on a résumé." As I realize what a big ask I've spoken, my eyebrows furrow and my already nervous stomach churns all the more. What am I thinking?

The sadness that fogged my boss's eyes clears as if a light bulb has turned on. "You know, Ms. Carlson, I think you just might have an idea. A pilot program to test the waters with your friend. I'm willing to take a chance on you." His head turns to the side as he focuses on something distant. "And I've wanted to do something about our city's homeless situation. Maybe this could be a start." He adjusts his glasses back onto his nose and looks at me. "Talk to your friend. Let me know when he can begin. We'll write something up—make it official, cover our bases, that sort of thing. Great thinking, Candace! As usual." He nods at me with his signature kind smile and knocks on the door. "After you finish up, you have a great weekend."

"I will. Thank you, Mr. Jacobs. You too."

He exits without disturbing his environment. After years hunting down insects, he's a masterful soft paw, appearing and disappearing without a sound. But his presence—a quiet, confident steadfastness—lingers wherever he goes. How amazing his response was! *God, thank you for my job and my boss. You really are showing me the way, aren't you?*

———

"I can't keep the good news in," I spout before Hank can even say hi.

"Hello to you too!" His eyebrows wiggle, making his glasses rise.

I drag him by the hand into my apartment and gently push him to sit. The couch lets out a soft *pff.*

"What's the news?"

"I got Lyle a job."

"What?"

"Not a paying job. But he can help me, and get work experience. That's something, right?" After I say it out loud to Hank, a rush of fear rises to my throat. What am I thinking? A job with no pay for a homeless guy who may not even be interested. Was it a stupid idea? I plop on the couch, discouragement washes over me.

A warm hand pats my knee. "It *is* something." Hank nods. "It's something."

"It's something," I echo.

———

I trudge through my emotional hesitancy, up a spotless walkway between lush green bushes and aspen trees trumpeting their vivid yellow glow. Of course Hank's sister lives in a high-end place like this. She must do well, to live here on her own. That thought causes my gut to go berserk. What will she think of me? Hank said Megan is his closest sibling. What if she doesn't like me?

Before we get to the door, it swings open to a beaming dark-haired woman with the broadest smile I've ever seen. "I'm so excited to meet you!" Her voice sparkles like her pearly whites. She rushes toward me with an extended hand. "I couldn't wait, have nooo patience. You'll learn that about me." She shakes my hand aggressively up and down.

"A little over exuberant, sis," Hank comments, resting a calming hand on ours. "Don't yank her hand off."

She throws him a brief scowl, then her smile softens to what I would consider normal and friendly. "Whatever you say, brother. You're the boss tonight." She turns toward me. "He told me to mellow out. Coached me to not scare you away. But I don't think you're the type to scare easily. He told me about your tree climbing. My kind of gal."

"Th-thanks."

"Come inside. I have something yummy going and we have so much to talk about." A gentle nudge from her hand on my back pushes me forward. "Hank's my favorite brother, you know."

"I'm your only brother," Hank says, swatting Megan's hand away from my back. I move toward the door, ignoring the muffled rumblings going on behind me.

As I expected, I walk into a beautifully decorated apartment, its turquoise color scheme complemented by pops of metallic gold in the artwork. Serenity washes over me as I survey the room. Everything blends and makes sense. This space was created to be tranquil. Much thought must have gone into it. Creating a space like this would make my brain explode.

"Your home is beautiful," I say, scanning the place in wonder.

"I love to decorate. It's what I do. Help people create homes that welcome them every time they walk in the door. It's one of the things I live for." She lifts a picture frame from a mahogany table and flashes me the photo. "This little guy, not so little anymore, is one of the other things."

Hank grabs at the frame and tries to take it away, a sibling game of keep-away ensues.

"Oh, don't be a spoilsport, Hanky-poo."

"You brought that picture out just to embarrass me."

"No, I didn't. I love this picture."

As they half-heartedly chase each other around the coffee table, she notes how cute Hank was at three, when the picture was taken. "Now look at him. What a booger. A boogersnot!" She aims the last comment straight at him.

"But you love me."

"Always and forever."

They both suddenly stop and sing in unison. "Always and forever."

It's a little weird, but I can tell there's some kind of inside joke. They both hunch over, grab at their stomachs and laugh. Again, I'm reminded how special and different Hank is. And how worth my time.

CHAPTER 30
MORE THAN A THING

CANDACE

S avory smells wisp through the air as we settle around the table. The gift of cooking must run in the family, because Megan's dinner could be served at any of the finer restaurants. Garlic steak bites with double-baked potatoes, and parmesan grilled asparagus. My mouth waters anticipating each buttery bite.

The chatter during dinner is full of teasing and laughter and silly childhood stories. Each time Hank blushes, my heart softens a meter, until it threatens to melt all over the floor. I wonder if his sister can tell. I worry he can.

"Are you as blessed as I am to have siblings?" Megan asks after Hank flings a snarky comment at her.

"Yes, two sisters. They live close to my parents, who still live in the house I grew up in. I'm the youngest."

"Do you get to see them much?"

I look toward Hank for backup but he gives me a curious look like he's just as interested to see how I'll respond.

"I haven't seen them in a while."

Megan's eyebrows lift. "Oh? Too busy with the bees? Busy bee." She wiggles her finger around. "See how I did that?"

"Yes." I scan from her to Hank and back. "And no. I'm waiting."

"Waiting?" She looks thoroughly confused. "For what?"

"To be ready."

Her brows furrow even more.

"I'm the youngest."

She nods. I already said that.

"I act differently when I'm with them. I'm trying to discipline myself, set boundaries, that sort of thing."

"By limiting your visits with family?"

"I turn into someone else when I'm with them." I fling my hands in the air. "Geez! I can't even cook for myself because I've let everyone take care of me." I ignore Hank's raised eyebrow and shaking head. "I want to take care of myself, be grown-up, all on my own. I don't want to ambush myself by turning back into who I used to be."

Megan stares at me intently, as if trying to see deep inside my motivation. "Candace, you *are* grown-up. You've gotten to where you are in life. I can't imagine not letting myself spend time with my family. We only have them with us for so long." Her countenance drops, and a knot forms in my throat. I need to give her a better explanation. I need a better explanation for myself.

"I'm tired of being the youngest. The one who doesn't quite fit expectations. I'm almost thirty, have a well-paying job, take care of myself. But every time I go home, I turn into somebody else. I get quiet and turn off and the accomplishments I admire about myself somehow don't seem to be enough." I splay my hand across the table. Wow, what am I saying?

Megan pats my hand. "The transition from childhood to adulthood is multifaceted." She sways her head toward Hank. "Truth is, he could say something similar. Poor guy, surrounded by four older sisters. He'll be bombarded with teasing and belittling for the rest of his life."

"I wouldn't have it any other way." Hank's affection for Megan warms the atmosphere.

"But you did have to stand up to us during one season." Both nod with a serious expression. "And we changed, a little." She gives him a half smile.

He looks at me. "I told you about my grandma."

I nod.

He fumbles his hands in front of him like he's attempting to open a package with too much tape. "When Gran was sick, at the end. Not remembering things, getting weak. Everyone knew how close we were and kept trying to keep me away, to protect me. I had to stand up for myself. For Gran and me. I knew I could step in and care for her. I was the one who had the time and the freedom." He pounds a fist on his heart. "I felt I was the one meant to be with her every day. Even for the undesirable things she couldn't do for herself."

My own heart expands as he continues. "At first, no one wanted me to take the responsibility. But when they saw how well Gran responded, they let me be a grown-up." He turns toward Megan. "That time was a gift to me. And, I believe, to Gran too. It was special."

Megan's hand slips from mine, and grabs hold of Hank's.

"It was a precious time," Megan agrees, then she turns to me. "Don't miss the precious times. I know there are times to stand up for yourself or gather yourself or whatever you want to call it. But don't let it take so much time that you miss opportunities while they're still possible."

"Work the works while it's still day," Hank says as if to himself, but the words catch in my heart, penetrating deep. What am I doing by staying away, torturing myself and my family? Distancing us? For what?

Megan breaks into my self-affliction. "Thanksgiving is right around the corner. Will you spend it with your family?"

My head pops up. "I don't know. I—"

"I'll go with you," Hank throws out like confetti, almost too cheerfully. "If you want."

Megan giggles. "Yeah, he'll help you stand your grown-up ground." She throws a wink at him, then looks at me, away from his glower.

"You two are together, right?" She nods toward him.

He tilts his head, his cheeks brightening to red.

"Are we?" I ask.

"Aren't we?" he responds.

"Is that what 'being a thing' is?" I giggle.

"Yeah, we're a thing." He nods at me and then toward his sister.

155

"Ahhh, you two are more than a thing." Megan snickers. "Much more than a thing."

She stands and begins stacking plates. I reach to help, but she stops me. "No. You're my guest. You and Hank can chat. I'll clean up and then we can play a game before we call it a night." She smiles so affectionately, I sense she is welcoming me into the family. It's nice to feel accepted, like I belong, at home.

Hank stands, handing her his plate and silverware. When her back turns, he leans over the table and, ever so gently and quietly, presses his lips against my forehead. I close my eyes to take in the rush of comfort. He is the sweetest man I've ever known. He gently takes my hand and I open my eyes. He escorts me to the living area, where we find cards in a bureau and set up to play.

Over a rousing game of Speed, the three of us laugh and slam cards on the table, bumping hands and just missing injury. Usually, I regret that I don't have long, manicured fingernails. In my line of work, they're too hard to maintain. But having long nails tonight would make me lethal.

As the evening winds down, Megan asks me one more time the question I've been considering all night.

"So, you'll take my little brother to spend Thanksgiving with your family?" She elbows him and wiggles her eyebrows.

Hank rolls his eyes and I laugh. I want my family to meet him and I've put off visiting for a sufficient amount of time. Now my logic for waiting just seems stupid. I nod my head.

"Yeah, I think it's time."

Why don't I feel at home with my family? I know they all love me, even if they can be a little patronizing of me as literally the littlest in the family, their Runt, Squirt, and Candy-Pansy. I guess I let years of comments about me being the baby get to me. Then there is the sense that I'm not ladylike enough, that my choice of career or activities don't suit the woman my mother hoped I would be, a woman she can relate to. A teacher and homemaker like her. Or more like my sisters, who spent time following her around learning to cook, bake, sew or clean. I always escaped outside and followed my dad or grandpa in the fields. Instead of making homemade bread I dug in the dirt.

But I've worked hard to get to where I am. I'm accomplished. I've reached my goals and pursued *my* dream job. I'm living on my own, totally independent and self-sufficient. Why do I still feel the need to prove myself? Is it to my family, or is it to me?

After we thank Megan for dinner and tell her goodbye, Hank opens the car door for me. "So, now that you are off Meg's hook, do you really want me to go with you to Thanksgiving? Or would you rather see your family alone?"

I lean against the metal ridge of the open door and stare up into the glare of his glasses, I wish I could see his eyes better to judge his expression. But the tone of his voice is full of compassion—not thinking of himself, just thinking of me. The smooth comfort of kind words, flowing from an unselfish heart, is becoming so familiar, like flinging off my shoes after a long hard day and dropping into the fluff of my overstuffed chair. Hank feels like home.

"No pressure." He steps back and rests his hand on the top edge of the car door. "Let me know when you figure it out."

I set my hand over his, keeping him from moving away. "You sure you're ready to meet my family?"

"Only if you want me to. You've made the first step, meeting mine."

"One sister isn't exactly meeting the whole family."

"Still—" He tilts his head. "She's a pretty good indication of what you're in for."

"I'd love for you to come. Since, you know, we are more than a thing." I squeeze his hand, and he leans in like a warm whisper of wind, his lips against mine sweep me into a dream under the starry night sky.

CHAPTER 31
SUNSET AND CAMDEN

CANDACE

"Here we are," Hank sings as he pulls into the guest parking space at my place. "Sunset and Camden."

I sit quietly and don't move, staring intently at the dusty plastic dashboard in front of me. Hank has to work tomorrow, but I don't and am not ready for this night to be over. Let's face it. I want to kiss him some more. Like, a lot more.

"Candace?" A warm hand pats my thigh. "You okay? We're here."

It's too dark to really see his dreamy brown eyes. "Do you want to come inside?"

His eyebrows rise. "Haven't you had enough of me for one night?"

"Not even." I tilt my head. "Just for a little while. I want you to myself. And not in the car."

He lets out a short laugh and an extended "'Kaaaaaaayyy." Then he bites his lip, and his car door explodes open as he shoots out like a rocket. Maybe he figured out what I'm really saying. A good sign, right?

My door opens and he extends a hand. "My lady?"

"Wow, so formal. I feel like royalty."

He squeezes my hand and doesn't let go until I need it to manipulate my key in the lock. I push the door open and flip the light switch. He follows behind, closing the door.

When we get to the couch, I playfully push him down, then plop next to him, slamming my thigh sharp into his. His arm wraps behind my neck and I drop my head onto his chest. I can feel the twitch of his heartbeat under his shirt. We sit in contented silence for a while, as if mesmerized by an ocean tide washing in and out. Then a low hum reverberates in my ear when his voice vibrates from his chest.

"How long have we known each other now? Three months?"

"Four. But I'm not a master chef yet, so you're not off the hook."

"Not sure I want off the hook." A nervous laugh echoes into my ear, now warm against his chest.

"What is 'more than a thing'? What does that mean to you?" I pull back to see his expression. A crooked smile grows across his face.

"Well. I'm not gonna see anyone else. Not sure if I ever will again." He startles, as if he didn't know his own thoughts. "I didn't say that to make you feel pressure. I just..." His fingers flail through his hair. "Candace, I like you. I've never known anyone like you, and I guess I'm curious to see where this might go." His head drops, then pops up again. "No pressure though. You don't have to say anything." His face is flush, and he looks panicky. "But you asked."

A giggle escapes. My lips pinch tight to hold back saying too much. Then I throw caution to the wind, plant my lips hard and fast on his, and let my actions speak for me. Our hands tangle in each other's hair, the demure standard of the past few months overturned like rogue waves. My torso presses against his chest, our body heat so intense that sweat droplets form on my skin.

Swept away, we let ourselves snog with no care for time. We're alone in our own cocoon, and it's sweet and passionate and right. Every ounce of what is happening between us fills me with pleasure.

After I don't know how long, we simultaneously take a breath. I sit back, giving him space to move.

"Wow." He runs his hand through his hair, then reaches for his glasses, which ended up on the floor somewhere in the process. "Not gonna lie. I've wanted to kiss you like that for a long time."

I reach for my glasses and straighten them on my face, residual warmth still pulses through me. "I've been wanting you too," I whisper, looking down at my hands.

Firm masculine hands encompass mine. "But you're okay if…" He takes an audible breath. "I hold myself to a certain standard. That's okay, right?"

He has the sweetest expression. If that's what liking me looks like, then I'll take it, because it's the closest thing to love I've seen in a man's face ever. "Hank, I don't care what anyone else thinks is normal. We decide what is right for us. And if we use old-fashioned standards, then I'm okay with it. I prefer it, if that's what you mean."

"I'm not sure kissing like that qualifies as old-fashioned." He leans back. "But, as my dad says, 'Keep your pants on, Hank!'"

I laugh as he turns the brightest red of the night.

"Sorry." He washes a hand down his face and pinches his lips, making fishlips. "I can't believe I said that to you."

"I'll take it as a compliment that you feel comfortable enough to say something so awkward." I giggle.

He reaches over and musses my hair till it completely covers my face. I grab his hands to stop further tangling and flip my head to whip the strands out of my face, bonking his chin with my head. His teeth clatter and I look up to him as he cradles his chin.

"Ow!" He looks at me in shock. "You have a hard head."

"Sorry." I pull his hand down to inspect the damage, then softly plant a healing kiss where his chin is the reddest, catapulting us right back into another round of making out.

"Okay." Hank cuffs my hands in each of his. "I gotta get out of here before every noble thing I said earlier goes out the door."

He's right. Heat and tingling are making their way to places that don't need to be awakened. Not now. We can wait. I want an old-school sacred first time with him. And something tells me I'm going to get it. *Oh my gosh! I think he's the one!*

CHAPTER 32
AN INTERESTING PROPOSITION

HANK

The library has a foggy glow as I float around the place and open the blinds. A dreamlike atmosphere is tangible, warm and soothing sunlight peeks through dusty wood slats as I turn the cranks. Slivers of light glisten against the short, looped carpet, and quiet serenity follows me around the perimeter of the building.

The strong scent of rich dark coffee wafts to the front desk, where I flip on computers and check the time. It's still early, but people are waiting outside. What am I gonna do? A countdown until I unlock the door? Not my style. My keys jiggle in my fingers until the right one is found.

"Don't you look cheery today?" Lyle gawks as he walks past me toward the percolator and pours himself a cup of steaming java.

George follows behind, a friendly guy who comes in to read the paper far from the frenzy of grandkids who have taken over his home this past year. He and Lyle chat it up on Saturday mornings before any others show up, then they retreat to their self-designated positions, never saying another word to each other until the next Saturday.

When the clock strikes nine, quiet conversation gives way to a new aura as the library fills with children arriving for story time and adults looking for their latest escape or doing research. I stand ready for any questions that might come my way. Lyle meanders into view and splays his fingers on end against the countertop in front of me, his arms stretched out like a tripod, a goofy grin plastered across his face.

"You had a date with Blondie, didn't ya? You got a crazy lovesick look in your eyes." He twiddles his fingers in front of his eyes, bringing attention to stringy hair in need of a good shampooing. "Well? Didn't ya?"

Heat rises to my cheeks as I think about last night in vivid detail. "Yeah, we were together."

"Something happened." He wiggles his eyebrows at me. "I can tell."

"This is hardly the time or place to talk about it. I gotta work."

He chuckles and points two fingers at his eyes and then mine.

I roll my eyes. "You're watching me? So what?"

He huffs a quick laugh and walks away as my first customer of the day wanders up. The guy taps on the counter as if it will jar his memory, then snaps his fingers and asks where to find late nineteenth-century literature.

Patrons roll through the checkout as if on a conveyor belt. I relax into the groove of the day, trying to be patient and not think too much about where I'd rather be and who I'd rather be with. That'll just drive me crazy.

As thoughts of Candace dance across my mind anyway, a familiar floral scent tickles my nose and there she is. I ease in a breath, willing my heart rate to slow down while I let a smile grow across my face.

"Hi," I whisper.

"Hi." Her blonde hair shines in the light breaking through the window. It lies in soft curls over shoulders hugged by a hot pink sweater. The bright color complements the turquoise in her glasses, making her blue eyes electric.

"Did you hear me, Hank?" Her voice startles me, then floats lightly once I focus. "I don't want to get in trouble for being too loud. Your boss might kick me out."

"Sorry. What were you saying?"

She leans in to whisper. "I'm going to pop the question today."

My eyebrows jerk up, making my glasses slide down my nose. I fumble to straighten them.

"Where's the entomology section?" she asks. "Before I ask Lyle about the job, I'd like to find some books to prep him."

I drop my hands. Oh yeah. *That* question. I hope I look natural as I again take a long breath, aiming to neutralize the adrenaline that just shot through my system.

"Can you show me? Or are you too busy?"

Never too busy for you. I look around to make sure no one is waiting for me to check them out. A familiar pain flares when my hip hits the broken corner of the counter as I move onto the library floor. "This way, ma'am." I wave my hand like a tour guide, and she giggles and follows.

We walk down the canyon of books to the place where we will find the subject matter she seeks. I scan the shelves and reach for the first strong contender. Her back is to the section where she should be looking. Instead, she sways and wears a coy grin, holding her hands in front of her like she's about to ask for a cookie before dinner. I have no doubt what she's thinking about, but I can't go there. "I'm at work."

"I know."

"Well, you can't do that," I say in hushed tones.

"What? I'm not doing anything."

"Oh, aren't you?" I shake my hand at her and the book almost drops out of it.

Her laugh is so sweet I can't stop my own grin from spreading, but a jumble of motion catches my eye in the periphery.

"Guys!" Lyle stage-whispers. "Big Boss Mama is coming."

Seconds after he disappears, Mrs. Jones turns the corner and charges toward us. "Hank, people are waiting in line. You're needed elsewhere." She looks Candace up and down.

Candace takes the book out of my hand. "He was helping me find a book."

The lead librarian eyes her, then looks at me with a condemning stare.

"On my way." Not daring to look at Candace and lose my composure, I straighten to my full height and walk past my boss, toward the front desk.

You'd think everyone at the library is on the same schedule. A rush floods to the counter, and then the tide rolls out, a quiet hush creating a sacred void until the next wave of checkouts. The ebb and flow sets a meditative rhythm, like breathing in and out. After a steady stream of checking out everything from Mary Oliver to Tolstoy, Dr. Seuss to Silverstein, there is a lull.

In the sudden quiet, I notice Candace and Lyle deep in conversation at the other end of the library, him leaning forward in his chair, her sitting on the floor in front of him. Her hands gesture ferociously, then she slaps them down on her knees. The sound reaches even me, and a sudden wave of shushes rolls through the place.

Candace shuffles to a stand, scowls at a few shushers, then beelines toward me. Lyle fumbles up from the chair behind her in hot pursuit. I watch her every step until she stands three feet directly in front of me, only the counter creates a separation.

"We need to talk." She looks at Lyle behind her, then back at me. "Without having to be so quiet. Lyle's not understanding, and obviously I'm making everyone mad." A frown pulls down at the corners of her mouth.

Even now she's adorable. She can't help herself. It's the way she talks and moves and—

"Hank?" She waves a hand in front of me. "Can you help? I don't want to go to McDonalds." She points to the currently unused patio. "What about out there?"

I look over to the gray courtyard. Clouds have rolled in and it's gloomy out there—not rainy weather, but the season has turned a corner. My boss breaks into my view, so I wave her over, despite the deep furrows etched on her face.

"Mrs. Jones, could my friends use the courtyard for a while? They'd like to talk, and it relates to the book choices they'll be making." I hope I have a sweet smile, not the doofy look that never swayed anyone when I was a kid. Candace threads her arm through mine, and a look of relief washes over Mrs. Jones's face.

"Wait. Is she your girlfriend?" She points to Candace.

"What?"

"Is this the girl you've been talking about?"

"Yes, this is Candace. And yeah, we're…" I look to Candace for proof. She seems interested to see how I respond. "We're together."

Mrs. Jones breathes out a quick laugh and looks at Candace. "Sure, honey, you can use the courtyard. Sorry for the mean-teacher bit earlier. I thought Hank here was getting involved with another…" She turns toward me and shakes her head. "But you're not like that, are you?" A pained look takes over her face while Candace whispers a thank you.

As I watch my boss walk away, the air thickens and creates a heavy fog across my shoulders. I thought she knew me better than to think I'd… I shake it off, look toward Candace, and sweep my hands toward the slider leading outside. "Free and clear. Can I join you on my break?"

She nods. Lyle's eyes are wide, his face squished up on one side. Of course he's not sure about what's going on. Skeptical even. Has Candace thought of all the little details?

My mind turns over those details during the twenty minutes I watch her and Lyle look all chummy through the dingy slider door. Finally, it's my lunch break. My boss moves to stand next to me, staring straight ahead, unfocused.

"You okay?" I ask.

"No, but I will be. Just something to deal with I'd rather not."

Could her frustration earlier have something to do with her son? She mentioned he's about my age and has made some bad decisions affecting their family. "Mrs. Jones?"

"Don't worry about me." She nods toward the courtyard. "You've been watching them this whole time when you didn't have someone at the desk. Why don't you join them for your break?"

"Just what I was thinking. Thanks."

She nods and I dart to the back room, grab my sack lunch and jacket, then approach the old glass door. Two heads jerk toward the sound of its swish.

"Hey, it's my lunch break. Mind if I join you?"

"Come on over, Glasses. This girlfriend of yours has made an interesting proposition. She's offering me a job without pay. Imagine that." He chuckles while Candace glowers at him.

"I was wondering if I could join you," I blurt out.

"We just said you could." Lyle wiggles in his chair. "If I see something interesting in your lunch bag, though, I may claim it."

Pulling one of the wrought-iron chairs across the concrete makes a horrific screech. I squint an eye, then relax, thankful, when the assault of sound is over.

"That was brutal," Lyle remarks.

"Sorry."

Candace offers a partial smile. "Lyle is questioning my tactics. And how this all might work out. Logistics and such."

I clear my throat. "Like I was saying, can I join you?"

Two sets of questioning eyes stare at me. They have no idea what I'm talking about.

"Maybe I can come count bees too—once a week, on my day off. I can be Lyle's ride. Heck, I'll even make his lunch and feed him breakfast and dinner." *Oh, Hank, what are you getting yourself into?*

A calm assurance settles gently in my gut as reasons to be part of this flood my mind. I can learn about Candace's passions up close and personal and help Lyle in multiple ways. Maybe my doing this is part of the answer to our prayers. Candace's smile tells me it is.

Lyle looks stunned. "You'd do that for me, Glasses?"

"Yeah. Sounds like fun to me. I want to learn about bees."

"Sure, that's what you want to learn about." Lyle laughs.

Thankfully, Candace seems too preoccupied to catch his suggestion. She looks seriously back and forth between me and Lyle. "I have to say something," she spits out, zeroing in on Lyle. "Although this is mainly fieldwork and could be messy, you're going to have to clean up before work."

Lyle's eyebrows rise like she's crazy. "You offer me a job that doesn't pay, and now you want me to figure out how to get cleaned up before said job every week." He huffs. "Blondie, you've seen where I live, how I live. What do you want me to do, dive into the creek in the middle of November?"

Candace huffs back. "No, I just...If this is going to go over with my boss and coworkers and with the visitors who observe, then you need to…" She shrugs her shoulders and closes her eyes. "You're going to have to smell better and look tidier. I'm sorry. It's just how it is."

She pops open her eyes. "I know! You can come to my house on work mornings and take a shower. And we can go shopping today. I'll buy you a couple of outfits for work. What do you say?"

"No." I swallow hard as she jerks her head toward me.

"Why not?"

"He can shower at my house, and I'll take him shopping."

Her glare rips into my soul. Oh boy, our first run-in. She's not going to just hand this win over.

"I already know where he lives," she counters, reminding me she's one up on me. So, this is how she fights. I don't want fisticuffs. I like her spunk, but I'm right. *Lord, can I please get some help here?*

I hold my palms up to her and take a breath to hopefully slow things down. "What if Lyle comes to church with us Sunday night, we all have dinner together, then he stays at my house overnight and I come to work with him?"

Lyle growls. "Do I have a say in the matter? Or are you two just gonna take over my life? Who said I even want to do this?"

Candace and I exchange a meek glance and turn toward him.

"You're right, Lyle," she says. "What do you want? I hope you say yes to the opportunity. I think it would be great. We could work together and get to know each other better. You could learn about something I absolutely love." Her eyes sparkle like Christmas lights. "It may change everything for you."

"Or nothing," Lyle says flatly.

"It's a good opportunity," I add. "What are you going to do instead? Everything as usual? If you want a change, you have to do something different. At least, that's what somebody told me."

"Great, Glasses!" Lyle wags his head. "Use my own words on me."

I got him. "So? What do you say?"

"Does church really have to be part of it?"

Shivers leapfrog up my forearm as Candace rests a hand on it. "What if we start with dinner together the night before?" she says. "Then you two can do the guy's sleepover and meet me at work

Monday morning. We could take one week at a time. Okay?" She looks at me.

I close my eyes. Ever the zealot—that's me. Pushing too much too soon. I look to Lyle. "I'm game if you are."

"Can't say the thought of a soft couch once a week isn't enticing."

"Enough to make counting bees all day appealing too?" Candace asks.

Lyle gives her a scrutinizing look. "I was interested even before all this." He fiddles his hands in between all of us. "I'm not completely stupid. At least, I'd like to think I'm not anymore."

Candace drops her hands in her lap. "You still need clothes. Which means shopping."

A *thud, thud, thud* echoes from the sliding door. Mrs. Jones waves at me. I look down at my dad's old watch on my wrist. Its Roman numerals indicate I should've been back on the floor ten minutes ago. I give Mrs. Jones an embarrassed grimace.

The chair screeches its complaint as I stand. But before I leave, I have to give my two cents. "How about we all shop together tomorrow afternoon before dinner?" So much for an evening alone with Candace. But I guess more than one big thing is happening here, not just finding my one true love.

"Sounds like a great idea!" The delight in Candace's voice is music to my ears. "Lyle, what do you think?"

"I'm in."

CHAPTER 33
COUNTIN' BEES

CANDACE

After two consecutive nights of cooking together, conversation, and Hank's goodnight kisses when Lyle wasn't around, I'm hyped up despite this foggy gray morning. I sit on the edge of my office chair, still bundled up in my double-layered flannel jacket and hiking boots. My hands fumble over each other so roughly I risk hurting myself.

Stop, Candace. It will be okay. It will all work out. My heart rate and thoughts heighten the buzz at the end of every nerve. Seeing Hank, seeing Lyle, and finding out how today will work out—it's all cluttering my mind. *It'll be okay, it'll be okay, it'll be okay.*

A warm weight settles on my shoulder as I stare at the glass double doors. "Candace, it will be okay."

My boss's low voice could calm a raging sea. "This is a pilot program. I know you want it to work, but face this with curiosity, not fear. This effort will educate us for the future no matter the outcome." His hand gently pats my shoulder, and then he moves toward the hallway. "Bring them by for introductions when they get here."

I'm able to force out a trembling "Okay." I look down at my watch and shine the face of it with my sleeve. The neon numbers glow at me.

Five more minutes. I hope they are on time. I rub the watch face again, then wintry air hits my forehead. I look up.

"Hey ya, Blondie." Lyle has cleanish teeth, combed hair, and tidy clothes. He looks…

"I see you don't recognize me. Let me introduce myself." He extends a rough yet clean hand. "Lyle Gilmore, at your service."

My shoulders relax as I grab hold of his hand. "Lyle, you're here, and you look…" I don't want to offend him. What do I say? "You look ready for the day. I'm so glad you're here."

"And me?" A tall presence hovers behind Lyle like a guardian angel. I don't remember Hank being so much taller than Lyle. Dressed for the outdoors, he looks strong, like he could knock over Hercules.

"Jaw-dropping gorgeous, aren't we, Blondie? Don't catch all the bees in your mouth before we get out there." Lyle chuckles as I clamp my mouth shut, a rush of heat washing across my face.

"Right. Yes." I stand. "Here we go. Let's go down the hall and meet my boss." I turn with a swish of my hands and lead the way toward his office.

I can't look at Hank. What is wrong with me? I didn't even say hi. Maybe seeing him carry a situation that could be so heavy with ease is throwing me off.

With each step, I sense my heart rate slowing, my composure strengthening. Am I walking taller? Everything is going to be okay. Hank is here—with me, with us. This is all going to work out.

———

Halfway into the day, I'm impressed with Lyle's ease in taking in information and then applying it. He gracefully swishes the net to capture a bee, uses the bee squeezer with precision, then marks its thorax with a paint pen, and takes a picture to log each insect before releasing it. I know every word I say is absorbed, because Lyle summarizes each point I make. I'm a little floored at how quick he is, how intuitive and, well, smart. How biased am I? He did say he was near graduating when his downward spiral started. *Lord, if only—*

"Blondie, check this out." Lyle has already sequenced the prints we made, organizing them by family. He points out identifying marks on each creature. "This one kept coming back for more, like we were new best buddies."

"They can recognize faces. Maybe something about you made her feel safe." I stop and stare into Lyle's green eyes. Deep in the dark pool of those eyes lives a man, a scholar, someone full of possibilities. I feel like I see him the way that bee might.

"Blondie?" Lyle waves his hand in front of me. "Don't go looking at me all starry-eyed. Hank'll get suspicious, and it's kind of freaking me out."

I shake my head. "Sorry. I'm just so impressed by how quickly you've picked up on this."

The corner of his mouth lifts in a crooked smile. "Didn't know I was this smart, did ya?"

"Lyle..."

"Okay, I see the sympathy thing." He flips his hand dismissively. "Don't feel sorry for me. I'm here and we're seeing where this goes. That's what you said. I'm doing you a favor, remember?" He laughs, then mumbles. "We both know you got an agenda."

"We needed the help," I say. "And be honest. So did you."

"Touché."

"Hey, you two! Sorry I took so long." Hank looks at me. "Your boss cornered me out there. Interrogated me with a tone. You know, like he doesn't think I'm good enough for you." Hank's eyes bug out under those dark frames of his. "Maybe I'm not."

Hardly. "You are just right." *Rein yourself in, Candy-girl. You're at work.* I smile, then turn toward the array of photos spread across the table. "Look what Lyle did."

"Wow. Bud, looks like you're a natural." Hank pounds Lyle on the back.

After lunch, we are sent on assignment. Well, I'm sent on assignment. Lyle and Hank get to watch me. No pressure. We drive out to a call of a swarm collecting in the wall of a barn. I have to transfer the bees to a hive. We all put on our white gear and netted hats. Lastly, I put on gloves and pull out my smoker.

After a few puffs, the white mist mesmerizes the bees. They let me press my hand through the wall of buzzing until I find the queen, the jewel of the hive. The worker bees will follow her anywhere she goes, and they instinctively know where she is. I set her in a bee house with the lid open, along with a palmful of vibrating bodies. Then the magic begins. The workers' little bodies wiggle and dance, relaying the information they all need. *The queen has moved. Gather round.* An army of striped bodies moves in formation into the bee house. The sight takes my breath away every time.

Dropped jaws and wide eyes let me know Lyle and Hank are taking in the experience with the same wonder. I love my job. Every single creature on this planet is so amazing when we stop to observe. We are all so connected. How I want to honor each one! That thought pulses across my mind as I look at Lyle. He is one of God's creations. *Lord, how do I help him be all he was made to be?*

You don't.

I choke on my own saliva and sputter.

"You okay?" Lyle pounds my back.

"Just swallowed wrong." I look at him. Those eyes say so much more than I ever noticed before.

"Blondie, I told you. No starry-eyes." He chuckles, then slaps Hank's arm. "Well, I guess our work here is done." Lyle taps his bare wrist. "Gotta be five by now. I'm starvin'."

Hank looks down at his watch, then up at me. "It's after five, but I'm guessing you have to get this bee house somewhere before we can call it a day."

I nod, then position Lyle and Hank to help me safely carry the hive to the truck. "We'll reestablish their territory far away enough so they won't want to return to this old barn."

CHAPTER 34
ONE DAY AT A TIME

HANK

"She was mesmerizing, wasn't she?" I'm not really looking for an answer from Lyle as I stare at his wide eyes. We ended up back at my place for debriefing after working all day with Candace and then the three of us made a quick dinner—spaghetti with sauce from the jar and salad.

"You've got it bad, buddy. But I don't blame you. There was something magical about watching her move those bees around like an orchestra conductor." He drops onto the couch, starts to lean back into the cushions, then scoots forward and perches on the seat's edge.

"You can stay here tonight." I collapse onto the couch's opposite end.

"I don't want to impose."

I shake my head. "Tonight's fine. It's been a long day, and I like the company."

"I'm not a cute blonde, though."

My hair drops into my eyes as I think about Candace. "I wouldn't want her to get tired of me. I'd like her to keep wanting to see me, ya know?"

"Buddy, I don't think you need to worry. She's as goo-goo-eyed for you as you are for her. You had to have noticed. She's bad at hiding it."

"You think?"

"I know."

Cat, who hasn't transitioned to Megan's house yet, paces back and forth under Lyle's hand, rubbing her head, nose to ears, under his fingers. He relaxes back into the couch.

"Today was like living in the trenches," I think aloud. "Not in a bad way. We just worked harder than I think I ever have. I had no idea how physical Candace's job could be. I'm a Pop Tart next to her."

Lyle's laugh is wry. "I was gaga for a girl like that, a long time ago."

Something inside tells me to keep my mouth shut and let him talk. It's an uncomfortable conversation. About how he was one of the unlucky ones who couldn't handle even one hit. He spiraled into addiction like a sinking ship. He lost the love of his life, his close relationship with his family, and what he thought were good friends.

"The year I learned to cook, it was all over. At least, for a long time." He smiles and points to his teeth, ravaged by his addition. "Evidence of how long and far I went. In and out, in and out. Rehab."

He shuffles his hands, then returns one to Cat's back. "My mom tried so hard at first, but I was a jerk. I wasn't myself. The stuff turned me into someone else, someone angry and violent and accusatory. My mom and family have never been anything but supportive and loving, but I accused them right and left of all kinds of things. Stole stuff from them and lied about it. The whole sad story, ya know."

I don't know, but I nod like I do.

He shifts in his seat as if the couch is suddenly made of thistles, and Cat scurries away.

"My mom wrote me a letter when she didn't know what else to do. It was her 'I can't do this anymore' letter." He looks up at me with a somber face. "Candace read it the day she was crying. I keep it to remind me." He tilts his head. "Even though Mom couldn't deal with me anymore, she still said her door would be open if I ever wanted to come home clean and change my ways. Said she loved me no matter what but had to set a boundary, for her own health and, she hoped, mine. No drugs in her house or inside me."

Lyle has my full attention. I want to say something but have no idea what. So, I say nothing, just stare.

"I know you don't get it, Glasses. You've never done drugs, have you? Probably never got drunk or even ditched a class."

I close my eyes. Yep, I was the "good boy" who followed the rules and stayed out of trouble. And in my case, it saved me.

"I was a good kid." Spoken to Lyle, those words feel like a confession. "I don't know why, but the stuff you're talking about never appealed to me. I stayed away from it and the people trying to push it on me. It didn't take long for them to get the hint and leave me alone. Except for getting teased. But if they were really my friends, they wouldn't have tried to push it on me. I found friends who respected my boundaries, I guess. Or we respected each other's."

My voice catches, and I study Lyle with caution, noticing no red flags in his expression. "And my grandma would've killed me if I'd gotten mixed up in any of that kind of stuff." I chuckle. "I'm sure Gran prayed for me every day, so much I couldn't have gotten in trouble if I tried. But I didn't want to try, maybe because of those prayers."

"Wish I'd had a grandma like yours." Lyle shakes his head. "Never knew mine. Gone on my mom's side before I was old enough to know her. Don't know anyone on my dad's side. He had some kind of big falling out with his family when I was little. Never saw or heard from them again. They didn't even show up for his funeral." Lyle shrugged his shoulders. "It is what it is."

"But what do you want it to be?"

"Whoa! That's a loaded question."

"But isn't it *the* question?" I want to pull my hair out. This guy has so much potential. I have no idea why he hasn't moved past this. He's worked to get clean, set boundaries in his own way. But he just stays stuck. "I'm willing to help, for as long as it takes, to get you into your own place and moving in the direction of a future you want."

He gives me a suspicious look.

"With my own boundaries. Like your mom. No drugs, no drinking. Showing up to do the work. You have to do the work, but I'll be here with you if you'll do it."

"You sound like the rescue mission." He scowls, then an acceptance dawns across his face. "For whatever reason, Glasses, you just might

175

have a deal. After today, I have a little bit of hope again. It felt good to do something right for once."

He grins and a thought occurs to me. "Lyle, I'm sorry for how you've struggled. But who you are now is not who you were back then." He squints and I tap my forehead. "You gotta change your inner dialogue. Today wasn't the first time you've done something right. I've seen you do good things in the library. Help older women or kids get books they can't reach. Pick up things folks drop and chase them down to give it to them. Heck, even being a friend to me and Candace. You're a good guy."

He shakes his head. "Don't get all romantic about the homeless guy. You don't know everything. You don't want to be let down."

My eyebrows rise, making my glasses slide down my nose. Maybe he's the one that doesn't want to be let down, by me or himself.

"Let's just take this one day at a time." The assurance in my voice reminds me of Candace and encourages me too. "For tonight, you can have my couch. In the morning, after a warm breakfast and a shower, you can help me open the library. How about it? One day at a time. Deal?"

I interpret the drop of his head as agreement and present him his sheets and blanket from the night before. He settles in and I retreat to my bedroom. Even though I trust him more than I ever have before, I still lock my bedroom door before turning out the light.

CHAPTER 35
DEEP BREATH, CANDY-GIRL

CANDACE

W hat's wrong with me? Walking through the front door of the office never felt so silent, almost like the air has been sucked out of the space. The fluorescent lights give off just enough buzz to let me know it isn't my ears ringing. I turn into my lab and sit on my raised chair to punch in numbers and other findings from yesterday's research. But my heart isn't in it as usual.

When I look up at the drab gray clouds outside the window, a light bulb comes on and I realize what's bothering me. Is this how every Tuesday is going to feel?

Going out in the field helps a little. The crisp fall air gets my heart rate moving past its slow idle. I let my fingers graze over the high brown grass still hanging on to the idea of summer.

I pull off a feathered tip and rub it in my hands, then raise it in my palms to my nose. The dry hay smell tickles my senses and reminds me this field will be green again once the spring rains begin. Then the ecosystem will roll with the change of season. For now, there are more insects to document, before my focus turns to what's next in *this* season.

———

The click of the light switch illuminates my living room with a subtle glow. Somehow even the light knows my melancholy. I tap the number of my most trusted friend on my phone and pace up and down the hall.

"Jillian, it's silly," I say into the phone.

"Why?" she demands.

"I don't know him well enough."

"Candy-girl, you don't need to know his shoe size to know what your heart is telling you. He sounds like a great guy. Not like some of those other—"

"I get it. I don't want to go there."

"Well, just because you've hit your magic line doesn't mean he won't surprise you. Sounds like he already has."

The magic line. The line in the sand where the guy is either going to keep my attention, and I his, or our relationship will teeter out. I've only crossed this line twice. Once in high school, with a relationship that barely made it that far and is the baseline for the magic line, and—

"What if he's like Pablo? Perfect in every way until it gets so serious you either have to get engaged or... Well, you know what happened."

"Candace, Pablo was a decent guy, just not the one for you. You learned a lot with him, right? Learned what matters to you and what doesn't. Learned you need a guy who has a better understanding of your stealth independence and fragile romantic heart. I know you're scared. But have a little hope. Have a little fun. Trust the process. *Enjoy* the process."

"Pfft!" I want to gag. An acidic feeling in my throat stirs the butter-flies already going berserk in my stomach.

"Candace, breathe." Jillian says. "You like him a lot. And you're welcome, by the way, for me not saying what I really think. You L. O. ..."

"You don't need to spell it out!"

"Can-Can don't sabotage yourself. Let this be what it's going to be."

"That's the thing." I slump into the bathroom and stare at myself in the mirror as I admit it to both Jillian and me. "All I want to do is be with Hank. I was a mope all day at work because he wasn't there. You know how I'm usually consumed with my job and stay late. But today I kept staring at the clock, listening to the droning tick of the second hand. And I don't even get to see him tonight. His family is having dinner just because."

"He didn't invite you?"

"He did."

"And you said no?"

I close my eyes and groan. I've already processed that decision. If I meet his family, his whole family, then suddenly this relationship becomes real. I don't want to have my heart broken by both a guy and his family. I've met his sister already. I know I'm going to fall for the whole family just like I'm falling for Hank.

"For now."

"Then don't complain of missing him in one breath and trying to pull the plug in the next."

"Wow, sassy pants, I appreciate the support."

"Candace, you know I love you. You know I support you. I also know you, and you have nothing to complain about. What's going on right now between you and Hank is exactly what you've been praying for."

As Jillian hits the mark for the win, it's like being shot between the eyeballs. I *am* right where I want to be. Hank is amazing, and I need to let it be. Worrying about what's going to happen with us is like stirring the rice when I just need to let it steam and soak in all the goodness of the broth, instead of making it a sticky goo. *Deep breath, Candy-girl. Just take it as it comes. Try to enjoy this.*

O Lord, I'm falling in love.

———

I hear a knock at my entry and mope over, knowing it isn't Hank. The door creaks as I open it and squint at the outside light and the moths knocking themselves out against the bulb.

179

"Candace?" The gentle fatherly voice of Neighbor Bob breaks through my fog. "You okay?"

With effort, I muster a smile. "Just tired. Maybe a little sad."

"Maybe?" He shakes his head, knowing better. "How about dinner and a card game?"

My sigh cuts through a haze I can almost see. "That would be great."

"Come on over. I have all the ingredients for my favorite goulash. Seems like a good night for something savory and comforting. There's a crisp bite in the air."

No kidding. Biting me in the butt. *Oh girl, get a handle on things.* "Fall is officially here. I'll be over in a minute."

As the sweet, huddled shape of my neighbor shuffles away, concern floods my mind. Has he suddenly aged ten years? I never noticed the shuffle or his shoulders slumped, his straight posture hunched over by the wave of years. My stomach clenches as the thought of limited time ambushes me. I try to shake it away and focus on tonight. We're going to have one of our special evenings together, just like we typically do. My feet drag, though, as I flick off each light switch until my little apartment darkens, heightening the sound of my scuffling footsteps.

"Door's open!" Neighbor Bob shouts. "Come on in!"

I follow his voice to the kitchen. Peony-splashed dish towels hang from the dishwasher handle, evidence of the life he lived with his wife. Everything about his living space sings of her, with its floral pillows and curtains. Pinks, lavender, sage, and baby blue tell the story of her gentle way. She is present even though she has been gone for several years. In a funny way, she comforts me as I enter this home. As does the gentleman hovered over the stove, stirring a worn wooden spoon around in a stockpot. Steam floats into his face, and he turns toward me with a funny grin and fogged-up glasses.

"Happens every time." He laughs. "Oh to have the eyes of a young'un like you. These stupid things…" He takes off his glasses and rubs the lenses with the cabbage roses in his apron's material.

Misty steam warms my hand as I reach for the spoon and stir. The simmering spices infuse and soothe my heart as I inhale the thick aroma. Being at my neighbor's and sharing our special times gives me a sense of home, reminding me of my childhood surroundings, my catalpa tree, my family.

Why do I insist on keeping my distance?

Because I've made a formula for what I will allow in the hopes of learning to be independent and stand up for myself, since no one seems willing to stand up for me when mom disapproves. I didn't want to remain the girl easily tossed to and fro by my family's opinions or what I have interpreted as their lack of faith in me.

"Honey, I think it's ready. You don't want to stir all the flavor right out of it." Neighbor Bob has a wry smile, and his eyes divert to the pot and my vigorous pummeling of our dinner. My hand slows and I let out an apologetic giggle.

"Guess I'm venting a little."

"We can talk over dinner." He pats my hand, then lifts the pot off the stove, transferring it to the already-set table.

Over goulash, I tell him everything. Ev-er-y-thing. His eyes are soft and exude compassion. I know he understands it all. I don't know how I've managed to be so fortunate to gain this extra grandfather. God must've known I needed him.

Bob sits up tall. "Candace, I have something I need to discuss with you. This may not be the right time, but I've put it off long enough. I don't want you to be caught off guard."

Like a fist clenching around my heart, pain sears through my chest. "What do we need to discuss?" Judging from the seriousness on his face, maybe I don't want to know. But I don't want my imagination to go to unnecessary places.

"It's time, honey." He pats my hand. "It's time for me to move to the next phase."

"Tell me you're not dying!"

His chuckle calms my nerves. "No, no. Not yet. At least not that I know of."

I let out the breath I was holding.

"But..." His pause allows me time to gulp in another breath, like

I'm readying myself to dive deep into a dark abyss. "It's time for me to move."

I feel my eyes bulge like they're ready to explode. But he doesn't notice because he won't look at me.

"I need a little more assistance. An easier way to connect with others. I know I have you. But honey, you work all day, and you have another life you need to pursue." His soft gray eyes look up at me. "It's time," he says as if hitting a nail flush with one single strike. "You understand, don't you?"

"Where are you moving? *When* are you moving?"

"I should have told you sooner. I've been planning this for a while. Put my name on a waiting list." He hesitates. "I've just learned there's an opening. I move at the end of the month."

"That's only two weeks away!"

He nods and his penetrating eyes reach into my heart. "You're ready for this. I'm ready for this." His head bobs up and down until the reality of what he's told me sinks in. Tears brim in my lower eyelids, then spill down my cheeks. Suddenly, I realize how much I've taken Bob for granted.

"We've been neighbors for this season for a reason." He squeezes my hand. "But seasons come and go. You and I have new chapters ahead of us. Let's embrace them and appreciate the past for what it has been. A saving grace."

I should be happy for Bob. Shouldn't be so selfish as to expect him to just be next door whenever I feel like a visit. He's right. Things change. Time marches on. And sometimes we have to let go of good things.

We reminisce for the rest of my visit. Warm memories float around the room as we play gin rummy. I am grateful for the easy ebb and flow of conversation, the history and shared stories, the laughter that rolls like waves through our conversation.

Ever the proponent of not wasting time, Bob says I'm dragging my feet and should jump full bore into a serious relationship with Hank, though he adds to not let Hank know of his approval. Then Bob retells his favorite love story, of him and his wife. I feel her presence so strongly when I'm with him. As if I've somehow known her all along, though she left this earth long before I met Bob.

The evening ends soft as a whisper. It may be the last dinner and card night we share in his apartment. But it won't be the last time I see him. I assure Bob of that. I vow to myself to schedule consistent visits with my dear friend.

CHAPTER 36
ONE STEP AT A TIME

HANK

"Time to wake up!" I shout. Lyle didn't budge at a normal voice level. Showered and dressed, I run my fingers through my still-wet hair and spatter the drizzle left on them onto his face since his eyes are pinched shut. "We have a deal, right?"

His grimace takes its time to soften, then he opens his eyes and gives me a forlorn look. "This early?"

"You're on *my* time now. Go take a shower while I make breakfast. I like to get to the library early. You're gonna learn my whole routine. Suck it up, buttercup." I chuckle as he rolls to the floor with a thud, then lifts to all fours before inflating to a full stand.

"You're ruining *my* routine," he grumbles.

"That's the idea," I singsong back to him. He gives me a dirty look and then lumbers down the hall to the bathroom.

"Gotta hit the loo anyway," he says over his shoulder.

Yellow fluff forms as I move my wooden spoon around the edge of the pan. The eggy smell isn't all that great, but the sausage sizzling in the neighboring fry pan makes up for it. As I turn the flame off, I hear a plop at the barstool on the other side of the counter. I slide the eggs onto two plates and fork us two sausages each.

"Breakfast is served." I scoot a plate in front of Lyle and stand with mine in one hand.

"You always eat standing?"

I don't know. "I guess I do in the morning. Never really thought about it. I usually cram food in my mouth so I can get out the door on time."

Lyle points his fork toward my wrist. "What time is it? It's gotta be earlier than the rest of the world considers a reasonable time to be awake."

The hands on my watch tell me. "It's seven. Right on schedule. We'll leave in thirty."

"Putting us at the library at?"

"Seven forty-five. Time to get the coffee going. Vacuum. Tidy up and open the shades. Maybe my early customers will be there, but the door opens at nine—no later. You know the schedule."

"My gratitude for your promptness has now been replaced." He stares at his plate. "By the other side of the coin."

We clean our plates and brush our teeth. Maybe I should get him to the dentist soon.

Lunches packed, we head out the door, and my ambition is suddenly kicked to the curb by apprehension. I never asked Mrs. Jones if this would be okay. I guess it'll be better to apologize later than to hinder a momentum balanced on a razor's edge.

———

Lyle is surprisingly helpful as he wisps a long-handled feather duster across the top of each bookshelf, swirling the plumes in a spiral over the empty space between bound treasure and aged wood. It's like he's made an art form of exposing deeper layers of the scraggly creature he presents himself to be. He's meant for so much more.

"Quit gawking, four-eyes. I'm just doing my job."

I raise an eyebrow. "Yeah, just doing your job." I gather the pile of books strewn in the overnight return, like a mother hen gathering her chicks. These precious babies need to be scanned and returned to their homes. I set them in formation, spines out. Red, green, and ochre stripes with golden etched lettering form a masterpiece on the rolling cart. The beauty of these books draw great admiration for the writers, artists, and creatives who grace our lives with their giftings. Oh, to spend my days with pen in hand, letting it take me to faraway places and people, and…

"Glasses, I've lost you."

I startle and notice Lyle standing two feet away from me, swinging dust motes in a circle as the light catches just right.

"Where'd you go? You're all dreamy eyed today." His expression is suspicious.

"Just a lot on my mind. Speaking of which, we need to get you to a dentist. Then a physical, then—"

"Hold on. I didn't say I wanted to do any of those things."

"Lyle, you need—"

"I need to take one step at a time." His eyes bug out at me with an expression clearly meant to shut the conversation down.

"Okay. You're right. Let's focus on today."

"Forgot this one." Lyle reaches for a book on the counter to put on the cart.

"No. I'm reading that one."

He turns it around in his hands. "Percy Jackson? Doesn't seem like the kind of book you'd read."

"I read everything." Do I sound too offended? "Candace likes them, so I thought I'd check them out."

He wiggles his eyebrows at me and drops the book on the counter.

"Aaanyway." I point to the rickety coffee table. "You want to learn my coffee-making secret?"

"Not really. You'd just make me brew the coffee from now on, and I wouldn't be able to say no one makes it like you."

Yeah, Lyle, this is the end of an era. Your life is changing, and whether you acknowledge it or not, you're going along with it.

Despite his complaint, I teach him my secret, a pinch of salt on top of the grounds. The percolator spouts its gurgling song as I hand the door keys to Lyle.

"You get the honors today."

He nods with what looks like gratitude, then shakes the keys at his morning buddies and lets them in.

"Welcome!" The early regulars give him odd looks. "Coffee's a-brewin' and books are a-waitin'," he announces. "Love the fedora, Bruce."

"Lyle." The gray-haired man with the rumpled argyle sweater-vest tips his hat. "I see you've been promoted."

"Who knows what's next?" Lyle chuckles, and I wonder if his vision of possibilities has broadened for himself, just as they have for me.

CHAPTER 37
IT'S OFFICIAL

CANDACE

The knock on the door makes me jump, then my heart revs its engine, sending heat to my face. He's here. Why in the world am I so worked up? The doorknob is cold against my palm as I turn it. Everything feels in slow motion.

I lift my face to dark brown eyes behind black-rimmed glasses. Suddenly, I'm kicked into real time. Hank's smile is the sweetest. Unpresuming. Like he's shy and still trying to figure out if I like him.

"What's so funny?" I must've giggled out loud. His first words of the evening make me self-conscious. I hope he doesn't think I'm rude.

"Sorry. I'm just happy to see you, is all." I love how his brown hair flops over his left eye and he has to comb it back with his fingers. I'm sure he has no idea how subtly sexy it is to me.

He jiggles the brown sack balanced in his elbow and points at it with his other hand. "Thanksgiving test run. I thought we could make stuffing tonight along with a chicken. A turkey seemed too much for just the two of us. And then—" He scoops his hand into the sack and pulls out a bag of green apples. "Apple Pie! You've hit the big time, Candace."

"Yeah, Candace Can-Can cook," I mumble.

"Candace Can-Can cook. I like that."

"Jillian and her kids call me Can-Can."

"I like it. It's cute, right? A vote-of-confidence kind of thing." His eyes suddenly change to concern. "Wait. I won't call you that if you don't want me to. If it is a special thing between you and your friend."

"It's fine." I snicker. "I like the vote-of-confidence *and* you feeling more comfortable with me."

A smile spreads across his face. "Yeah, me too."

We move to the kitchen to practice the test run of our Thanksgiving meal. He assures me the only significant difference between a chicken and a turkey is the size, affecting the amount of time we cook it. Once the stuffed mock turkey goes into the oven, we get to peeling apples. Lots and lots of apples. A sweet fruity and spicy scent rises from the bowl as sugar and cinnamon are sprinkled like mountains of snow over apple chunks. The smell forces me to steal a piece or two, until I get kindly scolded by a half-hearted frown on Hank's cute face.

Setting me up for success, he places a mound of pie dough on flour he dusted around on the counter. I stare at the white powder he just unconsciously wiped on his cheek.

"You can do it," he urges. I guess he thinks I'm hesitant again, but I'm not. Just mesmerized.

He moves behind me, sets his hands over mine, and wraps my fingers around the handles of the rolling pin. "Just move smoothly and apply downward and outward pressure." I'm not that dense, but I'm gonna let him think so right now, because the warmth of his body against my back is intoxicating. And the touch of his hands. How can he apply pressure and be so gentle at the same time? I can't help but let my head fall back against his chest, and the rest of the world drifts away.

"Candace?" His hands lift off mine and he moves away. A wisp of cool air grazes my back, returning me to reality. I turn to face him.

"Are you okay?" he asks.

I look down, he's wearing brown leather shoes. They're nice. He's also wearing a rust-colored button-down oxford and what look like new jeans. I glance up and grin. "You look quite seasonal. Fallish."

His eyebrows furrow as he tilts his head. "You went limp for a second."

"What?"

"You quit moving. I was concerned. Are you okay?" He runs his fingers through his hair, "I mean, you look okay, but you just suddenly stopped—"

"I'm fine." I stifle a giggle. "Really, really fine." I don't know if he finally can read the look on my face, but his eyebrows rise, and then he steps forward.

"Oh." His curled fingers slide down my left cheek. He chuckles. "You mean like in that movie, *Ghost*?"

My head drops and I stare at his fancy shoes again, willing my heart to stop pounding so hard my blouse flutters with every beat.

"Candace?" Warm skin brushes my chin, gently forcing it up. It's like a magnet pulls my lips to his. Soft bangs tickle my forehead as his lips press deeper. A swirl of heat and comfort cyclones around us, sweeping us away from my little worn-down apartment, off to another world.

Ding!

Like a couple of scolded teenagers, we jerk away from each other and look, in unison, at the oven. Stupid thing couldn't give us five more minutes? Hank quickly moves to the pie dough.

"We better get this assembled and in the oven." His gaze moves back and forth between the oven and the rolling pin. The scent of buttery onion, celery and carrots blend with the savory chicken and a revelation hits me. Maybe the smell of things has something to do with the success of a meal.

"Hank!" I bump his hip with mine, and nudge him toward the oven and reach for the rolling pin. "I want to do this. You can pull out our dinner, then maybe coach me from the other side of the counter. You are too distracting." I give him what I hope is a sly grin.

"Oh," he says almost sadly. Then a smile spreads. "Wait. You're saying I'm distracting in a good way?"

"Depends on if it's what you want or not." I raise an eyebrow as I press a mound of dough into submission.

"I'm starting to believe we want the same thing." A sweet look of contentment washes over his face. "I like you, Candace." He clears his throat. "I really like you." He nods as if willing me to divulge my feelings.

"I think you know how I feel."

"Well, if that kiss was any indication."

"We've had a few of those." How in the world can a kiss take you away like that and not mean something? Something big. Something I've never known before.

I look up at him, and his face has the swooniest smolder I've ever seen. "You better stop looking at me with those dreamy eyes or I'm going to climb over the counter, which will annihilate this pie for sure."

A sultry chuckle bounces around the room, echoing in my soul. Yep. It's official. I'm in love.

CHAPTER 38
COOKIN'

HANK

She must more than just like me. I mean, what else do all the sly vague comments and looks mean. And that kiss. Not that I haven't enjoyed kissing in the past, but when I'm with her it's something totally different than anything I've ever experienced.

She's buzzing around throwing the pie together like she knows what she's doing. Like she doesn't need me anymore. Once she disciplined herself enough to slow down and follow the recipe, she quit making silly mistakes and blowing up her pots and pans. I think she's just entertaining me now.

A gust of heat hits my face as she opens the oven door and carefully slides the pie in. She handled the whole thing. Wrapped foil around the edges of the pie and set the timer. Everything. She really doesn't need me.

"Hank, I was thinking." With the pie in the oven, she looks up from semi-fogged glasses. "What if we took the pie to Lyle's place?"

I fumble that ball from left field. "You mean, by the creek?"

"Yeah. I know the way. It's not completely dark yet. You and I can't eat all of this ourselves, and maybe he'd enjoy sharing it with his friends. Well, I'm not sure if they are really friends. There are a few people he hangs out with. He seems to avoid them during the day. But

I think they watch out for each other." She shakes her head like she's forcing thoughts out into the open. "I just keep thinking about him tonight. Like we're *supposed* to be with him. Is that weird?"

I stare at her, dazed. So much for a romantic evening. I guess I let my heart run ahead of me again.

"Hank? What do you think?"

About going to a back alley at night to take a pie to a handful of unsheltered people? Not sure it's a good idea. Even though one of those people is my friend. Is it safe?

"You're thinking too hard." Candace pats my shoulder. "What is your heart saying?" Her hand slides to my chest. It's over. She can have…

"Whatever you want." I rake my hand through my hair so hard it hurts.

Her countenance brightens. "Really?"

"Do you have any flashlights?"

"Yeah, I have flashlights. And paper plates, plastic forks—everything we need."

She scurries around the kitchen, gathering items and throwing them into the grocery bag I arrived with earlier. As soon as the pie comes out of the oven, she wraps it in layers of terrycloth towels and hands it to me.

"I'm driving, since I know the way."

She's so excited. Any trepidation I have needs to stay under wraps. Within ten minutes we pull into the parking lot of the Szechuan Diner. She bolts out of the car like she's in a race, runs around to my side, and opens the door.

"I'm excited we're here!" She gives a little jump and claps her hands.

I manage to balance the pie and the paper bag, and climb from the car without dropping anything. She leads the way around the restaurant and to the back alley, where a small group of people huddle around a big plastic trash can next to a grimy dumpster. Small flicks of light flare off and on. From lighters, I guess. A dark but familiar silhouette turns toward us. A knot congeals in my gut and my heart sinks. It's hard to see Lyle this way.

"Glasses? Blondie? What are you doing here?"

Candace takes the bundle of pie and towels from my hand and lifts it toward him. "We made a pie. We wanted to share it with you and your friends."

His head wags. I'm not sure he's too pleased about this turn of events. But Candace charges forward with a skip to her step. "It's apple," she sings.

"Oh Moody, it's apple," a woman snarks, then cackles.

Lyle looks back at the people around the trash can and jerks his head as if giving directions. They retreat to the other side of the alley and down the ditch bank. Candace stops as Lyle shakes his arms like a wet dog flicking off water, then meanders toward us.

"I'm not sure this is a good idea." Lyle's voice is low.

Candace's shoulders drop. "We were supposed to come here. To be with you. I know it."

"Blondie, it wasn't a good idea."

"Why? I've met your friends. They seemed harmless enough. And wasn't that Mindy?" she points an elbow in the direction of the retreating group, "I thought she might like some pie too."

"Mindy's not in the mood for pie." He says flatly and looks over her shoulder at me. "It wasn't a good idea."

Something's off. My stomach lurches as I attempt to squelch the bile rising to my throat. I look around, and recognition dawns as if a fog has burned off. Evidence lies on the asphalt around the trash can like dirty laundry. Foil, a blackened spoon, a lighter. Even worse is Lyle's look of shame.

"Lyle, what's going on?" I nod at what I see, and he knows I know.

"Nothing." He closes his eyes. "Yet."

"But you were in process? You've been doing so well. You have the possibility of two different jobs if you follow through long enough. What were you thinking? Do you want to stay here?" Hugging the paper bag, I use my elbows to point around me. "In *this*?"

Candace turns around and looks at me like a lost puppy. Lyle steps next to her and opens his fist, showing her a syringe. She gasps.

"Lyle! What were you doing?" Her hands drop. Amazingly, Lyle catches the pie before it topples to the ground.

He shakes his head, avoiding her eyes. "Just started cookin'. The old crew showed up. They had everything and were jerking me around... I get so tired of fighting." Stiff hair flops over his face like a dried-up mop as he releases a deep groan. "I'm sorry. I-I don't want to do this. I just... This is what happens. Over and over."

Candace sets her hand on Lyle's forearm with a gentleness speaking volumes. His eyes dart before settling on hers.

"Come home with us." There's nothing but determined compassion in Candace's voice. "Right now. Don't say bye to your other friends. Just come now. We'll have pie at my place."

Lyle looks down at the pie, then at me. I tap my forehead. "If you want to change, you've got to... ?"

He nods at me and then Candace. "Do something different."

She wraps an arm behind him and escorts him past me. I turn and watch, admiration rising to the surface of my jumbled emotions.

I think I just saw her save a life.

———

Lingering scents of sage and cinnamon surround us like a blanket as we enter Candace's apartment. We bask in the cocoon of it while we eat pie and play cards, Lyle half-heartedly participates.

Candace keeps what momentum there is going. No questions. Just flipping cards and commenting on who's ahead in the game. She doesn't let Lyle talk about what we saw him doing earlier. "What happened an hour ago doesn't matter," she says when he tries. "We're here now." She seems to be fighting the memory away, a lone soldier.

When the games are played out and we stand at her door, she looks like she's ready to burst into tears but catches it and changes course, determination written all over her face. "I hope you'll both hear me out. I have a plan, and here's what I know. Lyle, you can't go back to the creek tonight. And maybe not ever." She drops her head and grabs Lyle's hand. "Please, Lyle. Say you won't go back."

Amazingly, he nods. "I won't. If you don't want me to, Blondie. I won't."

Candace's determined look seems to manipulate its reflection onto Lyle's face.

"You're spending the night at Hank's. And we'll deal with other details tomorrow." She looks at me. "You're coming to church with me tomorrow." Then she turns to Lyle. "So are you. Hank's bringing you. Then we'll have lunch together and... What do you think? Will you? Please?"

I'm not sure what I think about everything that has happened tonight. It's all unbelievable. The last thing I want to do is let Candace down, and I hope Lyle feels the same.

I pull air into the depths of my lungs. *God, help me tonight. You know what Lyle needs. You know what I need. And once we leave Candace's place... it's on me.*

Lyle and I nod, eye each other, and walk toward the door. Lyle leads the way, and I follow, but a warm hand from behind stops me. I turn to see Candace's wide, sad eyes.

"I'm sorry." She whispers.

I shake my head and try to offer a reassuring smile. "We'll have our time." I lift her hand and press my lips against her soft skin.

"Thank you." She squeezes my hand before I turn to catch up with Lyle. *We'll have our time.*

CHAPTER 39
THE NECESSARY STEPS

CANDACE

W hat has gotten into me? I feel like a mama bear whose cubs have been messed with. The determination boiling inside my soul is consuming, like the heat that ruined my neglected pot months ago.

I will not be negligent. I must help Lyle, whatever it takes. I've never felt so sure of anything. Never had the confidence to demand actions from others like this. But something inside tells me I can't not.

Tan lace-up granny boots peek at me from under my maxi dress, its red and yellow pattern reminds me of falling leaves on a golden background. Focusing on clothing is usually my way of celebrating a change in season. Right now, it's helping me hold some semblance of sanity as I wring my hands and wait.

I jump when I hear a knock at the door. A low level of anxious energy has been pulsating just under my skin; worry Lyle might have run away during the night. *Lord, help me not to expect too much. Help me help him from falling over the edge of the volcano he's skirting.* Another knock pounds even louder. I smooth my dress and take the necessary steps to the door.

Yes, a voice from my heart assures. *Just take the necessary steps.*

Everything seems to slow down as I watch my own hand turn the knob and pull the door toward me. I look up and find my view of Hank blocked by Lyle, tidy and clean, his damp hair combed back. I scan his outfit. His thin body is swimming in baggy navy slacks and a striped, navy and white Oxford shirt.

"They're your boyfriend's," Lyle says, tugging at the clothes.

"You look nice."

"I look like a little kid in his dad's clothes."

I look at his face and cock my head. "You look nice. Thank you for being on time."

"Didn't have much choice now, did I?"

The rock hovering in my throat drops with a thud into my stomach. What did I expect?

Just take the necessary steps.

"Well, let's get going," I say, trying to ignore the emotional sludge we all seem to be trudging knee-deep. "I'll drive."

The car ride to the church is silent. I don't mind, because I need to pray quietly in my heart. *Please Lord, let Jillian and Matthew be at this service. I need them. Jilly's cheerful countenance and intuition will help me be brave, and Matthew's steadiness will keep all of us calm. The kids will lighten the weight I feel too, by being their silly selves.*

I park and open my car door as if dipping my toe in the Red Sea. The water parts when I spy two littles bounce toward me, their parents not far behind.

"Auntie Can-Can!" The kids throw their arms in my direction, giggling as they fight over who gets to hug me first.

"Hey Can-Can!" Jillian jogs up and tries to control the arms flying all around me. "One at a time, after me." Her arms envelop me, and my guttering courage reignites. She backs away and looks at me, concern flashes across her face before the lightning strike of her vibrant smile. "Love the dress!" She spins me around to face Lyle and Hank. "Introduce me to your friends." Her arm rests around the back of my waist. She knows I need her.

"Jillian, these are my friends Lyle and Hank. Lyle, Hank, this is my friend Jillian and her husband, Matthew. And these are their two kiddos, Hilary and James."

Gracious as always, Hank stretches out his hand to Jillian, then to Matthew and each of the kids. Lyle watches him and then hesitantly stretches his hand to each as well.

"It's so nice to meet you both," Jillian says, then she points to her watch. "I hate to be pushy, but we should get inside. Settling in is complicated with kiddos. Can you take them to Sunday school, Matthew? I'll save you a seat." She looks from me to Lyle to Hank. "Let's all sit together. Is a spot in the back okay?"

Thank God for Jillian. She knows toward the back is probably the only place Lyle is willing to sit.

We scoot into the miraculously open back pew. Hank, Lyle, me, then Jillian. She sets her bright yellow clutch purse next to her to save Matthew's seat. Music plays and the worship leader encourages everyone to stand and sing *A Mighty Fortress Is Our God*. We all rise except for Lyle. He hangs his head, closing his eyes, and I lift a quick prayer before joining in with the congregation.

I hardly get through the first refrain before the tears I managed to keep at bay for the last twelve hours will not be held back. Like a gentle waterfall, they consistently flow. Light. Freeing. Reassuring. A warm hand squeezes mine. I glance Jillian's way, but she simply nods once and keeps looking forward.

As the music fades, we sit, and she hands me a tissue. So much for my makeup. I dab my eyes, then set my hand with the wadded tissue on my lap, looking forward in anticipation of the sermon. A scratchy hand lands on mine. Lyle turns his palm up, leans toward me with an eye on the tissue, and nudges my arm.

His head is bowed, but his slicked-back hair can't hide the pained expression on his face. Or the tears. I give him the mascara-smudged tissue and watch him wipe his eyes.

"I can get you a clean one," I whisper.

He shakes his head and covers his face with both hands.

For the rest of the service, he doesn't move. Like a statue secured by a granite base, he isn't going anywhere. Then the minister starts the benediction.

"The Lord bless you—"

"And give you peace," I hear Lyle's mumbled voice.

We stand to leave, trying to be the first ones out, but a group of teenagers beat us up the aisle. Our row follows behind in single file until we pass through the foyer and emerge outside. When we enter the fresh air, I hear Lyle's loud gasp signal relief. He walks hunched over while Jillian corrals us in a circle and Matthew heads off to get the kids.

Jillian jibber-jabbers about the change of weather and other easy topics, until the kids run up and Matthew scoots into the circle. Child chatter takes over our cocoon, then Jillian excuses their family, saying they need to go visit Matthew's mom.

"I'm so glad you came." She purposefully moves her gaze to both Lyle and Hank. "I hope to see you again soon." She looks at me. "We should all have a game night. Pizza and Uno. You pick the date and time. See you then."

She herds the kids toward the parking lot, a mother hen gathering her chicks.

"You have nice friends," Lyle says.

"The best." I face the guys. "Shall we go back to my place and have something to eat?"

They both nod and we walk into a cone of silence, getting to the car and all the way to my apartment without a word.

———

The guys sit at my hand-me-down wooden table as I set the stockpot on the stained blue gingham hot pad in the center. Warm savory steam sends a fog of comfort around the table. Hank ladles the creamy soup into our bowls. Chicken and wild rice. A recipe from one of the cookbooks Hank suggested from the library.

"Wow, Blondie," Lyle says. "You really have learned to cook."

I haven't pushed the conversation toward deeper concerns yet, but after attempting a spoonful, I know it's time. I won't be able to eat if we don't move forward.

"Lyle, Hank, we need to all be on the same page."

"Blondie, I know you want to save me. And after seeing you cry today, I…" Lyle sets his spoon down and drops his hands in his lap. "I want to cooperate. I want to change. But you an' Hank got something special going. You don't need this messing that up." He points accusing fingers at himself.

"We've talked about this," Hank interrupts, "Candace and I have talked about what we are willing to do to help." He looks up at me with questioning eyes, "We're in this together. Right?"

"Yes," I drop my hand on his with relief. "We are in this together."

Lyle's head bobs back and forth as he eyes Hank and me. "I'm glad you have all that figured out, but I still have to go back."

"What? You can't! It's a bad idea." I protest.

"Where am I gonna sleep?"

"You can stay with me," Hank says.

"Don't say something you don't mean."

"I'm serious. Under specific conditions, you can stay with me. I've been doing some research and have some ideas to help you get into your own housing. But for now, you need a little extra support. I'm single and have the space if you don't mind my couch."

"Okay, but I still have to go back. To get my stuff."

"Do you really need whatever is back there?" I ask. "We can replace anything you need."

"No, you can't."

"What can't we replace?"

He looks at me, his expression more vulnerable than I've ever seen. "My mom's letter."

I drop my head and hide my face in my napkin. The waterworks leak out again, this time burning as they push pain to the surface. A whirlpool of fear that I might forfeit my relationship with Hank mixes with bittersweet relief that he is willing to go through all of this with me. And fear Lyle will lose what he's gained if he goes back is countered by knowing how important that letter is to him. How can I deny him that?

"Blondie," Lyle's voice breaks into the battle in my brain, "the letter's all I need. I'll just go back and get it and be right back. I promise I won't stay, won't do anything stupid. I mean it. I promise."

A muck of emotion muddles my thoughts. I finally push through. "Not alone. We'll go with you." I look up at Hank. "Right?"

A flood of thoughts seems to rush behind his wide brown eyes.

Lord, I need him.

As if Hank heard my prayer, his expression softens, and I relax at the sound of his steady voice. "Right."

CHAPTER 40
FIVE MORE MINUTES

HANK

W ind washes leaves across my windshield as I pull into the alley. Splashes of sunlight shower through the rain of reds, cinnamons, and browns. The contrast of bright color against a gray dingy street plays tricks on my emotions. I'm not happy about being here. But I agreed. I guess it's one of those times when God leads you somewhere you don't want to go.

Who in their right mind would go back to the scene of the crime? Especially if you don't know if it's been cleaned up or if the crime is still in play? But here we are, and I feel protective of not only Candace but Lyle. He's in no shape to protect himself right now. I don't even think he knows what he should guard himself from, which might be part of why he's been stuck in this place for so long.

The creak of my car doors warns me to my bones. We all get out, wander to the edge of the alley, and look down a well-trod path to the encampment where Lyle has been laying his head at night. He leads the way, Candace follows behind. Her boots and brightly colored dress don't fit in this environment but are a welcome distraction as I take up the end.

Tarps and cardboard clutter the edge of the creek with makeshift dwellings. A man sleeps in a camp chair next to an odd collection of household items and a heap of bicycle tires. Untied work boots stick out from the army-green sleeping bag covering him, face to ankles. At the other end, scruffy graying hair sprouts like a clump of grass.

Lyle continues past a couple of "homes"—I don't know what else to call them—until he gets to what apparently is his, two large boxes strategically connected and covered with tarps. A ragged broom leans against the front, where it looks like the dirt has been swept. Lyle pulls open a brown plastic sheet of a door and disappears inside. Seconds later, he emerges with one of the grocery bags he usually takes with him everywhere.

"Did you get what you need?" I ask.

He nods and we turn back as the guy with the sleeping bag shifts, then stands.

"Lyle, where'd you go?" The gray-haired man rambles over. "You missed the action. Mindy was having a high ol' time. She's out for the count, hasn't even come out to pee."

I watch Lyle's face turn white. "Did you check on her?"

"You know her, she'll be sleeping for days. Why bug her?" The man scratches the stubble on his chin, then picks at his arm. "Those buddies of yours kept her company before taking off last night. Thought it better to leave well enough alone."

Lyle draws his hand hard down his face and covers his mouth. He shifts his view down the dirt path to a faded green tent, hesitantly walks to the entrance, and lifts the flap.

"M-mindy?"

He kneels and reaches inside. Like a knee-jerk reaction I run toward him.

"Lyle! Don't."

He turns his head, his face sullen. "She's gone."

"What?" I drop next to him to make sense of what he said. His hand rests on her bare foot. She's not moving, not breathing, her body stiff.

I stand to block Candace as she tries to join us. I gotta give her something else to do. Distract her. She can't see this. "Candace, call 911 and go wait for them up at the alley."

"I know CPR. I can help." She exclaims trying to push past me.

"No." I hold her shoulders until she stills. "She's been dead for a while."

"Oh." She covers her mouth, and as if on autopilot pulls out her phone and climbs up the embankment.

"You sure?" The gray-haired guy asks.

I nod and ask him to help direct EMS when they come. He seems relieved to walk away. Then I turn to Lyle who hasn't moved.

"Come on Lyle. Come out into the sun. We can't help her anymore."

"Sorry Mindy." He whispers and slides his body leaving a swirl of dirt, sitting cross-legged, positioned like a watchman keeping guard. "I shoulda been here."

I drop to sit next to him and rest my hand on his back. He just moans, slumps his shoulders, and lets his face fall into his palms. I can't tell him I disagree with him, not right now. All I can do is pray in my heart thanking God Lyle didn't stay last night.

———

After a swarm of inquiries and statements, Mindy's lifeless body is taken away. We stand dumbstruck in a circle and stare at each other. I've been fighting off nausea for hours, and I imagine Candace and Lyle feel the same. I want to get out of here, and back to the world I know. A world that makes sense to me.

"Let's go. There's nothing else to do here."

Candace wraps her arm around Lyle.

"I'm so sorry." She rests her head on his shoulder and gently releases streams of tears down her cheeks. They match the tracks on Lyle's cheeks. He shakes her off and steps toward the opening of the worn-out tent.

"She's not there, Lyle. Come on, let's go."

He continues on like he doesn't hear me and though I figure it's most likely a bad idea, I follow him and watch from the opening as he picks through piles of debris.

"Lyle, what are you doing?"

"I gotta find it."

"There's probably needles in there. Don't just grab around. It's not safe."

"Who cares? I need to find… I gotta tell…"

"Lyle!" I pull him out by the collar. "What do you have to find? You can't afford to stick yourself with whatever she pumped herself full of."

The look on his face tells me how insensitive my last comment was. "Sorry." I press my hand down hard on top of my head. I've got to think straight. "Tell me what you're looking for and I'll find it. You stay here with Candace."

I look at her. She looks like she needs support. I look back at Lyle. Maybe they need each other's support.

A spark of understanding flashes across Lyle's eyes. He moves toward Candace and holds her hand, then looks at me. "She had a book, with a unicorn on the cover. A journal. With all her important numbers in it. It has her daughter's number. An aunt or sister or somebody is taking care of her. I gotta tell them."

I nod and try to let in as much light as possible, then gingerly pick through the mass of items this woman must've taken years to collect. Most of it looks like trash to me. Piles of stuck-together papers, sticky magazines, dead nursery plants in plastic containers, and… I stop. An exposed needle, a lighter, and a spoon dusted with loose powder light a flame in me. Wait, not just one needle but… I back away, thankful I didn't touch any of it. I take a breath.

Lord, I don't want to be stupid. Can you just show me where the book is so we can get out of here. I slowly scan from one side of the tent to the other. A book with a unicorn on the cover peeks out. Hunched over, I carefully approach the back corner and pick the book up with my fingertips, like I could be bitten at any second. I don't trust anything lying around here.

Sunlight dwindles as I exit what once was Mindy's home. A chill accentuates the gloomy atmosphere as if chanting a dirge. Lyle scrambles to take the book out of my hands. He leafs through it, opens it wide, and pats a page.

"This is it." He looks at me. "We have to call."

"The coroner said they'd contact next of kin."

"No. We have to call. I promised Mindy if…" he coughs and covers his mouth, unable to say anymore. I'm startled by what he's said, as if planning for this situation was common. Like setting up a will.

"We'll call. But let's get home. We'll take care of it there." Both Lyle and Candace nod in agreement, and I turn toward the gray-haired man who stands like a spectator at a distance.

"Sorry for your loss." I don't mean to sound harsh, but I barely have the bandwidth to take care of Lyle and Candace right now. The weight of everything settles on my shoulders and threatens to steal whatever strength I have left.

"Let's go." I lead the way up the ditch to my car and open the door for Candace while Lyle gets in the back seat. The realization that I could have been jabbed by some tainted needle or who knows what makes my blood boil. The shock from the last twenty-four hours has morphed into full-blown anger at being dragged deeper and deeper into Lyle's world. I have to be purposeful not to slam the door right off the car. I don't want to scare Candace.

As I drive to my apartment, fury bubbles under the surface, ready to explode. *Please Lord, help me hold it together.*

———

Silence looms like an offshore storm as we drive back to my place. *Just get home, Hank. We'll eat, make phone calls, make a plan.* I recite next steps like a mantra in my head. *Keep it together for five more minutes. Then the next five minutes, then the next.*

Focus on being a gentleman. Open Candace's door. I think through each move like parts in a mechanical process. *Unlock the front door. Gesture Candace and Lyle inside.* Thankfully, Cat has moved on to Megan's, so Candace should be able to breathe.

In the kitchen, I pull out a bag of chips and salsa and pour three glasses of water. Lyle and Candace start talking, and my defenses unravel. Molten lava outrage creeps up my neck. I don't want to explode on them. They have enough to deal with. I storm to the bathroom and hope they don't notice as I stomp down the hall.

Slam!

Shoot, I couldn't help it. I just want to punch something! A face of fury glares at me from the mirrored medicine cabinet. I swing it open and slam it, trying to change the face looking back at me. The door springs back open, triggering my razor and shaving cream to clank down into the sink. I hear footsteps run down the hall.

"Are you okay in there?" Such a sweet voice of concern. I gotta stop this. At least for Candace's sake.

"I'm fine. Just… give me a minute."

"Okay." She sounds sad. I'm sure she doesn't believe me, and she shouldn't. I'm not fine. None of this is fine. But I don't want to make a scene and can't exactly talk to her about it with Lyle around. I need someone to talk me down before I have to go back out there and be levelheaded.

I pull my phone out of my pocket.

"Hey, Hank!" Thank God Megan answered.

"Talk me off the ledge."

"Oh boy, what happened?" She knows me better than anyone.

"I'm mad."

"You're gonna have to give me more than that."

I huff and puff and hem and haw, then I tell her the whole ugly story. "And the worst of it is how mad it's making me. I should care more about Lyle and his loss, but I can't stop thinking about how I stuck my hand into who knows what, putting myself in harm's way. No gloves, no nothing. It's a health hazard out there. How can people live like that?" Oh, how uncaring and ugly I sound. Only thinking of myself. "I just don't get it." My head drops so hard it hurts. The flood of emotion and pressure behind my eyes thunders ready to break until Megan's voice calms my rage.

"Isn't that the point, Hank? You don't get it. It's not your life. You've never had to face it until now. It was unsafe. But sometimes we are called to go where it isn't safe. You know what dad says." Her voice deepens. "How do you stop someone from falling off the edge?"

"Get in their way," I respond automatically.

The question was one of our dad's broken records as kids. *"If your friends are jumping off a cliff, are you going to follow them? No! Get in their way.*" He'd say it like we had some responsibility to society to stop all the stupid choices others make. We didn't have time to make our own, we were too busy being examples and…

"Hank. Stop ruminating."

A whole lot of ugly swirls around in my brain.

"So what are you going to do about it?" Her inhale is audible. "You haven't punched anything have you?"

"I haven't punched anything since junior high."

"Yeah, but that time scared me."

"I punched the wall, not you."

"Are you that mad?"

"Yeah, but I'm older now. Give me some credit."

"So you locked yourself in the bathroom?" Megan laughs and suddenly I can breathe.

I let out a long exhale, thankful I can talk to the person who understands me the most. "What do I do?"

"The next thing, then the next." She sighs. "I'm sorry, bro, but you gotta get out of the bathroom and face your friends. You have to keep doing the hard thing. Candace and Lyle are waiting for you to call people you don't know and tell them someone they love died from an overdose. That's the first thing. Then you have to decide what you're going to do about Lyle. Are you serious about him living with you? Sure it's a good idea?"

"I don't know. I just can't think of any other solution right now, and the process of getting housing for him isn't just a phone call away—it's a whole long ordeal. If he keeps to certain expectations, having him here might be okay." I close my eyes, wishing I could see the future. But I can't. "I guess I just have to move forward with the only thing I know to do."

"Then that's what you do. And I'll keep praying for you."

"Thanks." I drop my hand over my face, willing its expression to lighten. "I better go face the music."

"I love you, bro."

"I know. Thanks. I don't know what I'd do without you."

"Say it. You love me too."

I laugh at how she makes me say it all the time, as if I need to learn to take medicine. "Yes. I love you too."

"Always and forever," we sing in unison.

I hang up the phone. My sister who tormented me as a child has become one of my greatest allies. Yet again, she has instilled in me the courage and fortitude I need for what's ahead. And here I go.

CHAPTER 41
DUST TO DUST

CANDACE

"How are Tara and her family?" I ask Hank as he enters my apartment, his hair covered with droplets of water from the incessant rain.

"As good as can be expected. But we did take care of the final details for tomorrow." He lumbers to the couch and falls onto the cushion as if a weight is pinning him down.

It's been two weeks since Mindy died. Hank has been a champ. He initiated the call to Tara, Mindy's sister, as Lyle and I sat around my kitchen table, our eyes fixed on him. Hank offered the phone to Lyle once he dialed the number, but Lyle let out a guttural sob and waved it away, dropping his head with a *thump* on the table. Hank opted for speaker phone. He and Tara were the only ones able to form words.

"I wish Lyle would talk to me. He just goes through the motions." Hank hunches forward, elbows on his knees. "He's had a hard time processing how Mindy died. But looks like a zombie most days and hasn't wanted to talk about what happened. Says he has to come to terms and will let me know when he's ready."

Hank runs the fingers of one hand through his floppy hair.

I sigh and hand Hank a fresh-baked oatmeal cookie from the platter I set on the coffee table. "At least Lyle's doing what he said he'd do, even if on autopilot." He tallies insect populations without a word. Pushes the paper into my face, then quickly exits at the stroke of five and waits outside the front door of my office building for Hank and me to join him.

"He's like a robot at the library each morning too." Hank wags his head as he chews and swallows the last of the cookie. "He shows up, not that he has a choice since I bring him with me. He does a great job cleaning, even unlocks the door for the morning patrons. But I miss him saying 'Hey, how's it going?' Or making smart comments as the people enter."

I nod and squeeze Hank's hand, grateful Lyle is showing consistency, but not sure I'm happy about what is happening. *Lord, is this a good thing? Our friend is just not himself.*

———

Rain drizzles on the dozen or so of us as we stand in a semicircle around the open grave. Droplets stream off the edge of our umbrellas and drill small holes into the ground around us. It's like a scene out of a movie. Surreal. The pastor reads through Psalm 23, then Tara shares happy memories she and Mindy had as kids. Mindy's mother and daughter stand solemnly, their oversized umbrella casts dark shadows across their faces. The little girl looks to be somewhat older than Hilary, maybe eight. She stares like a statue at the casket resting in the red dirt hole. Lyle waves a hand and asks to share something. Tara nods and he takes a step forward, eyes on the cherry wood coffin.

"Sorry, Mindy. It's my fault you're being buried in the dirt while I stand here. A slight change of events, and we'd be in opposite places. Please forgive me." His voice cracks as he looks up at her family motionless across from him. "Please forgive me."

Mindy's daughter doesn't move, but her mother nods. Tara covers her face with her hankie and nods as well.

"I wish…" Lyle lets out a groan. "I wish things were different." He takes a breath. "Mindy, you were as good a friend as I could have these past few years. I thank you for that, but this proves to me I gotta change. I gotta muster the courage to do what's right. For you, for your family. For me and mine. We talked about it all the time but never followed through. I'm sorry I didn't come to this sooner, for your sake. But I will now. For you and..." His gaze moves to the girl in a black dress and sweater, with black tights and patent leather Mary Janes. "For you, little one. So you know it's possible. It doesn't have to be this way. You can have better."

He skirts the gap in the ground and drops to his knees before Mindy's daughter. Both his hands grasp her forearms as he looks into her stony face. "You can have better. You will. I promise." His hands and head drop as if all his energy drains into the gaping dirt hole behind him, as if it's ready to swallow him whole.

The girl stirs. Her pudgy hand caresses the side of Lyle's face. He looks up, and there's wordless communication between them. Mindy's mom bends and draws Lyle up by the arm to stand.

"Mindy made her own choices." She nods at him intently. "And now you can make yours. We'll be okay. And Cassie here will be okay. Eventually." She pats Lyle's cheek. "You make this change like you promised. Do better for *you* and *your* mama. For Mindy's sake, for Cassie's sake. Whatever it takes."

Lyle mumbles something I can't distinguish, then walks slowly back to my side. The pastor says something about how we came from dust and return to dust—dust to dust. Each person from Mindy's family picks up a red rose and lets it fall onto the casket below, the sound echoing the pitter-patter of the rain. Lyle does the same. We all turn in the direction of black asphalt and trudge through the gray mist toward our cars.

———

"It's over," Lyle says, but his expression seems to look for answers from Hank and me as we sit around my kitchen table. Steam rises from our mugs of hot tea, and the scones I just pulled out of the oven. The air filled with the scent of warm cinnamon, offers a small sense of comfort.

"What do you mean?" I ask.

"What I said. I've been thinking about it since Mindy died. It could have been me. It should have been me. But it wasn't, and I don't know why, except you two got in my way." He shakes his head as if in disbelief. "Mindy was on a binge, and I... I was ready to dive in with her."

His eyes moisten. "I feel like it's my fault, but—" He gulps in air. "Something in my heart says I can't let myself think that way. Or maybe it's something my mom said once. 'No matter how good their upbringing, people make their own decisions. Some good, some bad.' Either way, I gotta make good on what I said. I'm done."

He looks back and forth between Hank and me. "Whatever you say to do, I'll do. I haven't figured this out on my own. So tell me what to do. I'll do it."

"That's a lot of trust." Hank sets his mug down and squints at Lyle. "You do have a say."

"Well, that's what I say. Tell me what to do, Glasses. I trust you more than me."

"Trusting someone else isn't always the safest choice."

Lyle raises his eyebrows. "Right now, I know it is. At least until I'm on my feet. You two have kept me afloat these last couple of weeks. I hope someday I can trust myself again, but I can't right now."

My hand instinctively reaches for Lyle's. "You can. What you said, what you've come to realize—all of it shows something is changing. You are changing."

I close my eyes, willing myself to focus. *Lord, what do we do now?*
Just take the necessary step.

"Lyle, if I were to ask you what your next step would be, what would you say?"

Lyle lets out a soft chuckle. "Blondie, why is it you make me laugh just by the way you say things?" He moves his hand out from under mine, gives mine a pat, then folds his hands together in front of him. "Okay. If I were to ask myself what the next step would be, I'd say..." He lets out a huff. "Talk to my mom." His fists knock gently on the table as if hammering the idea into place.

"Okay." Hank slides his phone in front of Lyle. "Here you go."

"What, right now?"

"No time like the present."

Hank and Lyle squint at each other. Lyle reaches for the phone and punches in numbers. When a ring sounds, he fumbles the phone and it falls on the table with a rumble like thunder. He slams a finger on the touch screen. "I can't. I'm not ready."

He races down the hall toward my bathroom. *Slam!* I cringe. Tight-lipped, Hank pushes his chair away from the table and drives his head back against the kitchen wall.

CHAPTER 42
MAN YOUR STATIONS

HANK

Less than a week ago we stood in the cold drizzle around Mindy's grave, now we're dancing in the kitchen at my complex. An interesting mix of scents, sounds, and people I may have never put together before fill the space where we gather. Marcus and his mom are in charge of the music. Festive mariachi trumpets in the background. Cooked pork, chiles and cumin somehow complement the smell of apples and cinnamon. We are here for one purpose, to support each other as we cook our portion of our separate Thanksgiving offerings for tomorrow.

Marcus signed up to participate in community service for school, so he decided to join Lyle and volunteer at a local outreach to feed the unhoused for the holiday. Marcus and his mom fill softened corn husks with masa dough and shredded pork, one of their family's traditional go-to recipes, while Lyle, Candace and I fill several pie crusts with crisp chopped apples slathered in cinnamon and sugar. How the atmosphere and generosity in each of our hearts has changed.

Marcus has taken me up on every assignment I've offered him. I guess the way to his heart *is* through his stomach. He even comes to the library just to hang out and read. Through an interesting chain of events he and Lyle started talking about community service and volunteering while Marcus waited for his mom to pick him up. She joined the conversation with Lyle, I think at first out of concern. But the three of them decided they'd volunteer together. So here we are, all of us dancing around the kitchen. Laughter and flour swirl through the atmosphere like wisps of dandelion seeds.

———

CANDACE

Nervous jitters overtake my stomach. At today's lunch I will meet the rest of Hank's family, then he'll meet mine at dinner this evening. Thank God I learned how to cook. At least I know my offerings for both gatherings taste decent and won't poison anyone. The five of us sampled the sweet potatoes, tamales and pies last night and we all agreed everything turned out amazing.

A knock at the door makes my heart jump. I hurry to open it. Hank is particularly handsome in dark blue jeans, and his rust-colored shirt which makes the gold flecks in his eyes sparkle. His hair looks like his mom fixed it for school pictures—perfectly in order. But I know strands will break free any minute and fall over one eye. A smile takes over his face, and my smile reciprocates, making my cheeks hurt. Why am I so excited and terrified at the same time?

"You ready?"

"Um-hmm." I close the door behind me and we walk to the car.

"We haven't been just the two of us in a while." He laughs. "Do you think we'll know how to act?"

I was wondering the same thing. "We'll find out." I hope that sounded like I was joking, but I'm not so sure of my delivery.

We get in the car, and even before we hit the main street, we're chatting like we did before Lyle's presence took over every waking moment. Lyle is safe, busy at the outreach with Marcus and his mom. We get to spend the day free from the cloud of worry that colored the atmosphere when we didn't know where he was or how he was doing.

I'm a half step behind Hank as we walk up to a large ranch-style house. The lawn is well manicured, even though the cool fall air has told the grass to let go of summer's vibrant green. The door flies open and a rush of chatter washes over us from inside. Meg throws her arms around Hank, gives him a quick squeeze, then pushes him inside and reaches for me. She wraps an arm behind me and pulls me to her side, avoiding a collision with the pie in my hands.

"Don't worry. I'll protect you from all of these hoodlums."

"Hoodlums?"

She laughs. "Not really. I just like to sound dramatic. Come on in but watch out. We are a family of huggers. You wouldn't know it from Mister Discreet." Her foot taps Hank's. "But the rest of us are very affectionate."

Meg takes the pie and ushers me into a room glowing with golden light. My view fills with bodies swaying in conversation as if dancing. Smells of roast turkey, stuffing, and cinnamon-stewed apples waft through the air. I think I've walked into a Norman Rockwell painting with the sound turned on. Meg introduces me to each sister and husband, niece and nephew. The brothers-in-law muss Hank's hair like he's still a kid, even though he towers over all of them.

An older, fuller bodied and distinguished version of Hank strolls up to me. Not that Hank isn't distinguished, but his dad's eyes have a similar look to my dad's. As if life has taught him secrets he carries like fragile jewels to pass down to future generations. He introduces himself with a generous "Nice to meet you." Then Hank is sidelined by other family members, and Meg links her arm into my elbow and ushers me into the kitchen.

"Here she is, Mom!" Meg says, a little too excited.

A willowy figure in a honey-colored turtleneck and tan suede pencil skirt stands before a steaming pot, stirring vigorously. Her hair is pulled up into a French knot. She looks like an old-school actress. Her smile is gentle as she floats over to me, wooden spoon still in hand.

Meg swoops in and pulls the utensil out of her mom's hand like it's a magic wand. "I'll take that." Meg resumes the stirring.

Hank's mom pauses for a brief second of what I assume is an assessment of me, then quickly stretches her arms wide. "It's so lovely to meet you." She draws me in, and I accept the hug she offers.

Sudden comfort envelops me, and I linger in her embrace long enough to take in her soft floral perfume. Though gentle, her firm arms exude strength. It all makes sense now. Hank's dad and mom convey the same steadiness, security, and safety I feel when I'm with him.

I take a deep breath as Hank's mom steps back, and places her hands on each of my shoulders. She gives me a wink. "You're so welcome here. We've been on this boy's case to bring you over." Hank meanders over and she musses his hair. "I guess he wanted to keep you all to himself."

"Mom, even you?" A rush of red splashes across Hank's face.

He looks at me. "They love to razz me. Although mom usually has my back."

"Oh honey, it's the holidays, time to loosen up." She radiates the most beautiful laugh and turns toward the stove. "Okay everybody, man your stations." Her voice turns to surprising firmness. "Dinner will be ready in five minutes."

Each family member assumes a position, the group acts like a well-oiled machine. Hank's dad marches to the turkey to carve it. Each of Hank's sisters puts a side dish into a glamorous serving piece. The sons-in-law keep the littles entertained and out of the way, while Hank puts ice in glasses and fills them with water. I stand back, afraid to mess up the fine-tuned orchestration.

Hank nudges me. "Hey, ask Meg for a spoon for the sweet potatoes we brought."

My lips pull into a smile and my cheeks rise. I guess I'm welcome to be a part of this machine too.

HANK

"Ow!" I rub my side where my nosy sister jabbed her finger.

"You love her." Megan swarms behind me through the doorway.

"Meg, I'm in the bathroom."

"Oh, hold it. You need to dish." She pushes her way in behind me.

"Have you told her yet? You can't leave without telling me. I see how you look at her. We all do."

"I'm almost thirty years old and you still won't give me privacy in the bathroom without a fight?"

Megan's laugh is one reason I can't stay mad at her. It's so bubbly and fun and somehow says she loves me.

"You haven't told her? Please tell me you've kissed her. You do hug her and hold her hand, let her know in that way, right?"

"That's not the only way to show someone you care." I think Megan's own concern about her relationship with Mike is influencing this conversation, but I'll let it ride.

She yanks my collar. "You aren't good at showing affection. If you want to keep her, you need to make sure she knows. Tell her. Show her." Her eyes bore into mine. "I really like her, and I like you with her. Don't you?"

"Do we really have to talk about this now?" My knees knock into each other doing the I need to take care of business dance.

"You two are walking out the door soon, so yes. I must know. You've been keeping your cards close even with me."

"Tell ya what, you'll be one of the first to know *after* I tell her. Now can I please go to the bathroom by myself?" Her feet finally unstick as I nudge her toward the door.

"Gotcha, loud and clear. You said *after* you tell her. So you *do* love her!" Megan cackles down the hallway.

"Please don't embarrass me," I whisper. I turn the lock of the bathroom door and knock my forehead against the solid wood. Megan wants my relationship with Candace to work out almost as much as I do. I just don't want to say something too soon and scare Candace away. "Ever the zealot"—that's what my last girlfriend accused. She said I was always "too much, too soon." When I look back, I think maybe we just weren't a good fit.

I walk down the hallway to find Candace surrounded but smiling. "You ready?" I ask.

She nods, and while we gather the dish we brought, my family gets in a single-file line to give goodbye hugs. I'll get one too, but I'm aware they care more that she knows how much they like her. I'm glad they like her.

Megan, last in line, serves up commentary with her hug. "Now Candace, my brother isn't as easy with affection as the rest of us. So please be understanding."

I roll my eyes at her, which she mimics right back at me.

"I love you, bro."

"Yeah, I know."

"Say it… "

Megan is insufferable, but— "I love you, sis. I love all of you. Thank you for a lovely dinner."

"Thank you for such a wonderful time," Candace chimes in. "I'm so glad I got to meet you all." She's so sweet. Fits right in but still acts a little shy. Far from the sassy girl who murders water. They'll all see that side soon enough and love her even more. Just like I…

I gotta stop. Gotta quit letting my thoughts get ahead of things. *Meg, what did you do? Planting ideas in my mind. Now I can't think of anything else.*

CHAPTER 43
HONK THREE TIMES

HANK

After I settle in the driver's seat, I look over at Candace. A soft serene smile washes over her face, already turned toward me. "I like your family. They are so lively and fun and friendly." She looks amazing sitting next to me in her autumn-themed dress and boots. She even changed out her glasses frames for the holiday. They are burgundy now. She says she likes to change with the season.

The drive to her parents' home takes us onto the freeway and then through rolling hills. Of course she grew up in the country. She needed trees to climb and bugs to chase. Red, orange, and amber leaves line the roadsides like picture frames highlighting meadows of grazing livestock. She points to a long gravel drive hemmed by pastures with several oak trees, mounds of dropped leaves circling each ancient trunk. Old white fence posts show the way to a two-story Victorian complete with antebellum columns.

"This is it." Her hands slap into her lap. "You ready?"

"Sure. It'll be nice to see where you came from."

She looks at me shyly. "I haven't been here for a while. Haven't seen my family in a few months. They don't know about everything we've gone through with Lyle. I don't know if I'm ready to tell them."

I rest my hand on both of hers. They are so soft and feminine. "I'll follow your lead."

"It'll be okay, right?"

"Why wouldn't it be?" I don't understand her apprehension. "It'll be great." I try to reassure her. I'm not going to tell her I'm nervous about meeting her family. That's the last thing she needs right now. After a quick hand squeeze, I get out of the car and jog around to open her door, then gather our contribution out of the trunk. The wind picks up, tickling my nose with the scent of damp, trampled leaves. The faint blue sky wanes toward dusky gray. It'll be coat weather soon.

We walk toward the red front door bookended by large planters on either side filled with burgundy, tangerine, and sienna-colored mums. Candace reaches for the gold lion-faced knocker, knocks three times, then steps back, bumping into me.

"Sorry."

I don't mind. Her soft shoulder sends a warm zing across my chest. "Not a problem."

She gulps in air right as the door opens. A neatly dressed man in a plaid shirt and tan sweater-vest greets us.

"Hi, Daddy."

"Candace, so glad you could come." He pats her arm then looks toward me, "And this is your friend?"

"Yes, this is my friend Hank," she says.

So, I'm her "friend" here. Okay. I pull my heart up by its bootstraps and offer a smile.

Her dad reaches out a hand and shakes mine firmly. "Come on in. Dinner is almost ready."

I follow Candace, and her dad pats my shoulder as I pass him. "I'll introduce you to the rest of the family."

"Thank you, sir."

"Call me Al. No need to be formal."

"Thank you, sir...I mean, Al."

He lets out a low chuckle and I'm put at ease, but Candace's shoulders are still pressed up practically to her ears. Wallpaper striped with moss green and soft burgundy makes the living room seem formal. Everything is clearly in its place, and soft piano music plays in the background. Candace takes the pie plate out of my hands and leaves me with her dad.

"Please have a seat, Hank. Make yourself comfortable and I'll gather the family to meet you. May I get you something to drink? Hot tea maybe?"

I sit on a sand-colored linen couch, making sure my back is straight. "Tea would be great." I bite my lip. Should I have said "fine"? Oh boy, I feel *my* shoulders travel up to *my* ears.

Al exits the room, then returns with a teacup and saucer in hand. He offers the steaming cup and backs up to introduce the small group behind him. Candace's mother, two sisters, and her grandparents, Henry and Candace. As Al mentions his parents' names, I'm reminded and amused by the coincidence. I hope I don't have a stupid look on my face.

The whole family is all dressed up for the occasion and all very congenial, but I'm a little relieved most of them have to get back to the kitchen to help. Only her grandparents stay and sit in the two wing-back chairs across from me.

"I'm guessing Hank is short for Henry," Candace's grandpa says.

I nod.

"Quite a coinkydink." He chuckles and wiggles his eyebrows. I'm not sure if he's making a funny face on purpose, but it does lighten the atmosphere. "Our Candace is a very special girl, don't you think? I'm sorry to say she hasn't shared much about you. Just that you are dating, and you work in a library. I love that you work in a library *and* met there. That will be quite a story to tell someday."

So, I'm *not* considered just a "friend" here.

Candace's grandma smells like peppermint and roses. Somehow it works. I guess because it reminds me of my grandma. "Henry and I have quite the story. Don't we?" She reaches a paper-thin hand toward her husband, who gently takes it into his.

"My favorite story. But we don't want to bore this young man with it right now. We want to get to know *him*. Find out what Candace is too independent to tell us." He looks me in the eye. "That's what she says, you know. 'I need to be independent. I need to grow up for myself.'"

He wiggles his torso. "I think she needs to lighten up and just say what she thinks. She's too worried about pleasing some folks in this household." He points his thumb back toward the kitchen.

"Now Henry, don't get all up in arms over our Candy. She's a sweet thing and just finding her way." Candace's grandma has a kind face, her pink cheeks framed by loose silver curls that escaped her hair bun. She has Candace's eyes. They gleam like a turquoise lake. I imagine what Candace might look like in fifty years.

"It's ready." I don't think I've ever heard Candace speak so softly, so fragilely.

We all nod and stand up. I wait for her grandparents to exit the room. Candace watches them pass her, then turns toward me and sighs.

I brush my hand over her shoulder and down her back, resting my palm at her waist. "It's going to be great." She leans on my arm ever so slightly, then steps with a little more determination than I've seen since we walked in the door.

We enter a formal dining room. A crystal chandelier hovers over a table set with china and goblets, teacups with saucers, and silverware on either side and along the top of each rose-lined plate. Each goblet has a thin gold line around its circumference, and burgundy napkins in gold rings lie in the center of each plate. This does not look at all like my family's casual holiday wear. I'm a little surprised by all the luxury, since I know one of Candace's favorite things is climbing trees. Everyone stands behind a chair, and her parents stand at either end of the table.

"Shall we?"

Candace looks up at me apologetically. "I'm sorry," she whispers. "I should've warned you."

"Candace?" her dad says like a teacher who calls on the kid who isn't listening. "Do you want to begin?"

She bows her head. "I'm thankful for my new friends and for renewed holiday traditions."

Quiet agreement sounds around the table. One by one, each person shares what he or she is thankful for. I'm last. With seven people ahead of me, I've had plenty of time to unscramble my thoughts and come up with something acceptable to say, like...

225

"I'm thankful for Candace." *That's what comes out?* I hear a giggle from across the table.

"Thank you, Hank," her dad says. "We're all thankful for Candace too." A crooked smile covers his face. "Enough of formalities! Let's sit and eat."

The rest of the evening plays out a little more like I anticipated. Family stories, especially curated to embarrass Candace. The red in her cheeks deepens by the minute, but I'm eating it up. She was a tomboy. Yep, I could see that. Cut her pigtails off at eight so they'd be out of the way and the boys would quit pulling them. For the two years she was taller than most of the boys in her class, she was called to the principal's office often, for tripping or kicking or punching the kids she found particularly annoying.

"Good thing you got cute as you got older," her sister Malory says, letting out a loud laugh. "Instead of getting even, the boys ended up asking her out."

Candace sinks in her seat and covers her face with her hand.

"What was that particularly persistent one named? Tommy?" Malory sings.

Candace sits up. "What about you and Jerry?" she flings back, and the sibling sparring begins, much like what happens at my house. I'm happy to recognize the girl sitting next to me again. After a minute, the parents step in.

"Okay, girls, that's enough."

"We do have company."

"Mom, he doesn't count," Candace's sister Teresa says.

"Honey, don't be rude."

"I'm not." She raises an eyebrow. "Hank and Candace have been dating for how many months? Past the magic line." She sets air quotes around the last two words.

Her mother clears her throat and turns toward me. "I'm sorry for my daughter's rudeness. Please don't take it personally."

I laugh. "I have four sisters and I'm the only boy. I'm used to this."

The sisters gasp in unison, and I think I see newfound respect in each one's eyes. "I don't know what the magic line is, but either way, I'm glad I'm past it."

The fragrance of buttery apple and cinnamon floats around the table as Candace helps her mom serve the pie we made. Everyone oohs and aahs.

"This looks and smells quite good," Candace's mom comments as she takes her seat.

"Hank, you're good for Candace." Malory lifts a fork full of syrupy apples and crust. "She never had the patience to make something this good before."

"I'd be a good student too if my teacher looked like him." Teresa elbows Malory.

"Girls! How old are you?" Candace's mom tries to keep up airs, but ineffectively.

I'm having fun with all of it, and as each minute ticks by, Candace's shoulders sink a little closer to where they belong. After all the dishes have been hand-washed and put away, she pulls me into their vast backyard. She wants to introduce me, she says—leaving me to guess who I'm meeting next.

The porch light and moon offer just enough glow to save us from tripping over gopher mounds as we venture through a pasture to an old wooden fence. She gathers her dress up to her knees, climbs through a wide opening between the wood slats, then looks back at me.

"Your turn."

Folding my body in half, I will my legs to make this look easy, then I thread through the opening and look out over the moonlit field. "You're going to introduce me to a cow?"

Laughing, she points. "That one with the white ear and brown body is Bessey. She's my favorite. But this is why I brought you out into the mud." Candace sweeps her hand toward a large, gangly-looking tree. "My thinking tree."

She pats the trunk and looks at me. I sense she wants me to do the same, as if the act is comparable to shaking hands. So I rest my fingers on the scratchy bark.

"Nice to meet you." That seemed the right thing to say.

Her giggle lights up the night. As she takes in a deep breath, her shoulders drop to their natural position. "I need you to know this tree, my catalpa tree."

She points up to a stalwart grouping of limbs thirty feet high. "That is where I'd sit and read and think." Hiking her thumb over her shoulder, she grins. "And escape."

A magical bubble floats around us as we quietly walk back toward the house. The last five minutes were sacred somehow. Like Candace opened a secret door to who she is. And now I'm aware of a new depth in my own heart.

We say our goodbyes. Candace's grandpa and dad shake my hand vigorously, and all the women awkwardly offer me a hug.

We walk across the gravel drive to my car and I open the door. Candace settles in. I wave to the small crowd highlighted under the front porch light, jog around to my side, and get in. I'm not sure why, but I honk my horn as I drive away.

"Why'd you honk three times?"

"I don't know. Thought it would be fun. A see-ya-soon kind of thing."

Candace sinks back into her seat, her shoulders low. "My grandpa honks three times every time he drives away. He says it's his way of saying 'I love you.'"

"Huh. I like that."

CHAPTER 44
WE'LL HAVE OUR CHANCE

CANDACE

A cornucopia centerpiece filled with plastic grapes, gourds, and pumpkins decorates each russet-colored tablecloth. Neighbor Bob pats the back of a chair, motions for me to sit with him and several other silver haired residents of his new home. Sprinkled around the dining hall, family members share the day-after-Thanksgiving lunch with loved ones. The stories Bob's friends share fill my heart with gratitude. There are so many valuable stories in this world. So many experiences I've never known and, honestly, some I don't want to know. The wars they lived through, the tragedies. Some of the stories evoke tears until, with a dab of a napkin, the conversation changes course to brighter days.

The sense that I've just encountered history in person rushes over me like a flood. My arms gently envelop the hunched shoulders of my dear friend, the scent of savory gravy and stuffing linger on his tweed jacket.

"Thank you for coming to share Thanksgiving with us." He gives a pillowy pat on my back. "I'm not that far away. You know where to find me if you ever want to visit."

"You can count on it." I straighten and offer a smile. My heart swells. *God, thank you for neighbor Bob.*

At home, I light cinnamon candles and look out my living room window until the sky darkens. Headlights glisten from the guest parking space in front of my apartment, Hank and Lyle are here to pick me up for Friendsgiving. The candle wicks let off black swirls of smoke after I blow out the flames.

This is the gathering I've been most excited about. Dinner and game night at Jillian's. Why is it we want our dearest friends to get to know each other, like it's the completion of a circle? I know they are all going to love each other. I'm banking on it, because I think Hank might be in the picture for…

Knock. Knock. Knock.

"Blaaawndie," Lyle sings from the other side of the door. I laugh to myself, grab my purse, and exit. Lyle bows, rolls his arm in a circle as if in a play. "Lover Boy is waiting in the car. Sent me to gather the princess."

"You're in rare form."

"Feeling better every day. More like the guy who was hidden in here." He pats his chest.

Without thinking, I wrap my arms around his rigid shoulders. Like melting butter, they soften. Warm arms wrap around me too, but only for a second.

Lyle lets out a dry cough. "We don't want to make Lover Boy jealous."

"I didn't mean to make you uncomfortable."

"No, I'm fine." Lyle brushes his hand through neatly combed hair. "I gotta get used to normal interaction." He straightens and gestures for me to go before him toward the car.

Pleasant recollections of the last few days flow easily as we drive. It's not late, but the dark curtain of a fall evening surrounds us like black velvet. The second Jillian opens the door, brilliant light floods the atmosphere.

We sit around her large oak table. The kids scamper around and show Lyle and Hank every toy action hero they can find. A loud debate ensues over who is better, Wonder Woman or Spiderman.

"Apples and oranges," Jillian says. "They don't compare." She sets pizza boxes in the center of the table. "Kids, sit. It's time to eat." Her mom voice causes Hilary and James to jump into their chairs, even as they wrestle over who gets to sit between their new friends Hank and Lyle.

Just as I expected, my dearest family friends have taken in my new friends as their own. Contentment washes over me as I sink into the chair next to Hank. His squeeze on my knee takes me by surprise. His smile reflects my feelings.

Without a hitch, the night is filled with laughter, conversation, and Uno. Jillian and Matthew let the kids stay up late and play with us. Lyle banters back and forth with the littles so easily. His silly puns and knock-knock jokes send the kids into fits of giggles, as we adults give each other looks of awe at how well he seems to be doing.

After devouring a plate of chocolate chip cookies and cocoa, we say our goodbyes so Jillian can get the kids in bed before Kraken can catch them awake past bedtime. Laughter and screams echo down the hallway as Hilary and James run to jump in their beds. Then they sneak back, wrap their little arms around each of us, and say they love us before we walk out the door.

On the way home, Lyle talks over the hum of the engine. "That was fun. I like your friends, Candy. That Jillian is a firecracker, and the kids…"

Startled by Lyle dropping "Blondie" and calling me by name, I turn in my seat to look back at him in the shadows. His head shakes as he looks out the window.

"Those kids said they loved me." Light flashes across his face from oncoming headlights, and I think I see serenity.

Hank pulls up to my apartment and puts the car in park.

"You gotta walk Candy to her door," Lyle spouts from the back seat. "I'll close my eyes, Lover Boy. So you can kiss her."

"Thanks for the permission." Hank gets out of the car.

He opens my car door and leans in toward me. "Sorry." He bends around me and looks at Lyle. "For the romance being completely taken out of the evening."

Lyle laughs. "Not completely. Just go kiss her. You'll get your romance despite me."

I pinch my lips and scoot around Hank, trying to pace my way to the door. Our relationship has gotten to a place with consistent good-night kisses. Nothing crazy hot and heavy, just acknowledgment that we are now…something more.

A hand presses against the back of my waist. "Sorry. I hope this isn't too awkward."

When I get to the door, I turn toward Hank's tall silhouette. I can't distinguish the look on his face in the shadows, but his shoulders are tense.

"I had such a fun night. Lyle razzing us doesn't bother me." I let out a small laugh. "Just kiss me."

Cold hands press against my cheeks and draw my face up into his soft lips. The night hums a lullaby in the background, then swirls around us with kiss upon gentle kiss. Sweet, soft, dreamy kisses. A cool breeze whispers across my face as Hank pulls back. His hands remain on my cheeks, now warming my skin.

"I…" Hank clears his throat and drops his hands, straightening up. "I guess I better go. Lyle's waiting." He steps back and looks toward the car, then to me, then to the car again, as if he can't move his feet. "I wish…" He looks at me again. "I wish I didn't have to go. I want…"

I don't know what's going on with him, but something seems to be stuck in his throat.

"Hank, I had a lovely time tonight. With all of us." My fingers trickle down his cheek, beckoning him to believe me. "We'll have our chance."

He huffs. "Okay." His hair flops over his face as he drops his head.

Lifting onto tiptoes, I kiss his cheek. "Goodnight." I unlock my door, step inside, and shoo him toward his car.

"Goodnight, Candace." His baritone voice sings to my heart. He smiles, then glides over the pavement as Lyle gets out of the car and moves to the passenger seat.

CHAPTER 45
JUST GIVE IN ALREADY

HANK

The chill of the Formica countertop prickles my forearms through my long sleeves as I hold the latest greatest murder mystery between my hands. Outside, the wind whips the last remaining leaves in circles and howls at the clouds that block the morning sun. Lyle doesn't seem to notice the chaos outside. He buzzes around the library, dusts the tabletops and makes the coffee. I'm just his ride, so I read until my workday starts. He earns a paycheck as the library's official cleaning service. It didn't take much to convince my boss to hire him, once she saw how efficiently he reduced the amount of dust motes glistening in the air when the sun shoots through the windows.

The sunlight brings out the red tinge in his hair. I didn't know it was anything more than dirty brown. But consistent showers and the outdoor work with Candace have made his hair almost shiny. He looks so different. With the weight he's put on, his pants don't hang off his hips the way they used to. His face is brighter, almost rosy, and he smiles more.

"It's that time," Lyle announces as he reaches over the counter to grab my keys, jingles them like a tambourine and practically dances a jig on the way to the door as he officially opens the library for another day of business.

"Morning George. There's a new *Reader's Digest* just waiting for you." Lyle almost sings and backs up for a few more early risers. One he nods at and receives a reciprocal head bob without a word though the silent conversation speaks volumes. I notice the familiar layered unkempt look of the man and wonder at the unspoken interaction.

I've watched Lyle's daily metamorphosis. He's even cooked dinner with Candace and me. The three of us bob around the kitchen dodging each other while music blasts. I hope he knows he belongs. I really do consider him a friend, not a charity case. Maybe at first he was, but that's not the situation anymore.

He still reels from losing Mindy. On several occasions, I've sat on the floor by the couch as he lays there with the blanket over his head. His muffled voice pummels through the dam of thoughts that threaten to drown him. But then he blasts like a rocket out of the dark chasm, determined to learn from Mindy's demise. And somehow honor her with his choices now.

We've had late-night talks. Sometimes with Candace, but mostly just the two of us. The heavy stuff he's revealed led me to encourage him to find a counselor. He goes to Celebrate Recovery to seal his abstinence and church with Candace and me to build hope and community. I don't remember what the pastor preached the first time we went to Candace's church, but something broke through to Lyle that day. I don't want to miss this ride with him *or* Candace, so I've adopted her church as my own. It's not much different than the one I grew up in. Anyway, we're all family, one body, right?

"You gotta stop that, Glasses. You're looking at me the way you look at Candy." He musses my hair and chuckles. "Don't go rolling your eyes at me."

"Don't flatter yourself." I push my glasses up my nose. "You are nothing like Candace." I laugh.

"I should hope not. By the way, one of the guys from my recovery group said he'd drive me tonight, so you're free for..." His eyebrows dance around as he gawks at me.

I ignore his comment. "At least I won't develop an ulcer tonight as you practice driving across town. No gritted teeth, or fear of losing life or limb."

"You're the one that wanted me to get my license again." He grabs a cup of coffee and returns to the counter.

"Hey." I pull out a folder from under the counter. "Since it's quiet, you want to finish up the rest of this paperwork? One more form and you get on the shared housing list."

His brow furrows and he rests his hands on the counter. "Hey, that guy," he nods his head to the back corner, to the chair he used to claim every morning. I nod. "He wants to get off the streets, but said all the paperwork and whatnot is overwhelming. Could he just watch us to get a better idea of what he'll need to do? Maybe it would help him find his way."

"Yeah, of course."

Wow, I guess this is paying off, like a ripple effect. Now Lyle wants to help someone find their way from unsheltered to having a home, safety, and healthy self-sufficiency.

The way Lyle bounces to the back of the library reminds me of his Monday mood, as he calls it. He's all about Mondays with Candace. Loves her boss, Mr. Jacobs, who has taken him under his wing, become a mentor, and even offered him a part-time job. Underneath Lyle's grungy exterior hid a brilliant mind. The opportunities Mr. Jacobs has presented have helped Lyle come to life, shown who he truly is and was under all the shame that had overtaken him.

It takes a village, as they say, each of us doing our part, working together. Candace and I did what we could, blindly most of the time. Lyle has done his part. I guess sometimes faith is like walking across an intersection holding a white cane. Man, I have so much more respect for people with the courage to venture into the world without the gift of sight. They've helped me to recognize the faith it sometimes takes to move forward. The things God can use to wake us up are crazy, huh?

What if I hadn't pushed past being uncomfortable and hadn't pursued Candace? I was dorky and awkward about it, but I did it. Because of her, we built a relationship with Lyle that helped him, and we've all created a friendship. Of course, Candace is more than a friend. More than a girlfriend even. I think she could be an important part of my life for a long, long time. Maybe forever.

"Let's get to this." Lyle's voice breaks through my rambling thoughts. I look at him, then at the man next to him.

"Hank, this is Joe, you probably don't remember him. He usually hides under a brown sleeping bag. He was there." Lyle clears his throat, "Well, you know when."

Joe frowns and drops his head.

"Joe." I offer my hand across the counter. "Nice to meet you." His countenance changes as he says. "Hey, I appreciate that lasagna you sent with Lyle the other day."

"You can thank my girlfriend, that was her idea. But I helped." I chuckle and then look down at the paperwork. "Okay, well, let's get to this before it gets busy."

"Yeah, before it's time to let the animals in."

"Animals?" I turn to look at the flyer Lyle's pointing to. He's right. Today's story time features a local wildlife group that will be showing the kids different critters. Man, I love my job.

———

"Don't wait up," I say as Lyle gets out of my car. I watch him head up the walkway, a spark of light bouncing off the apartment keys he pulls out of his pocket. He has the place to himself tonight. He's proven trustworthy, and I'm aching to go out alone with Candace.

Dinner and Christmas shopping. She's supposed to help me find equal but unique presents for my sisters. A crazy challenge each year, since their personalities are so different. Plus they dog me like I have a favorite no matter what I get each of them. Bringing Candace into the mix will kill two birds with one stone—give me ammunition my sisters won't be able to argue over and help me get an idea of what Candace might like for Christmas.

My heart rate increases as I walk up to her apartment. This is a real date. Just the two of us, no extra company. For the last month, we've either had Lyle with us or been at gatherings with family or friends. We haven't spent much time just us. Each step sends the butterflies in my stomach in a whirl, until I knock and she opens the door.

The butterflies settle as if finding the perfect flower to drink in nectar, the sweetness of her smile and bright eyes. She tightens the belt around her coat and pulls the door closed behind her. I back up to give her space, though I really want to throw my arms around her.

"What?" she asks with a shy smile.

"You look great." What this girl does to me!

"I wanted to be dressed in something other than mud-covered dungarees since that's how you saw me last." She giggles and my breath escapes slow and steady.

The stars shine bright even though it's barely six. Despite the regularity of the seasons, I'm always surprised by the early evening darkness this time of year. Candace changes everything about that dark feeling. She is a light walking next to me. Who cares how black the sky is with her by my side.

"What's wrong?" She raises a suspicious eyebrow. "You're looking at me so oddly. Do I have something stuck in my teeth?" She rubs her finger across her front teeth. "Is my lipstick smeared? I don't usually wear it." She fumbles her finger around her lips, drawing my attention like a neon sign flashing "Kiss Me."

Focus, Hank. Focus. I look away and stare at my car's shiny door handle like I'm asking it for help. The door creaks as I open it.

"You really should get that fixed. It only needs a little oil." Candace points to a hinge, then looks up at me. The car tried, but it got intercepted by starshine glinting from Candace's eyes. As if drawn by a magnet, my lips meet hers briefly, then I pull back.

"Sorry." My eyebrows must be in my hairline. "I couldn't help myself." *The truth.*

Her smile doesn't make this any easier. "I don't mind. It was nice." She slides into the car seat, and I lean into the door as I close it. I want to bang my head on the roof of my car, but then she'd really think something's wrong. All the feelings and thoughts I've repressed the past few weeks are exploding like confetti in my brain.

My warm breath creates a small cloud of white as air escapes my lips, leading my gaze up. Even the moon, bright in the sky, seems to laugh at me. *I am* over the moon for this girl, and there's no way back to earth.

As we sit across from each other and enjoy a meal neither of us had to cook, I pull myself together and keep my silly emotions out in the distance where they belong. We talk about Lyle's progress, about how Thanksgiving went well with our families, and our upcoming Christmas plans.

"Christmas lights. I love Christmas lights." Candace's face glows. "I'd love to drive down Christmas Tree Lane. We could put on carols, sing along, and see all the amazing decorations in people's front yards." She looks at me like she's asking for a cookie. She could have anything she wants as far as I'm concerned.

"Fun."

"Well, you don't sound very enthusiastic. It's almost like you're trying to not get excited."

Exactly. "I am excited. I'm just trying..." I take my glasses off and rub my face. "Oh, brother. I'm sorry, Candace. I'm trying to be cool. I've never been good at it." I can't tell what expression is on her face. She's slightly blurry as I stare, squinting.

"You don't have to be cool for me. I like you just as you are." She wags a blurry finger at me. "And while I like you in glasses, removing them shows off how gorgeous your eyes really are."

I fumble my glasses between my hands, then awkwardly put them on. She called me gorgeous. I mean, my eyes. But they're me.

"Yep, jaw-dropping gorgeous." She taps under her own chin with the back of her hand and I close my jaw. Her laugh dances around the table. "And now you're turning red." Her lips purse and her cheeks rise, reminding me of when we first met.

"Hank, don't act so surprised I like you so much. Ours hasn't cooked up to be a typical dating experience, but besides the obvious attraction, we talk easily about almost everything, and the hard circumstances we've faced together have only made me appreciate you more. All the ingredients are there." Her face suddenly drops, as if she said too much. "Or do you not think so?"

Words to match hers escape me. I squint one eye. "You do remember the kiss?" I look at my watch. "Around an hour ago?"

"I remember." Her shoulders relax and she tilts her head. "It might be nice to hear what you think, though... about us. With the whole Lyle thing, we haven't had much chance to talk about . . ."

Did her eyelashes suddenly grow? They are batting up and down and I can't see anything else.

"Hank?" She looks at me with expectation.

A black apron and hands fumbling for a pad and pen appears in the periphery and draws my attention. The waiter asks if we need anything else. We say no, he leaves the tab, and I pull out my wallet and scribble on the receipt. When Candace and I walk out into the cool night air, I give her a sideways glance. Mercifully, she seems to have moved on from the relationship conversation.

"I know the stores close soon," I say, "but I have a general idea of what I want to buy and am hoping for your guidance with the details. Are you sure you don't mind helping with my Christmas shopping tonight?"

"This works perfectly. I like to look around and get ideas, think about them for a while, then go back with a plan. I'm not a meander-type shopper."

Why does that description delight me and not surprise me at the same time? "Thanks." I open the car door for her and quickly turn so we don't have another kissing casualty.

That sounds so dramatic. *Kissing isn't wrong, Hank.* I take a breath, look up at the stars, and circle around the car. The problem is that I don't ever want to stop. I want to kiss her for the rest of my life.

I imagine the moon shaking its head at me. It knows I can't hold back my feelings from Candace much longer. I'm a lost cause. There's no turning back.

She's the one, Hank, and you know it. Just give in already.

CHAPTER 46
BEE CHARMER

CANDACE

"Jewelry?" I ask. Not all women are into jewelry. I'm not. It always gets in the way. My accessory motto has always been "simple is best." I may wear earrings, but definitely not a necklace unless it's a special occasion. At work, I'm bound to strangle myself. The wooden corner of a bee box, branches, tools of the trade, who knows what. There's too much to get tangled in. Plus, I'm weird about things around my neck. Even collars on a shirt can make me feel like my esophagus might close.

But if Hank wants to get his sisters necklaces, okay. I'm up for the challenge.

"I know they all like jewelry," he says.

He knows them better than me, so I will need to put on my "if I were in their shoes" hat.

"Do they like *necklaces*?"

"The way you said that makes me think you don't."

"I'm typically not a necklace girl." I wrap my hands around my neck and make a choking sound. Thank goodness he laughs.

"Okay. I won't buy you a necklace. But I want to get each of my sisters one, each about the same price but with a unique design. I think you could tell at Thanksgiving how different they are."

I nod and picture the big bauble earrings with matching necklace on one sister, only silver on another. Meg's more my speed. A funny turkey face dangled from each of her ears, but she did wear a pretty petite ring, antique gold with etched flowers.

We wander around looking at the glass displays. Hank points out options and I agree or disagree. After glancing through each case, we find a gold chain with multicolored miniature ornaments all around for his oldest sister and the same thing in silver and rose-gold for his middle sisters. Next, Meg.

"Don't tell the others, but she's my...I can't say 'favorite,' so I'll say she's the one I'm closest to. While I want all the gifts to be equal to avoid arguments, I want hers to be special, particularly since Mike— well, you heard the story. I just want to remind her she's special." His brow furrows. "Do you get what I'm saying?"

"I do."

His shoulders relax as we approach a glass cabinet with vintage jewelry. We're in our own little shopping bubble, until a clerk who's been wheeling and dealing with other customers advances.

"Can I help you?" The salesman asks with too big of a smile.

"We're good." Hank forces through gritted teeth.

"Vintage." The salesman's expression looks far from sincere. "I know a lot about the background. I'm sure I could help."

"I just want to see what you have. I care more about whether it fits the person I'm giving it to than what its background is."

The salesman shifts his approach. "Tell you what, I'll unlock the cabinet, and you can point out anything you'd like to see up close. I'll stand back and keep my mouth shut."

Hank nods with a gracious smile, then steps toward the cabinet. I follow suit, scan the display. One of the necklaces catches my eye.

"If I were to wear a necklace, it would be something like that." I point to an antique chain with tiny autumn leaves in various metals every inch or so. "It's kind of like the other ones you chose, but a little more Meg's speed, I think—if I read her right."

"Huh?" Hank stares at the cabinet a few feet away and points at something for the salesman to take out. I guess Hank found something else.

The salesman sets an open black box in front of Hank. I move over to get a look at what caught his attention.

"That's a ring," I say, not really paying attention to what it looks like. "I thought you wanted a necklace."

The look on his face is indecipherable. "What size is your finger?"

"What?"

Hank reaches for my right hand and puts the ring on my finger.

"It fits." He smiles, his eyes focused on my hand.

My heart beats in my throat and my palms start to sweat.

Oh gosh, I'm sopping his hand with my nervous sweat. What am I gonna do?

I gulp in air and make a horrible gag sound.

Hank looks up at me. "You okay?" He lets go of my hand and I shake it at him like I'm shooing a bug. Which I wouldn't do if it were a bug, but something foreign is on my finger and I didn't say it could be there.

"Candace, it's just a simple ring. Not even expensive. Look at it." The look in his eyes shifts from concerned to sparkling, and I realize he's amused at my reaction. "I'm not asking you to marry me. I grabbed your right hand on purpose. I just thought…Well, look at it. It's perfect. Like it was made for you."

Still freaking out, I straighten my arms penguin-like. Then I raise my right hand as if lifting fifty pounds and risk a look at this ring said to be perfect for me.

"Oh!" I pull my hand closer to my face and swirl the antique gold ring to see the sunflowers around its whole circumference. A little bee rests on the center of one of the flowers. "How cute! It's a bee and my favorite flowers."

Hank's face lights up and a broad smile replaces all remnants of the look of concern I caused him seconds earlier. "Look inside." He points to his ring finger and twirls his pointer finger around.

I slip off the thin gold ring and look inside. Etched in the center in cursive are the words *Bee Charmer*.

"Because you're my Bee Charmer." His face almost glows as he turns to the salesman. "We'll take it."

"Hank, you're shopping for your sisters, not me. I'm helping *you*. You don't have to get this."

"Don't be silly. It's meant for you. You can't deny that."

The salesman grimaces at me as I hand him the ring and shake my head. Hoping to redirect Hank, I point to a different display. "Let's focus on your sisters."

Again, I can't read the look on his face. Disappointment? Disgust? Frustration?

Resignation wins out. "Okay. Let's focus on my sisters." He agrees the necklace with leaves would be perfect for Meg.

I wander around the store while he makes his purchases. Minutes later, warmth radiates next to me as he stands by my side, a little black bag embossed with gold writing in his hand. He's back to his smiley self, so he must've gotten over the whole embarrassing ring situation.

"Sisters done. Thanks for your help with my list."

"You're more than welcome." I smile shyly, feeling stupid. He was trying to be sweet. And he's right too. If he wasn't here with me, I'd buy that ring for myself.

"Want to pick up some ice cream before we head home?"

I nod. As we meander down the walkway, a warm palm slips into mine. My eyes peek toward the tall dark-haired man next to me. He doesn't look at me, but he smiles like he knows I'm checking him out. A sigh escapes my lips and I hear him chuckle. I giggle too and he gently squeezes my hand as we navigate a crowd toward the pink-and-white striped awning covered doorway of the ice cream shop.

After we order, we find one of a few available tables, with a pink-and-white checkered tablecloth, and a white fringy Christmas tree in the center. Ice cream fueled chatter consumes the atmosphere which means we yell to talk.

Our conversation is safe—about how mild the weather is and whose names are left on our Christmas lists. A teenager in a chocolate-smudged white shirt and pink apron sets our order in front of us and takes the plastic placard from our table. Peanut butter and chocolate in a cup for me, a brownie sundae for Hank. The hot chocolates we ordered as chasers arrive in white mugs with pink ice cream cones painted on the sides.

TESSA BURNS

A swig of rich chocolate warmness fills my mouth just as Hank puts a black box wrapped with a gold bow in front of me. I gulp and my throat hurts like I swallowed a rock.

"Hank!"

He shakes his head at me like he won't have any complaints.

"Here's the deal." He pushes the box closer to me. "The ring is made for you. You know it. I didn't want anyone else to nab it before I could. And now seems the best time to give it to you. It's not an engagement ring. Not yet anyway."

His thick hand slaps against his forehead. "I'm as bad at saying how I feel as my sister seems to believe. I do care for you more than I have anyone else before."

He rubs his face. "Okay, the point is that I wanted to give you something special. Something you would like. But it's also my way of saying you're important to me. So…Well, here."

He takes the ring out and grabs my right hand. A crowd begins to gather around us. He quickly slips the ring on my finger, then looks at one particularly close gawker. "It's not an engagement ring. Just a present."

"Way to be a bummer, dude," the guy says. "False alarm," he announces to the room. "You can put your phones away. No engagements happen'n here."

"Oh, too bad," says a nearby voice. Several groans ring out around the place.

Hank looks at me. "Sorry. I guess I've got a gift for de-romancing things."

"You're fine." I struggle to hold back a giggle. "Do you want to get out of here, away from prying eyes and phone cameras?"

He looks dignified as he stands and then pulls out my chair. I slip my hand in the crook of his elbow. I'm on his side, even if the whole ice cream shop isn't.

CHAPTER 47
HENRY LOVES CANDY

HANK

My stomach does loop-de-loops, even though I've been to Candace's family home before. We're only driving out there to help put up Christmas lights, but something causes my heart to race and jets to zoom through my stomach at Mach 1. Thank goodness for the distraction of the Christmas carols blasting on the car radio.

Candace sings at the top of her lungs while she taps on her knee to the beat. Occasionally she points out someone's front yard and ooh's and aah's. Her red sweatshirt features a dancing Christmas tree wearing a comical grin. Mine has Rudolph with a red pom-pom for a nose. I should've thought that through. My seatbelt keeps either pulling at the pom-pom or rubbing it into my chest. I'm sure to have a bruise by the end of the night.

"My mom assigned us to string the lights for one of my favorite trees," she blurts out as I turn into the long dirt driveway. "It's that one." She points to a stout ancient oak. I've never seen one so tall and sprawling.

When we enter the house, Candace's dad, Al, shakes my hand firmly, the reason behind his grin indiscernible. Candace's mom places her hands on my shoulders and pulls me toward her but not too close, for what I think is meant to pass for a hug. Her sisters fling themselves at me. I guess I passed whatever their test was at Thanksgiving.

"The light boxes are labeled by location." Al points to red and green plastic tubs, then scratches his stomach where the Grinch on the front of his shirt displays a red vinyl grin.

"After we all finish our jobs, we'll have my famous peppermint ice cream cake and hot chocolate," Candace's mom says. "Then we'll vote on who wins the ugly sweater contest." She sweeps her hand in front of her shirt, as if the cute white bunny wearing a Santa hat passes for ugly.

From the way Candace rolls her eyes at me, I can tell she's thinking the same thing I am. She points to a container labeled "Family Tree" in bold block letters. I lift it and follow her out the front door.

The leaves crunch under our feet, and small clouds escape from my lips each time I breathe. On one hand, the cold air makes me want to finish our outdoor job quickly. On the other hand, I want to be alone with Candace as long as possible. Which could be pretty long, since Lyle is at a Celebrate Recovery meeting tonight and I don't have to pick him up. This could be the night I tell her.

There's been a tug-a-war between my heart and my head all day, which may be why my pulse is bounding and my stomach's in knots. Meg's voice keeps running through my head telling me I have to tell her how I feel. I don't want Candace to deal with the kind of disappointment Meg is having over Mike. But she freaked out over a simple ring. Is Candace ready to hear what I have to say? Am I?

She sweeps her arm in front of me, drawing my attention back to our assignment.

"This is one of my favorite trees. And do you know why?" Candace's eyes light up as she looks at me. "We call it our family story tree."

"What does that mean?"

She runs a finger through seams in the bark. "I want you to figure that out. Once we get started, you're sure to find the secret." Her right eyebrow rises and a sly smile spreads across her face.

"Let's get started then."

An old wooden ladder and an extension cord lie waiting on the ground. Al must've set them out earlier. The ladder has clearly had years of good use, its struts worn smooth by boots climbing up and down. We string the lights at the bottom of the wide trunk and circle up and around, the string spirals off the orderly roll. I've never seen Christmas lights this organized. My family's lights are always a tangled mess and take longer to untangle than put up.

"This is going to be quicker than I thought," I say.

"Just wait." Candace holds either side of the spool, letting the tension unwind the lights as she circles around. My job is to make sure each spiral is approximately three inches above the one below. Apparently, her mom will measure if it doesn't look right. "There's also a string each for two of the main branches, to make the tree look like a cross from a distance."

Candace points out the first branch. I retrieve the next roll of white bulbs, and she holds them while I climb the ladder. She looks up at me with a funny grin.

"What's wrong?"

"Nothing," she says, then giggles. "I'll hold this string for you 'til you get to the branch, then pass it to you."

Near the top of the ladder, I secure myself by wrapping one arm around the branch. As I catch my breath from the climb, the sun casts its last golden glow and turns the bark of the trunk in front of me to a shimmering tan. I see a heart etched in the tree and blink several times at the names carved inside.

"Henry loves Candy?"

Below me, Candace hugs the roll of lights close to her chest and grins. "My grandparents. Grandma used to go by Candy. That heart's been there for over fifty years."

Cold air slaps my face as the wind picks up. My nose burns, threatening to drip. This is not the time to wipe snot on my sleeve, but I don't want it to rain down on Candace as she looks up from below.

"There are more stories too," she says. "I'll let you find them." She tilts her head shyly. "I thought that one would be a fun surprise."

"Henry loves Candy."

Those three words on the trunk in front of me shine like the star of Bethlehem, pointing to something greater. Even this tree knows how I feel. My heart lurches into my throat and reminds me of all the times I've wanted to say it but held back. Is it too soon? Will Candace think I'm nuts?

I am nuts. Crazy nuts for her.

"Just keep looping this string around the way we did the trunk." She hands me the roll of lights. I lift the roll and spiral it around until it runs out. Then I zip-tie the end around the branch so the string will stay in place.

"Not too tight. We don't want to hurt the tree."

Can trees feel? "Your grandparents already carved into it. I'm not sure the tree knows what's going on."

Candace's scowl is recognizable even at this distance. "You'd be surprised. This tree has seen a lot—knows things I can only imagine. It watched my grandparents raise my dad and then my parents fall in love." She hugs the trunk. "It's heard a lot of secrets. Not just mine."

A hush falls as the sky turns to dusky blue. A whip-poor-will calls in the distance, transporting me to a memory I've never lived. In my mind's eye, I see a little blonde girl as she sits on the branch I just wrapped. I imagine her finger traces the names in the heart on the trunk. *Henry loves Candy.*

"Hey dreamy eyes, I'm cold. We need to get our job done."

"Be right there." I look down at the little blonde girl. *My blonde girl* and my heart picks up a beat again.

I hop off the last rung of the ladder, it clatters as I place it on the opposite side of the tree, where Candace waits to wrap the second branch. My puffy coat deflates into her when our arms meet, and I turn and look into her face. "I didn't mean to put your tree down."

She laughs. "You're fine. I know I can be a little dramatic about certain things." She pats the tree. "Two more rolls. For this branch and then the middle one." She squints and points toward a gnarled branch stretched high through the tree's center.

The ladder lets off a little screech with each step. At the top, another heart appears on the trunk. "Your folks?"

If it wasn't getting dark, I'm sure I would see her face redden. "My dad carved it into the tree the day he asked my mom to marry him." She hands me the string of lights and I start to wrap. "It's hard to believe, but there was a time my mom climbed trees too. They sat on that limb like they would often do back then, and he proposed. She accepted and he carved their names into the tree right then and there."

When we finish stringing the lights, I return the ladder to the ground next to the tree. We connect the plug into the extension cord and step back to admire the sparkle of lights against a midnight-blue backdrop. A gasp escapes Candace's lips, drawing my eyes toward her.

"Aren't they beautiful?" Her hand reaches into the crook of my elbow and she snuggles into me. Warmth radiates from deep in my core, and I lean into her and drop my head onto her soft cool hair.

"Candace?" What am I doing?

"Hmm?" Her voice comforts like a purr.

"Henry loves Candy," I say.

"Don't you just love that story? It's so romantic." She squeezes my arm, but I have to pull away to look at her straight on.

"No." I place my palms on each of her shoulders, then slide them down her arms to hold each of her tender hands in mine. I look in her eyes, full of questions.

"You don't think it's romantic?"

"It is. I just want you to know..." I look down at her hands, so fragile and cold in mine, then up into her eyes.

"I love you." I pull her hands into my chest. "Henry loves Candy, times two."

CHAPTER 48
PROOF IS IN THE BRISKET

CANDACE

The crinkle of the overstuffed brown grocery bag as it bumps the stainless-steel counter warns the paper might rip apart any second. Anxious jitters coursing through my arms say the same about me. I get the bag up on the counter just in time for its contents to fall there instead of onto the tile floor.

"I-I'm nervous."

"Don't be. You've got this." Hank's warm hand brushes down my arm, then pulls me close as he plants a soft kiss on my forehead.

"I don't know, this is a lot of people to feed." An extra stressor, since I have stupidly invited everyone I can think of to a Christmas celebration. Hank's family, my family, Jillian's family, Marcus's family, Lyle, Neighbor Bob, even my boss. Once it dawned on me that my place couldn't hold that many people, Hank came to the rescue and reserved the clubhouse at his apartment complex.

"What was I thinking?" I step back, plant my feet, and stare cross-eyed at all the bags we've toted into this industrial-sized kitchen. "I'm in over my head."

"Candace, you've got this. And you've got me." Hank snickers, which doesn't help. "Everyone coming loves you. I love you. What can go wrong?"

"Pfft!" He's got to be kidding! I fling my hands out. "I single-handedly murdered water not so long ago."

Big warm hands envelop mine. "You've come a long way since then. This is what you wanted. Like a big race you've trained for. We've practiced every dish and they turned out great. We've already done the prep work." He squeezes my hands as if to make the flimsy words stick. "Tonight is a celebration, and we are all going to have great food, great fellowship, and a great time. I promise."

Oh, now it's all on me and my lack of faith.

Hank shrugs his shoulders. "A wise woman once told me to just take the next step."

Ugh! Struck between the eyes. It's almost as if he can read my mind.

I pull in a big gulp of air. "Well. No turning back now. Let's cook!"

Anxious paralysis still threatens to stick my feet to the floor. I take a purposeful step toward the shiny silver counter. The gleam of the metal shouts that it can take whatever I dish out. My confident naivety of a few weeks ago forces me to prove that I, Candace, can-can cook.

Oh Lord, help me!

The list of to-dos and time frames I've written out will help. *Take a breath, Can-Can, and follow the plan.* I pull out the sheet of lined stationery and iron out its creases on the counter. The poor paper has been folded, opened, and read over more times than I'd like to admit. Now I must trust the plan to walk me through to the finish line of a meal fit for royalty—in this case, my friends and family, and my boss. My *boss*.

What was I thinking, inviting Mr. Jacobs? He doesn't even celebrate Christmas! But he did say he wanted to come—that it would be an honor. A slow breath escapes as I redirect my thoughts back to success.

Fumbling through a bag filled with miscellaneous items, everything from a backup spatula to a screwdriver, I pull out tape and secure the crumpled game plan to an upper cabinet, front and center. I will follow the plan and tonight will be great. I *know* it will. Maybe.

A stuttered breath escapes, which Hank responds to with a gentle swirl of his hand between my shoulders. "We've got this." He turns me to face him, places a hand on each shoulder, and looks deep into my eyes.

I poke his chest and giggle. "You better watch out. Lyle might get jealous if he sees you getting all googly eyed."

Hank pulls me into a bear hug and laughs. "That's why I love you. Comic relief when we need it."

I draw back and raise an eyebrow. "Not always on purpose, mind you."

His deep chuckle warms the air along with the preheating oven. "No more delays, Candy-girl. We've got a feast to prepare!" He lifts a fist toward the ceiling like a charge and the atmosphere fills with energy, kicking us into gear for the task at hand.

We place the four briskets we prepped yesterday with an amazing spice rub into the ovens. Yes, four. *Aye-yai-yai!*

We pull tables and chairs from the storage closet, then position the red tablecloths and centerpieces. Thanks to Megan, round mirrors and round vases filled with red marbles hold red and white carnations and pine accents. A few tea lights will reflect off the mirror and create a cozy mood. The hall has already been decked for the season with festive garlands accented by red, gold, and white ornaments. A tree sparkles from one corner, next to the upright piano. I wonder if anyone will play carols tonight?

We finish the table settings with candy-cane-striped paper napkins and silverware. Basic white plates will be left on the buffet table, so everyone can serve themselves and choose their seats.

"Hey Candace?" Hank calls from across the room as he folds another striped napkin and places it.

"Hmm?"

"Let's pull another table."

"Did we not count right?" I count each place setting again. Checkin' it twice. "I think we have enough seats for the people we invited."

He straightens and drops his hands to his side, at attention like a Von Trapp child from *The Sound of Music*, which we just watched together last night. "Permission for one more table, miss."

"What are you up to?" Suddenly, I think I know. "Oh, you want more *room* at the table."

At the last church service we attended, the pastor talked about inviting the stranger, entertaining angels unaware, that sort of thing. A vision crosses my mind—of Lyle's friends, Mindy's family, Joe, and any number of people whose names I don't know. My goal to prove to myself and others that I can cook a beautiful meal without making people sick gives way to the real purpose of Christmas. To share the gift of love.

I meet Hank's eyes and know we are on the same page. The welcome sound of chairs scraping into place around another table gives both Hank and me a spring in our step. I knew there was a reason we bought an extra tablecloth. I wanted backup since I'm prone to make a mess, but now the real reason hits me. We needed to make room.

My phone alarm sounds to remind me to put the potatoes in the oven, then the trays of green bean casserole. The savory smell of brisket fills the hall, and my mouth waters. This get-together might just turn out beautifully.

The last half hour before our guests arrive is the most nerve-racking. As we turn our attention to preparing the gravy for the brisket, the grand panache. Hank bumps his hip against mine. I look at him, and his eyebrows rise, making his glasses slide down his nose. *Man, he's cute.*

"I'll be your gallant knight this time," he says apologetically.

"What?"

"Remember our first time cooking together?" He nods like I should know what he's talking about. "You sliced the onions." He reaches for the onions in my hands.

"Oh." I let go willingly. "Thank you."

"You can slice the apples." He gives me a wink.

My heart flutters. A rush of memories from the first time I cooked with the cute guy from the library overtakes me. Back then, in the unknown of what would come, I would've never imagined a day like today. Yet here we are. Cooking side by side. Still bumping into each other—only now on purpose. His hands brush mine. A rather loud sigh escapes before I can stop it.

"Yeah." Hank laughs. "Slicing onions sure is romantic."

I giggle and get back to the task at hand. Who knew a simple visit to the library would change my life?

———

Loud greetings announce our time alone is over. A rush of adrenaline spikes and then drops like a rollercoaster, draining all the energy out of my arms. Hank reaches for my hands, but they just flop back down to my sides.

"Guess I have to hold on tight." He lifts one eyebrow. "Candace, it's going to be okay."

The kitchen door swings open and hits the back wall.

"Hey! Where do I put these?" Marcus holds a huge aluminum pan toward us, the holly-printed hot pads on his hands uncharacteristic. "Ma and me made tamales. Lots of tamales."

I squeal. "They were so good last time."

"Yeah, we make them for Christmas every year and hand them out to everyone whether they want them or not." Marcus closes his eyes and shakes his head. "Ma says it's tradition. I told her you said we didn't have to bring anything, but she wouldn't have it."

"I'm so glad!"

Marcus's green sweater is the perfect color for his complexion. "Nice sweater," I say and direct him to one of the serving tables.

He shakes off the compliment. "Ma picked it out, and I don't dare cross her, especially at Christmastime."

Hank's cologne tickles my nose as Lyle plants next to me and splays his hands toward the almost empty table.

"So, Candy, is this where the extra food goes?"

"Yep."

"Okay, got it. I'm on the job. Go get Glasses and do the host thing. I'll take the service part from here." Lyle lifts his head to Marcus. "You ready?"

Marcus nods and they stride toward the entry door, ready to

retrieve casserole dishes and cookie trays from the flood of friends and family making their way inside.

I balance on the balls of my feet so I don't slip in my heels and clip-clop toward the kitchen to get Hank and turn up the Christmas music. Here we go.

CHAPTER 49
POSSIBLE FOR ALL OF US

CANDACE

Frank Sinatra is singing "Happy Holidays" in the background as I scan the room. Animated gestures at each table look like flapping fishtails as the buzz of chatter splashes energetic joy off the walls.

Marcus receives a gentle pat on his arm from his mom as his grinning sister and nephew look on. They and a beaming Neighbor Bob sit with Mr. Jacobs and his chattering wife. Lyle's friends from Celebrate Recovery and a few comrades he lived with by the creek occupy the extra table.

My parents and Hank's parents have gathered at the same table with Megan and Jillian's family. A stitch pricks at my stomach as my eyes meet my mother's. In one smooth swoop, she scoots out of her chair and heads straight toward me.

I slowly inhale, then notice the genuine smile on her face. She reaches toward my hands and holds them gently, like she did when I was a kid in need of encouragement.

"Honey, everything is just wonderful. And the food!" She squeezes my hands. "I've never had such a tasty brisket. You really have learned to cook. And to cook well at that!"

"Th-thanks."

Her head tilts. "You were always so bored in the kitchen and opted

256

to play outside. You'd beg me not to *have* to cook. I gave up trying, since your sisters were more interested." Her eyes veer and focus on some past memory, then move back toward me. "You were much more interested in climbing trees and getting dirty back then. But look at you now, look at all of this!" She sweeps a hand toward the tables of lively conversation. "You made this happen. And it is all quite lovely." My mother's arms envelop me and pull me into a warm hug. She holds me long enough to smell a hint of Shalimar, her favorite perfume.

She releases me and moves to return to her table.

"You'll catch flies if you don't close your mouth, Blondie." Lyle nudges my arm with his elbow.

I snap my mouth shut and turn toward him. His eyes shine brightly as he offers a toothy grin and waggles his eyebrows in true Lyle form. My shoulders automatically drop and a giggle escapes.

"That's better." He plants both feet and gets a serious look on his face, "I want to thank you. This event..." He shakes his head. "I haven't had a Christmas like this in a decade." He closes his eyes and takes a breath before continuing. "You and Hank made a difference." His green eyes glisten as he looks back at me, washes his hand down his face, and flashes a signature smile. "Hey, I haven't told you. Mr. Bossman—"

"Mr. Jacobs, you mean?"

"Yeah. Mr. Jacobs has offered me a scholarship to finish school and a part-time job for the duration, as long as I hold up my end of the bargain. I'm turning over a new leaf. I guess that whole future-and-a-hope thing can be possible for me too."

"Oh, Lyle!" I can't help but reach for his rough hands and squeeze them. "Of course it is. It's possible for all of us."

His hands lightly wiggle free, and he swishes his eyes to the sky. "Yeah. Anyway, I just wanted to say thanks. Oh, and to let you know I called my mom. She's in remission. And," he clears his throat, "I'm going home for Christmas."

Flinging my arms around him, I sway him side to side. His stiff body gives a little until he sways with me. "I'm so happy for you!"

He pulls back with a laugh. "Yeah, I'm happy for me too. But..." He looks around. "We don't want to get Glasses jealous."

We laugh together, then he turns to where a crowd is gathered around the piano. Voices sing joyfully, demanding figgy pudding.

Seconds later, Hank is by my side. "I guess we blew it."

"What?"

"Well…" He points toward the piano and jogs his finger to the beat of the music. "We don't have figgy pudding. And I'm not sure I even know what it is."

We laugh as he reaches his arm around me, warm against my back. I nestle into his side and rest my head on his shoulder.

"You did good, Can-Can."

"We did good. I think we make a pretty good team."

His head drops onto mine. "Yeah, we do. I'm glad we found each other. And guess what? Candace can-can cook." He chuckles.

"Yes! I can cook, can't I?"

Hank slips his hand in mine and leads me toward the piano. Our eyes dance around the eclectic group of friends and family assembled there, then meet. And at the top of our lungs, we join in and sing, "We wish you a Merry Christmas! And a Happy New Year!"

ACKNOWLEDGMENTS

Being a writer can make you an odd duck at times, and so I would like to especially thank those who have put up with my oddities. Thank you to my family and friends who have listened to me talk about my characters and their experiences as if they were real. I appreciate your patience as I've obsessed over their stories.

I am grateful for Women Fiction Warriors and Inspire Writers critique groups who have read many of the words in this novel and offered encouragement and sound advice. I especially want to extend my thanks to Laura Joy Lloyd who gave so much time and support through the process of writing this book, and Jill B. Wilson for her meticulous editing skills.

A big thank you to Ginny L. Ytrupp for her encouragement along the way and for creating her Words for Writers Cohort which helped me find my tribe and hone my skills. I'd like to thank Paula Pierce Brown for spending several hours with me sharing her experience, feet on the ground, with our local unsheltered friends.

Thank you to Keri Wyatt Kent who walked me through the publishing process to bring this manuscript to my readers.

And thank you to my readers. I am grateful you have picked this book to read. I hope you have found something valuable and lasting while being entertained along the way. You are the reason I write.

www.ingramcontent.com/pod-product-compliance
Lightning Source LLC
Chambersburg PA
CBHW060626260626
47161CB00008B/2816